TO THE RESCUE

"Are you hurt, Miss Edwards? I am so sorry that oaf put a hand on you." Jeremy stood near her to offer his assistance and support.

"T-thank you, Lord Carruthers. He did me no harm other than to my dignity," she said with a small smile.

"I must say you have a bruising right, ma'am!"

She smiled in earnest at his teasing and breathed a heavy sigh. Clara just now realized she was alone on the terrace with this intriguing man.

He moved a half step closer to brush a lock of hair away from her face. The slight movement gave her a start, and she looked up expectantly into his face bathed in moonlight. He tilted his head down to hers and gently, so gently touched his lips to hers. His arms seemed to find their way around her shoulders and she shivered at his touch.

Could this man truly have feelings for her, as her aunt had said?

A Proper Introduction

CHRISTINE LOCKSY

ZEBRA BOOKS
Kensington Publishing Corp.
http://www.kensingtonbooks.com

To my wonderful parents, Elaine and Bill,
who have always inspired me to my best.

ZEBRA BOOKS are published by

Kensington Publishing Corp.
850 Third Avenue
New York, NY 10022

All Kensington titles, imprints and distributed lines are available at special quantity discounts for bulk purchases for sales promotion, premiums, fund-raising, educational or institutional use.

Special book excerpts or customized printings can also be created to fit specific needs. For details, write or phone the office of the Kensington Special Sales Manager: Kensington Publishing Corp., 850 Third Avenue, New York, NY 10022. Attn. Special Sales Department. Phone: 1-800-221-2647.

Zebra and the Z logo Reg. U.S. Pat. & TM Off.

First Printing: October 2004
10 9 8 7 6 5 4 3 2 1

Printed in the United States of America

ONE

AN EVENTFUL MEETING

Clara finished adjusting her hat at a jaunty angle and moved with haste to dress for an errand before luncheon. She wore her favorite habit—the beautiful green one that matched her eyes. The gold braids of the military trim accented the flecks and sparkles in those eyes. Colors were such a small thing, but she knew how to use them to advantage in her wardrobe and her watercolors. The habit was a few seasons old and showed some wear, but she couldn't bear to part with her favorite.

She had plenty of time to ride into town and be back for her late meal this afternoon, but she wanted to travel the long way and enjoy the countryside. Maybe she could take a bit of a detour on the way home and really put her horse, Sparkle, through her paces? It had been a few days since she'd had a good ride.

Clara was anxious to be outside in the beautiful early spring day. The sky promised a bright sun and even some warmth and was a welcome change from the earlier rains. She gazed quickly out the window and saw just a few clouds above the garden view she enjoyed from the house's east side. She loved to sit and stare out into the garden when the morning sun made it all so alive. The jumble of colors in the spring flowers just begged for a paintbrush. *But I'll have to save that for another day she thought with a sigh.*

Clara left her room with a decided bounce in her step. She had sent Meg down a good fifteen minutes ago to have Willie saddle Sparkle, so the horse and groom were undoubtedly at the front steps waiting for her. She'd just stop in to let Mama know that she was leaving. She made a quick turn into the drawing room.

"Mama, I am off to town to buy the new half gloves before our dinner at the Thompsons' tonight. Oh, hello, Lady Winters. I am so mad at myself for ripping my best pair last week. Did you decide if you needed anything?"

"Why yes, darling," her mother replied, "I do need some new blue ribbon to match to the gown I wore to Cousin Belle's wedding last spring. You're such a good judge of color, dear. Do see if you can find just the right one."

"Of course, but then I'd better have Willie bring the buggy 'round. I can't very well carry the dress while I ride! But wait, isn't there a sash I could fit inside my pocket?"

"Yes, but it does not come off the dress. I'm afraid you do have to carry the whole thing. You can have Meg put it in a box for you. I'm sorry to be such a bother."

"Not to worry, Mama," Clara laughed, "you know I love to drive as much as ride. It makes no difference to me. I'll be home in time for luncheon."

And with the errand settled, Clara kissed her mother

on the cheek and smiled a good-bye to Lady Winters as she left the room.

"Such a lovely girl, Marie," Lady Winters said. "You are so lucky to have both a boy and a girl. Not that I don't love my three boys and their wives," she hurriedly added, "but I do regret missing the girl talk and friendship you share with Clara. And she has such style."

"Yes, she is a joy, Helen. Why you should see the watercolor she has almost finished of the summerhouse and gardens. You would think it a museum piece, and that's not just a proud mother talking!"

Helen laughed with her. Clara's watercolors were the pride of the parish. Many people counted themselves lucky to have one of her "dabs," as she called them, hanging in their drawing rooms or a sunny morning room.

"And she has always seemed so happy and joyful during all the years our families have been neighbors and good friends. Now, if only we could find the perfect man for her . . . Any chance she'll accept your sister's invitation this year to come up to town for the Season?"

"Oh, Helen, she's already sent her regrets. Right after Harry went back to school this Tuesday last she wrote to Sheila. She said that she was too happy in her country life to muddle it with a trip to town. I really thought she'd finally go this year what with Emma Thompson all excited about her first Season. But no, it's not to be, and now with Harry returned to school she's back to her quiet life. Every time he leaves, it takes her a week or so to get over missing him. For a brother and sister, they are just the closest of friends."

"Well, she is just turned two and twenty. Not past her prayers at all. Why my Gerald married Charlotte after she turned three and twenty! We'll just have to come up with a plan to entice her to the city. Do you think

Harry could convince her? He seems such a considerate boy."

"That may be a good idea. He has matured so much the past year. Harold and I were remarking on it just after Harry left this time. He does seem to have a greater sense of purpose and appreciates his studies. Oxford has been the making of the man, I think. Perhaps I'll write to him to slip in a good word to Clara in his next letter. If he were to add his voice to those of her mother, aunt, and good friend, maybe our combined forces would see her to her first Season. Sometimes, Helen, I despair of her ever marrying. And now she's taken to sometimes dressing in drab colors and calling it her 'spinster look.' It's not like her, no, not at all. Why that riding habit is the most colorful thing she's worn this week."

"Surely we're not at that point yet! She is a treasure, and we have only to put her in the way of some eligibles to turn the trick."

"But she's already turned down three offers!" Helen exclaimed. "And all of them very eligible. Though I must admit that Johnny Trent is two years younger than Clara, besides being Harry's best friend. And William is her second cousin. But I don't know what came over her to turn down Butterfield during that fortnight we spent in Brighton two summers ago. It would have been a fine match, even if he is a trifle dull."

"Plus being *twenty* years her senior, don't forget. And I'm sure she feels more sisterly to Johnny and William than any kind of love. Why those three and Harry were inseparable all through childhood with their pranks. Every time someone deserved a setdown, those four stepped up to do the deed."

"Perhaps Harold and I indulged her too much in her tomboy ways as a child. Harry was always their ringleader and the instigator of the fun, and with so few other girls her age when she was young, well, it had seemed unkind to deny her the pleasure of Harry's friends. I must confess that we had a hard time disciplining the two of them when we laughed so hard at the results of their antics. Oh, Helen, I didn't tell you their latest adventure when Harry was here. It will so delight you!"

"Marie Edwards! No wonder the girl doesn't take life seriously if you still condone these pranks. Honestly, who's the adult in this household?" But Helen's words were spoken with a smile and not meant to hurt.

"Oh tosh, you know you enjoy hearing the stories as much as I do telling them. Now, quiet while I remember all the details." And Marie sat back in her chair to begin the tale.

Oh the sky is lovely, Clara sighed. She drove the small buggy at a sedate pace, especially for her. She was just so enjoying the panorama as she came down the drive. The Edwardses' family home, Waverly Manor, sat at the top of a modest hill and afforded a striking view of the surrounding countryside. Clara paused as she reached the end of the drive to pluck an early rose from a tall bush. Even nature seemed to blossom in full color for her today.

With her mother's dress securely boxed beside her on the seat, Clara felt a bit less frivolous in her errand. At least she was helping her mother and not just buying some frippery for herself. Really, it seemed she spent all her time these days in these short trips to town, the odd evening out with her parents, and visits with tenants and neighbors. She often times found herself longing for some purpose—or a little excitement. Especially now that Harry had returned to school again.

The household had been surprised when he came home mid-term. She smiled as she remembered her father's horrified glare when first presented with his supposedly studious son. Harry had hastened to assure them that his visit had a scholarly tone—he had long considered it a mark of pride and resourcefulness that he and his cronies had never been caught in some prank. This visit was purely legitimate, as he needed to review some of the local records in research for a paper. The two of them had found lots of time for fun, and life was sadly flat now that he was gone. And another dinner tonight at the Thompsons' held little allure for her.

Clara was lost in thought as she rounded the bend. Her view was blocked by the tall grove of trees alongside the road, so she missed seeing the approaching curricle. Had she been attending to the drive at hand and not woolgathering, she couldn't have missed hearing the barreling vehicle in its headlong approach.

Fortunately, her ears finally picked up the rollicking song coming from the curricle's unknown occupant as he bellowed at the top of his lungs. What was that racket ahead of her? Perhaps just instinct made her pull over slightly towards the side of the road, but that small space gave her the maneuvering room to avoid the disaster that surely would have sent her tumbling to a frightening injury.

Rounding the bend fully, Clara gasped as she saw the curricle heading toward her at a terrible speed. What was the driver thinking? Her quick wits and abilities saved a crash as she deftly signaled the mare to veer further off to her side of the road. Her buggy turned almost perpendicular to the road as it slowed. Unfortunately, the other driver seemed to be pulling his horses to the same side! Was he daft? She couldn't abide shoddy driving, and this clown certainly had no business on the open road. And such beautiful horses, too.

Clara's buggy came to an abrupt halt just as the curricle swiped the back of her small vehicle. She craned her neck around to see the right wheel of the curricle resting against her buggy wheels. Her view also included the very ignominious flop of the driver as he slipped to the ground. Crumpled was more like it, and he didn't move when he landed.

Clara jumped quickly to the ground to rush to him. He must have hurt himself badly with that fall, the poor man. Unmindful of the mud on her skirt from the night's rain, she knelt quickly to listen for breathing. But what she heard sounded like a snore. She didn't understand and knelt more closely to check for his pulse. The smell of brandy forced her back on her heels.

Why he was drunk! And at only eleven o'clock in the morning! All her sympathetic feelings quickly evaporated into thin air at this oaf in front of her. No matter that he was quite finely dressed in beautiful blue superfine and gleaming, if smudged, hessions. He had passed out right in front of her, and she didn't have a clue how to revive him.

Clara glanced back and forth on the road hoping for another carriage or even a donkey cart to aid her. *No one in sight,* she groaned. Now, what would she do with him? He could be hurt from that fall. At least the horses all seemed docile after their ordeal, so she didn't have to worry her head about them. Well, she could try to lift him, she supposed, and put him in the buggy for a ride into town to the doctor. She moved around to lean over from his side, carefully placed her hands under his shoulder and lifted. Mistake number one.

"Get your filthy hands off of me!"

She gasped at his menacing tone and dropped him the small distance she'd managed to move him. Unfortunately for him even a short drop felt like the length of the cliffs of Dover to his spinning head.

"What the devil! Are you trying to kill me now, since you missed with your blasted cart?"

"Why, I never! I was only trying to help you, you drunken fool. You could have been hurt." Clara's fright turned to an anger to match his.

"No thanks to you and your foolish driving. I could have been killed when I was thrown from my curricle."

"*My* foolish driving! *You're* the one going at the breakneck pace on a quiet country lane. And I'll have you know you weren't 'thrown' from your seat. . . . You slipped out in a drunken stupor, you old sot!" Clara's anger did seem to rather affect her usually polite speech, but she didn't even notice the change.

"I've *never* fallen from a carriage you—you harridan! I'll have you know I'm a champion driver and have raced with the best of the Four in Hand Club. Beat them all, too," he boasted.

By this time he had managed to sit up straighter and leaned against his precarious carriage wheel. He would not give her the satisfaction of seeing how sore his backside was from the fall. His quick glance took in her rather magnificent riding habit and the frayed braid. Probably a castoff from her mistress, he thought, but she did fill it out quite well. And her lovely blond hair had slipped from its pins and cascaded down her back—he did so like blond hair.

"Well I'm afraid you didn't distinguish yourself today. Are you hurt?" Clara asked. Her anger seemed to dissipate with his boasting. Why, he was nothing more than a drunken town boy in fancy clothes. She couldn't help but notice his broad shoulders and finely shaped calves as he sat in front of her. And the way his dark hair fell forward on his forehead—she had to grab a handful of fabric from her habit to keep her hand from gently brushing it back. *For a drunk, he is most pleasing to look at,* she giggled to herself—silently, or so she thought. Mistake number two.

"Well I'm so glad to have afforded you some amusement today, young *lady.*" His sarcasm was even stronger than intended in his still slightly inebriated state. "Perhaps I can find a mud hole left over from these infernal rains to wallow in and please you even more. Or maybe you had something even more enjoyable planned for us?"

His leering voice didn't register with Clara until she looked into his eyes. Then she jumped up and stepped back from him as she frantically looked around for someone to help her.

"Oh don't worry yourself. I wouldn't bother with a country miss like you. I like my women prettier, with a little more flesh in the right places." He pointedly directed his insolent gaze at her bodice.

Thoroughly frightened now and blushing furiously, Clara could only think of fleeing. Why he was so insulting and coarse. No kind of gentleman, even one with the fine clothes and address of a member of the *ton,* could act in this manner. It truly stunned her to think that someone like this had accosted her so close to home.

Home. Clara turned without another word and fled to her buggy. She quite ungracefully leapt into the seat, turned the horse back to Waverly and raced across the field, with all thoughts of her errands in town gone from her mind.

"Wait, you can't just leave me here!" he yelled to the quickly departing girl. Well, apparently she could, and had. Even in his fury he noticed she handled those reins quite well, but the knowledge did nothing to ease the pain in his aching backside or in his throbbing head. What kind of predicament had he landed himself in now?

TWO

CONFESSING ALMOST ALL

Clara's hands shook uncontrollably as she continued her mad race across the fields to Waverly. Anyone who might have seen her would have thought she sat behind a runaway horse, so quickly and wildly did her buggy careen. The jaunty riding hat had long ago fallen to the ground, with her hair streaming down her back in riotous blond curls mixed with tangles—neck-or-nothing driving certainly did little for one's coif!

Her thoughts were in no better shape than her appearance. How dare the man! Who was *he* to treat her so? So what that he did not know her name or station? No one had the right to speak and act so cruelly to another person. And she did feel cruelly used and abused by his behavior. How would he have liked to have his insults thrown back at him? Since she had little experience with the effects of liquor, it did not occur to her that brandy could have so affected a person's usual manners and deportment.

Clara had not calmed down in the least as she barreled up the drive. She jumped down from the buggy before Willie could run around from the stables to help her. She barely saw the boy as she hurried up the steps to the front entrance. Gerald quietly opened the door to a firestorm.

"Mama! Wh-where are you?" she stammered in a most unladylike holler.

"The madam is in the drawing room still with Lady Winters, miss." His glance took in her disheveled appearance and heightened color. "Miss Clara, are you all right?" The concern of a longtime family retainer was evident on his usually stoic face.

"Oh my, well I am a bit of a wreck, aren't I?" said Clara as she looked down for the first time at her muddied gown and saw her tousled hair in the hall mirror. The so totally inappropriate picture she presented tickled her funny bone and was a small measure of enjoyment in this horrendous morning's events. She calmed just the tiniest bit as she ran upstairs to find her mother.

Mrs. Edwards and Lady Winters had hurried out of the drawing room at the sound of Clara's earlier cry. The three ladies met at the top of the stairs, and Clara took comfort in her mother's arms.

"Darling, what has happened?" said Mama in a concerned and comforting voice.

"Oh, Mama, he was just so rude and mean to me!"

A decidedly panicked glance fell between the two older women over Clara's shoulder. What had happened to Mrs. Edwards's precious angel? Luckily, she had the presence of mind to guide Clara back into the drawing room. Even loyal servants such as theirs would find it hard to keep back what looked to be a very juicy, and heaven forbid, scandalous story. Gerald could be counted on to bring a restorative tea to the unhappy girl.

"Now, Clara, just come here and tell me calmly what happened. Are you hurt?"

"No, I'm not hurt, not physically at least. He just insulted my driving and abused me with vile language, and he called me a h-harridan!" The last words were said at a wail as her voice broke and she crumpled onto the settee to cry. The danger had gone, to be replaced by anger mixed with mortification.

"Start at the beginning, dear. I take it you met some man in town who was less than a gentleman?" The soothing tones of a voice she had always counted on to heal all her hurts made Clara one tiny bit calmer. So she began the tale.

"But you have no idea who this supposed 'gentleman' is?" asked an intrigued Lady Winters as Clara came to the end of her story.

"Helen, they hardly exchanged introductions," said an amused Marie.

"Mama, you don't seem too worried about all this. Why I could have been seriously hurt in the carriage accident, or even abducted by that vile man."

Now, the look between the two women over Clara's head was all amusement and relief. Their earlier panic had given way to the absurdity of a drunken gentleman and a sheltered country miss verbally tangling on the roadside. Marie was only glad that no one had come along to witness the fiasco.

As Marie poured out more of the now tepid tea that Gerald had brought at the start of Clara's story, she did acknowledge, if only to herself, the real danger Clara could have faced with a more unscrupulous adversary. Or perhaps a less inebriated one. She would speak to Harold this evening about Clara's driving and riding off their estate without a groom or companion. He was too trusting in Clara's abilities and had never seen the need when a concerned wife had raised the proprieties with him.

"Now, dear, you know I am concerned. Heavens, the

man was a brute and hardly the sort we will associate with at the dinner table tonight. But, I think we can just take more caution in the future. Willie or Meg can go with you on your rides from now on." Marie knew that the unwelcome prospect of a chaperone would take the girl's mind off her close brush with danger, and she wasn't wrong.

"A chaperone! Mama, I am a grown woman and in no need of someone to coddle me on my rides. And you know Willie can't begin to keep up with me when I give Sparkle her head. I'd be positively poking along if I were saddled with him. You can't be serious!" But Clara could see that she was.

"We'll discuss it later. Now I think you should go upstairs and have a nice hot bath, a bite of luncheon, and a good rest. And if you don't feel like going out to dinner tonight, I can send Emily Thompson our regrets this afternoon."

Clara had little interest in the dinner, even without today's excitement, but she knew her mother enjoyed the gossip and conviviality of her neighbors. And if Clara stayed home pleading a fatigue or nerves that weren't even there, her mother would feel compelled to miss the evening's fun.

"Oh, don't be silly. Let a little thing like bad manners keep me home! Why I'll feel wonderful after that bath, even without the nap." And she smiled a true grin of affection at her mother.

Clara's mind could not shake the picture of the dark stranger as she soaked in the tub. She realized it was a most improper place to be thinking of a most improper man, but that just made him even harder to forget. She wished she could remember what color his eyes might be. Despite her love of color, black eyes were her favorite, and the deeper the color the better.

Her anger, too, had calmed some more to a point where she began to think rationally about the morning's events. Hard as it was to accept, Clara had to acknowledge that her mother was probably right about a chaperone for her rides. She would have truly welcomed another person in her buggy today to help her to face him. She supposed she'd make a token gesture of complaint when the subject next came up and then relent on taking a companion on future rides. *It wouldn't do to be too docile,* giggled Clara. After all she had her independent reputation to uphold!

Clara could feel the water cooling after her continued soak. Playing the invalid was a bit of fun, but not when it meant turning into a prune!

"Meg? Can you bring me a towel?"

"Oh yes, Miss. 'Tis toasty warm from the fire. You just stand up now, and we'll have you dry in a trice. Then the madam says you are to lie down and rest for at least an hour."

"I know, Meg," sighed Clara. "But I am positively famished. Can you run down for my luncheon tray? I'll dry myself by the fire and slip on my nightgown while you're gone."

"You make sure you don't catch cold. I'll hurry back, and I expect to find you snuggled under the covers," said a concerned Meg as she slowly turned to leave for the tray.

"Yes, Meg." Clara couldn't help but smile at the possessive tone in Meg's words. She was a devoted servant, and Clara was happy for the attention. She didn't want to admit to anyone that she still felt edgy from her close brush with danger.

* * *

Meanwhile, the man so occupying Clara's thoughts was having a considerable amount of bad luck trying to repair his damaged curricle. Had he even tried, Lord Jeremy Carruthers, heir to the Marquess of Sutherdown and a sizable fortune, couldn't have bought his way to a mended axle using twice the family funds.

Shortly after the girl's hasty departure, a local tradesman had ambled down the lane to find him still propped up against the damaged wheel. During the wait, Jeremy hadn't moved except to rub his ever-aching backside. With transportation at hand, he managed to stand up and bumped along in the cart for a ride back into the village. He wasn't sure if he wouldn't have been more comfortable astride one of his cattle, but the thought of another fall kept him in the relative safety of the cart.

His problems continued when he learned the village wheelwright had closed early on this particular day. He was to attend the very mill that had brought Jeremy into this part of the countryside. And with all businesses shut down for the Sabbath tomorrow, he was sure the day couldn't get much worse. He was right—the day would only get better, but the night held more surprise in store.

Jeremy had resigned himself to spending two more nights at the local inn, and this time he didn't have the pleasant prospect of relieving the good proprietor of any more of the fine brandy that had gotten him into today's trouble. Too bad he'd finished off the lot as the sun rose on the morning just past.

With the horses stabled at the livery, he began a slow and limping walk across the main street to the inn. It served him right for traveling without Martin again. Each time he left his valet for one of his short country jaunts, he had to deal with stern looks and protests. Now he'd have to face an "I-told-you-so" attitude along with the usual harangue when he returned to the city. The anticipated verbal scuffle brought a lopsided smile to his face.

"Jeremy? I say, Jeremy old chap, is that you?"

"Why, Roger, what are you doing in these parts?"

"I live here, you idiot! I think that question is a better one from me to you. What *ever* are you doing here and in such poor dress? Just look at your boots, man! Don't tell me you've sacked the amazing Martin? Why, he's a legend!"

Jeremy crossed the street to meet Roger, and they warmly shook hands. He was glad to see a familiar face in this good friend of his father's, but the hardy clap on his shoulder brought a sharp grimace to his face.

"Are you hurt? Come sit down in the tap room and refresh yourself with some home brew. Mighty good stuff, too." Roger guided him through the door and over to an empty bench as he called for two pints.

"I had a bit of an accident with a buggy this morning. My curricle saw the worst of it and is right now waiting for the blasted wheelwright to return from the mill I was here to attend." Even though Jeremy tried to put a humorous tone to the short tale, some bitterness crept into his voice. This was supposed to have been a fun weekend to help get his mind off the traitorous Colette.

"My coachman is a fine stand-in for the Colverton wheelwright if you're not busted up too badly. I'll send my man back to the house to have John come look at it. If he can fix it, you can be on your way tomorrow. And if you want, you can borrow one of my rigs today for the ride to your mill. See, all's not lost my boy, so cheer up!"

Jeremy was surprised at this quick generosity. Even if Roger were an old family friend, it was deuced nice of him to offer the services of servant and carriage to someone he had only a passing acquaintance with. But then, he knew his own father would help out one of his son's cronies if he happened upon one limping across the street in Sutherland.

"Why, thank you for the kind offer. I don't think the wheel is too much the worse for the crash, but the axle seems a little off. I would appreciate any help your John can offer. I'm a trifle sore to jaunt off to the mill, though. I managed to fall off the seat after the crash. The girl told me I ought to be ashamed of my drunken stupor. It seems it was not a pretty sight."

"Girl? What girl? Are you traveling with someone?" asked an intrigued Roger.

"No, no. I, ah—well, I sort of hit someone else's buggy," said a sheepish Jeremy. He hastened to add, "She wasn't hurt and took off in a terror after I yelled at her. I'm afraid I was suffering the hair of the dog from the brandy this good landlord offered me last night. I wasn't in the best form, and the crash didn't help my manners much. 'Fraid I rather insulted her, whoever she was."

"By gad, a regular scoundrel in our midst. Well, you'll stay with us tonight if you won't press on to your mill. A good soaking in a hot tub will help your muscles, I'm sure. And if it doesn't, I have more of that good brandy." Roger winked at Jeremy.

It was a pleasant prospect that Jeremy readily accepted. A quiet evening in the country wasn't his usual style, but it would surely be welcome after today's excitement.

"Come then, we'll head home and send John back to look at the wheel and axle. My Emily will be in alt to add a new and mysterious young man to her table tonight. Perhaps it would be best, though, if we didn't tell her about the scoundrel part." They both laughed as they headed out the door.

THREE

THE PLAN BEGINS

The Edwardses' carriage rolled to a gentle stop in the Thompsons' drive at Hadley Abbey as Willie jumped down to open the door for the ladies. The night was chilly and clear, and Clara took a deep breath of the fresh air to give her energy for the evening ahead. While she wasn't nearly as upset as earlier this afternoon, she would have far preferred to spend the night curled up by the fire with her new novel.

They left their cloaks with a maid and headed into the drawing room at the top of the stairs. The room's warmth radiated from both the blazing fire and the air of good feeling from its occupants. Clara saw they were not the first to arrive—probably more likely the last—as her eyes quickly scanned the crowded room to take in the people gathered before dinner. She spotted Johnny Trent by the window mooning over Emma Thompson and headed over to rescue her friend. Really, Johnny could be so predictable sometimes.

"Emma, you look lovely," Clara said, "Have you done your hair differently? Hello, Johnny."

"I say, it is capital, Em. How-to-do, Clara," piped in Johnny.

"Oh, Clara, thank you for noticing," Emma said as she raised her hand to touch her hair. "Yes, I had Amy try something from the latest copy of *La Belle Assembly*. You like it?"

"Certainly, yes, it gives you such a regal air. Much too elegant for all of us here. It will be all the rage next month in London, to be sure."

"Oh, stop! You'll make me blush here in front of everyone." But Emma wouldn't have been a normal girl not to enjoy the compliment and the attention.

Clara gladly took a cool glass of punch that the footman served from his tray. The larger than normal crowd had started to make the room noticeably warm. She took a delicate sip and wished it could have been an unladylike gulp. Well, another quick sip wouldn't be noticed. Fickle Johnny had wandered off in search of another damsel to distress.

She enjoyed Emma's company and had counted her a good friend these past seven years, despite the almost four years' difference in their ages. The Thompsons had moved to the area around Colverton when a great-uncle had left them the estate. Ever since Emma had returned from Miss Phillips's Academy two years ago, the girls had been especially close, and now she would be traveling to London in just a fortnight for her come-out. The big day had almost arrived, and Clara could see that Emma couldn't have been happier. Why, she positively radiated, and it couldn't be just the new hairstyle.

"What's put you in such a wonderful mood, Em? You seem to be glowing."

"Haven't you seen him? Even though dark hair isn't my preference, I could make an exception in his case. He's positively perfect! I never knew Papa had such wonderful friends, and, best of all, he's going to be in

London next month for the Season. He's over by the piano talking with Mama and the vicar."

Clara smiled at her enthusiasm and looked over in the direction to where Emma had tossed her head. She had no inkling of foreboding and expected to see a rather dapper, refined gentleman. Instead she gasped in shock and was sure the whole room could have heard her cry. How could *he* be here? What would she do?

"Clara, oh Clara, what is it?" asked Emma. "You're white as a ghost. Are you feeling all right? Here, sit down on the window seat and rest. Shall I call your mother for you?"

Clara made a less than graceful plop onto the window seat. "Oh Em, it can't be! The man's a brute and called me some horrible names today when he crashed his curricle into my buggy. Why is he here?" she wailed.

"Shush! Heavens, people will hear you. Do you mean to say you know him? Why, Clara, how lucky you are!"

"*Lucky?* Emma Thompson, if you aren't the meanest friend a girl could have. Didn't you hear me? The man insulted me and doesn't deserve to be in this good company and fawned over by a silly girl."

Clara hardly realized how cruel her small speech had been, so upset was she by this unexpected turn. Fortunately for her, Emma was the best of friends and didn't take the words to heart. She immediately came to Clara's defense.

"Well, I never! Imagine the blackguard darkening our door. I'll have to tell Mama immediately, and she'll have Papa throw him out on his ear. Would that make you happy?" Emma rose to go to her mother.

"Emma, no!" Clara grabbed her skirt to pull her back down next to her on the window seat. "You mustn't make a scene. I'd be mortified if everyone here knew what had happened. I'll just tell Mama I have the headache from the crowd of people. She'll understand

and not make me stay for dinner. Please walk with me while I find her. And try to appear normal!"

The girls began their walk across the room to Clara's mother. She was on the far side talking with two other women, and awfully close to the piano and him! It would be tricky to reach her mother without coming into view of the man she most wanted to avoid. As they walked, the girls were stopped a number of times by friends saying hello. *Will we ever reach her?* wondered Clara. Just as the prize was near, Mrs. Thompson called to her daughter.

"Emma, darling, please come over. I want to introduce Clara to our guest. I've seated them together at dinner and feel they should at least know each other first with a proper introduction." Little did she realize the irony of her words—"Proper introduction," indeed!

"Ignore her," whispered a desperate Clara.

"I can't just keep going. She knows I heard her. She saw me looking right at her. Oh Clara, we're doomed!"

"Emma, dear. Did you hear me? Please come here." Mrs. Thompson's voice carried a tone that did not allow for disobedience.

Clara pushed Emma over to the calling woman but kept walking to her own mother. Had he seen her yet? She must find some way to leave without causing a scene, and one seemed to be developing right in front of her. Would she ever be able to go home?

"Clara, didn't you hear Mrs. Thompson asking to speak with you? That was quite rude, dear, and not at all like you." Marie Edwards had left the women she was talking with to come over and admonish her daughter.

"Oh Mama, it's him!" Clara hissed under her breath in desperation.

But before she could explain any further, Emily Thompson was at her side.

"Clara, you are a slippery one. Marie, Clara, may I present Lord Jeremy Carruthers. His father is a long-time friend of Roger's. He's staying with us for a few days. Jeremy, this is Marie Edwards and her lovely daughter, Clara. They are our neighbors, and Clara is a bosom bow of my daughter, Emma." Emily fairly crowed the words as her matchmaking mind worked overtime.

The two central characters to this melodrama finally looked each other eye to eye. As Jeremy stared down at Clara's face, something seemed familiar. Awfully odd girl to be looking at him so strangely—almost like she wanted to do him harm. And her blushes seemed out of place as well. Oh well, these country folk could be a bit different sometimes.

"Pleased to meet you ladies." He executed a small bow of introduction.

"Good evening, my lord," said Marie.

Clara felt her mother's elbow poke into her side, and hard, too. She had to say something or the small crowd around them would think her a ninny.

"Good evening, my lord." She hoped all her hurt and anger came through in those four uninteresting words.

"Well, now that's settled, and I see Horace at the door. Dinner must be ready," said Emily.

And as she finished speaking, the butler announced, "Dinner is served."

Marie could see that her daughter was upset but was at a loss as to why. She had seemed fine during the carriage ride. What could have happened to overset her so and cause her to blush at a simple introduction?

Harold came over to offer his wife his arm for the walk into dinner. Marie introduced the two men, and the short interlude gave Clara a small amount of time to collect her dignity. She could only hope the warmth of her face would cool shortly.

"I understand we are to sit next to each other. May I escort you into the dining room?" Jeremy extended his arm to Clara.

She was trapped and could see no way to extricate herself from such a horrible prospect as four hours in his company. Would she be able to endure it?

He felt a fool with his arm out to this silly girl who seemed to ignore him. What was wrong with the women in these parts? First that charmer this morning and now this one. *Must be related,* he laughed to himself. Most everyone had already moved out the door toward the dining room, and they were left in relative solitude.

"I will sit next to you since I must, but I cannot make polite conversation. I consider your behavior to me this morning on the road as inexcusable and insulting. You do not deserve my attention." Clara was proud she could say the words quietly and calmly.

Jeremy drew in his breath with a start. *Damn!* It was the same girl. No wonder she had looked familiar. How was he to know? She looked vastly different in this charming evening gown. He made a hasty attempt to mend his fences.

"Please accept my apologies for this morning. You are right, it was inexcusable and insulting, and I am truly sorry to have caused you embarrassment or discomfort." He didn't know how he could apologize more sincerely. He only hoped she would understand he did mean what he said.

Clara couldn't just forgive and forget, as he seemed to feel she should. The hurt and humiliation were still too fresh in her mind and only intensified with every glance at him. She would have to find a way to get through this evening and only hoped he had a lively conversationalist at his other side.

"Shall we go in to dinner?" She finally took his arm and turned them to the doorway without acknowledging his apology.

Jeremy looked down at her as they walked into dinner. She just stared straight ahead and continued to ignore him. Well, it looked to be a less than interesting evening with this statue at his side during the meal.

As they seated themselves at the large table, Clara immediately began making small talk with the gentleman to her right. At such a large gathering, protocol allowed for conversations with only the two people seated on either side of you, and it was considered quite bad *ton* if you pointedly left out one of them. Well, she expected she would be labeled any sort of ill-mannered mouse for her upcoming behavior, but she couldn't force inconsequential drivel from her mouth with the beast to her left.

Happily, the delightful Mr. Robbins sat at her right. He was something of a local curiosity as a retired Oxford don who continued his passion for ornithology in their county. It was to him that Harry had come calling just a fortnight past, so Clara could find much to talk about that interested them both. She only hoped the woman on the other side of Mr. Robbins would not try to talk to him too soon.

Clara felt she had won a small victory when she finished the first course with nary a word to the odious Lord Carruthers. She did acknowledge it was ever so small a victory, since Emily Thompson was known for her endless dinners which often threatened to burst many a stomach. Seven courses each with four or five removes were not uncommon, and Clara had long ago learned to pick daintily at her food.

Jeremy could see she was true to her word, or promised lack of them to him. So she planned on giving him a silent treatment, did she? Well he'd play along with her game, but not from any sense of defeat at her hands—he just didn't know what to say to the chit. Oh, he did feel guilty enough for what he'd done and said this morning and recognized it for extremely bad *ton*. But he had tried to apologize after all, and didn't that count for something? Unfortunately he knew he carried all the blame in this incident and the apology was a small recompense for her wounds.

The middle of the second course proved to be Clara's undoing. Mr. Robbins's attention moved to his other companion, and she was left staring at her plate. As she sipped her wine and glanced at the other guests, she noticed silence at her left side. Apparently his lordship had no one to talk with either.

"Well, Miss Edwards, are you enjoying this tasty meal?"

She continued to eat in silence. Her eyes pointedly ignored his presence, but fortunately everyone else was so involved in their own conversations and gossips that their small drama went unnoticed.

"Miss Edwards? Are you feeling well?" He kept his voice low—no point in calling attention to this idiotic situation.

At this question, Clara turned to stare him in the eye. She refused to say anything to him as long as it was possible, and with no audience to their one-sided sparring, she felt her confidence grow. *My plate was quite interesting,* she smiled to herself as she turned her eyes downward once again.

Why bother with her? thought Jeremy. She wouldn't say anything unless forced to by others to save face.

Clara was wrong in her assumption that no one noticed their strange *tête-à-tête*. Both her mother and Emma had kept a watchful eye on her end of the table. While Mrs. Edwards had no notion as to the problem, she did see that Clara seemed to ignore that new man next to her. Where were her manners? Why, this was the second time tonight she had been so poor in her behavior.

Emma, however, felt helpless as she watched her friend suffer so. She recognized the silent treatment as Clara's defense against a man she could not bear to be around. Emma's heart went out to her, but there was little she could do from across the wide table. When she glanced over as the second course was cleared, she saw that they continued to eat in silence. Would anyone else see?

At the first lull in the conversation to her right during the third course, Clara fairly pounced on Mr. Robbins for attention. The poor man would have his fill of her prattle by the meal's end. And even Clara could see that she had started an inane conversation this time—the route to Oxford was in all the guidebooks, for heaven's sake!

This strange meal continued in this strange vein for two more hours, and Clara and Jeremy spoke no other words to each other. At one point Clara caught her mother's eye and read disapproval in her look. Her nerves were close to a frazzle as she readily stood up with the other ladies to remove herself to the drawing room. She was happy to leave the gentlemen to enjoy their brandy and cigars. She had survived!

The drawing room was abuzz with the strange behavior they had witnessed at the dinner table. As the meal had drawn on, just about every lady there had found a reason to glance at the charming and handsome newcomer. It was hard not to notice that he spent half his meal in silence and often Clara had sat just as silently next to him. Something was afoot, and the ladies were anxious for a good story. While Clara was a favorite in the parish, a good gossip was impervious to its central character among country folk. With all eyes upon her, Clara hardly realized she was headed for just the attention she'd hoped to avoid.

As Clara entered the drawing room, she looked for an empty spot away from the center of the room. She saw the window seat she and Emma had occupied before dinner and headed towards her haven.

Marie saw her daughter enter the room and noticed the haggard look on her face. What was wrong? Well, enough of this mystery. She would get to the bottom of this strange situation, and now! As Clara sat down, her mother reached the window seat. She joined her daughter and with a stern look shooed away the nosy onlookers.

"Now, young lady, I want an explanation for your behavior at dinner tonight. Everyone saw that you and Lord Carruthers were at odds—why, you might have just worn a sign that said, "'I'm rude and unmannered.'"

"Oh, Mama, I tried to tell you before Mrs. Thompson introduced us before dinner." The pain of the uncomfortable evening was evident in Clara's quiet voice.

"Tell me what, dear?"

"Why, Lord Carruthers was the man who treated me so shabbily this morning!"

"No! It couldn't be! How could this gentleman have so forgotten himself and abused you so? Has he no manners?"

"Oh he apologized in the proper way, but just looking at him was too much a strain for me. Dinner was a fiasco and quite the worst meal I've ever experienced."

"Well, you'll just have to put him out of your mind. You won't have to see him again after tonight, and no one here need ever know."

"But I already told Emma when we first saw him before dinner. She won't say anything, but her mother is sure to ask her if my behavior was so remarked on by everyone. Oh, I just want to die!"

"Nonsense! You'll do no such thing. You're in the right of it here and can hold your head high. Any lady would simply ignore a person not worthy of her notice—you did just the right thing, my dear. You mustn't let him defeat you with his boorish behavior this morning. I realize you don't want to face him again, but you'll put all these gossips to rout if you behave as if nothing were amiss."

"You mean talk to him? Oh Mama, no, please don't make me!" Clara's voice came dangerously close to a wail and attracted notice from the ladies nearby.

"If it would pain you so, well, I suppose you can just take part in the rest of the evening's entertainment. I don't imagine he will seek you out, and you can stay here on the window seat until we can make a graceful exit."

"Oh, thank you! I promise to be quiet and a model of good manners for the rest of the night. I'll sit with Emma, and we can talk about her Season or some other triviality."

Mrs. Edwards arose from her seat and headed over to her hostess. She had but a few seconds to come up with a plausible reason for her daughter's behavior these past hours, and her mind worked furiously as she walked. She passed Emma as the girl hurried over to her friend to offer comfort.

"Oh, Clara! Are you all right? How ever did you manage to survive such an ordeal?"

"I'm fine, Em. Mostly mad that he is here and I've had to face him. Much as I don't want word of this morning's meeting to get out, I would so enjoy for him to be recognized for the scoundrel he is. Masquerading as a gentleman among these good people—why, he's a fraud and should be exposed to all."

"You mustn't," said a scandalized Emma.

"Oh, don't worry. I'll behave myself tonight. I plan on keeping my distance from the man and staying here in the background. Tell me about your plans for London."

As the girls continued their conversation, the other women in the room could only wonder at the mystery at dinner. No one wanted to be so rude as to come right out and ask Marie why her daughter had behaved so strangely, so the buzz soon turned to other topics. Shortly, the vicar's wife was coaxed into playing the pianoforte, and the ladies settled into the usual evening entertainment. The men would soon join them for the tea tray.

Clara's embarrassment had abated much by the time the doors swung open to admit the men. She was content to sit quietly and leave for home as soon as it was polite. Unfortunately, she hadn't counted on a mannerless Johnny to spoil her calm.

"I say, Clara, what was that spectacle at dinner with you and Carruthers? He was mum in the dining room, but I knew you'd tell me."

"Hush, Johnny! Oh, do go away, and be a little more circumspect in your questions. Can't you at least try to be a gentleman and leave a lady alone?" asked an exasperated Emma.

"Well, I say, Em. What are you so touchy about? Clara was the one making a cake of herself at the dinner table, not you. Who ever heard of someone not speaking to her dinner companion? Bad *ton*, Clara, bad *ton* indeed."

"Who made you the arbiter of fashion tonight, Johnny Trent? Now go away! And I mean now," Emma snapped. As Johnny ambled off, she turned her attention back to Clara only to find her near to tears.

"I have to leave here before I disgrace myself. Please,

Emma, vouch for me if my mother asks about me. Say I tore my dress, anything to explain my absence for a few minutes while I compose myself." And Clara slipped out the side door to escape the crowd and the man.

Jeremy had watched her all the while he was in the room. He could see that young cub Trent had bothered her. Drat the boy, but what could he do? He'd already apologized once tonight, and he didn't want to call attention to her antipathy with another rebuff. At least Trent was moving away from her now. But where was she going out that door? Jeremy stood near to the back of the room and neatly exited during the applause that followed the end of the song.

He came upon her in the library. Every candle was lit as he quietly entered the room. Empty except for the two of them. Jeremy thought he could try one more time to offer his regrets for the morning's behavior. He cleared his throat in anticipation, and she jumped at the sound.

"You! Please, leave me alone. It has been hard enough to endure this evening without having to talk to you."

"Please, Miss Edwards, I have to speak with you. Can't you believe me when I say how sorry I am for my ill-mannered behavior and coarse language earlier today? I can have no excuse for the way I treated you, and the whole miserable incident was entirely my fault."

He looked at her with a true expression of regret and obvious embarrassment. She could see that in his face. She also noticed the dark hair falling across his brow and clasped her traitorous hands behind her back. She didn't break the silence between them.

"I can see your distress, and I would take back the morning if I could. I should probably start by taking back the night before and the brandy I drank. You were quite right to accuse me of drunkenness at eleven o'clock this morning, Miss Edwards, but it is not my usual style. The liquor made my manners disappear, and the fall didn't help my dignity much either. I can only tell you that I am normally a gentleman who respects a lady and treats her with proper honor and kindness."

More silence, and it just drove him to say more words. Words better left unsaid.

"And if you had had a maid with you, or even a groom in attendance, I would have known you were not just a country miss. But with your frayed habit and solitary state, I mistook you for, for—well, not for yourself. You obviously haven't had much experience with men, and my behavior came as something of a shock. More of a shock than I had realized for someone of your years. Oh, I'm making a mess of this." And Jeremy pulled his hand through his hair as he tried to think of some way to extricate himself from the muddle caused by his errant tongue. What was it about this girl that made him make such a cake of himself, and twice in the same day?

"Very well, my lord. I accept your very honorable and kind apology for your actions this morning." Clara struggled to keep her voice even and hoped her tears wouldn't start now. She had responded in a monotone but couldn't help stressing the word *kind* as she acknowledged the rambling apology. Really, the man would just get into deeper trouble if she let him keep talking! Maybe he would just be quiet and leave her be if she cut him off with her own words.

Such an overwhelming acceptance! Well, he supposed it was better than her silence from before. Certainly a far cry from the fawning mamas and marriageable daughters he usually experienced in the *ton*.

"Thank you, Miss Edwards. I appreciate your own

kindness. Now, may I escort you back to the drawing room where we can rejoin the party?"

Such correct words now from the oh-so-correct Lord Carruthers. She supposed he thought everything was all right now. She could just imagine the gossip were she to reappear on his arm at the drawing room door. No, she would have to slip back in as she had exited—through the side door, and by herself.

"Thank you, but no. I prefer to remain here for a few more minutes."

"As you wish." He nodded his head in farewell and took his leave.

Clara could hold back her tears no longer, and one small droplet slid down her cheek followed by another, and then another. Why did she let this man unsettle her so? She should put it all behind her, since it was obvious to her that he had no further qualms after his apology. Were all men so cavalier in their dealings with women, or maybe just the women they wronged in some way?

Clara moved over to the French doors and parted the draperies. The night sky glittered brightly with the stars. She stared for a long time at those faraway stars, and it calmed her tears. She thought about the day's events and this unlikely conclusion. Would she be able to just forget, as he now seemed to have done?

But the things he'd said both this morning and tonight were etched on her mind. Her foolish driving! Harridan! Liking prettier women with more flesh in the *right* places! Inexperienced with men! Her solitary state! Someone of her years! As she remembered each phrase, it only added fuel to her returning anger. It didn't matter to Clara that perhaps some of the comments about her might be true. Oh no, the more she thought about him, the more she realized he was a pompous lord too used to getting his own way. And she had done just as he'd expected when she'd accepted his apology so quickly a few minutes ago. Oh, she could just kick herself for making it so easy for him! He really deserved a setdown.

An angry Clara was not someone to be trifled with, but the unsuspecting Lord Carruthers had left the library with no knowledge of the coming storm. And had he known, he was powerless to stop the plot forming in Clara's crafty mind. For a plot to give him that setdown began to consume Clara as she stood at the window.

It must be something to do with driving, she thought. He seemed to set such store by his wonderful driving ability. She could maneuver him into a race, beat him, and show him up for a clumsy hack. But no, he'd never agree to race a mere miss, and her reputation would suffer in the bargain. She'd probably come out the loser no matter what happened in the race. And it would be no fun if he lost a race to someone else, even if she had arranged the meet.

What else held a high place in his regard? *Obviously himself,* she thought. But what could she do to lower himself in his own eyes? Compromising a lady might do it, but if she weren't willing to sacrifice her reputation for a horse race, she'd hardly do so just to take him down a peg. No, nothing quite so drastic. Really, this scheming was quite fun, and it was too bad Harry wasn't around to share the plotting. She'd have to write to him with the details—once she figured them out herself, that is!

Back to her plan. He set quite a store in his appearance and dress. Was there a way to maneuver him into falling off his horse into a large mud hole? Oh, the visual picture was delicious and did much to restore Clara to the good spirits she'd had when she set out on the fateful ride so long ago this morning. Perhaps she could talk to Emma about arranging a ride or a picnic tomorrow. There were sure to be wet patches on the ride. But how to make him fall? Oh, this was difficult! Harry had always been the one to think up their schemes, and here she was trying to do all the work herself. Well, she was an intelligent and capable woman, and she'd think of something to make him fall.

But maybe she was plotting the wrong kind of fall. He'd said this morning that he preferred prettier women with more flesh in the right places . . . could she be that woman to attract his fancy and then turn him down flat? What a wonderful fall that would be. She could go right back into that drawing room, turn him up sweet, and see him fall under her spell. Then turn him down flat!

Oh, who was she fooling? While she might look well in this evening gown, she was hardly the type to sweep a man off his feet. Those accolades belonged to her Aunt Sheila. She had been the beauty and quite a dazzler to the six-year-old Clara when she'd made her come-out. Now, if she could only outfit herself in a stunning gown with the lights of a thousand candles in a London ballroom, then she might have a chance to catch his eye.

Well, why not? Could she still accept Aunt Sheila's invitation to come to town for the Season? It would make perfect sense with Emma going up for her first Season, and Emma had said he would be there. And Sheila had such style—she could offer all kinds of help to make Clara into a beauty to catch his eye. Aunt Sheila need never know the real reason for her visit. And when he developed a *tendre* for her, it would be such fun to hold him off and squash his overtures. His fall would be doubly sweet when she reminded him that she was not his "usual" kind of woman. Oh, this plot was developing into a lovely setdown. She pushed aside any nagging fears about facing the matrons of society in London.

Clara had lost track of time as her plan had taken shape in her head, but she knew she should return to the drawing room. Emma's excuses could only last for so long before someone would come to look for her. With her tears long dried and her spirits restored, Clara left the library and slipped quietly back into the drawing room. The recital had ended, and she immediately saw Emma talking with him—the man she most wished to avoid.

No one seemed to notice her as she returned to her seat. She'd just sit here a few moments and then move over to join a conversation. If she appeared as calm on the outside as she now felt on the inside, no one would be the wiser for the horrible thoughts that spun through her head. She could mouth polite and amusing inanities for whatever amount of time she needed to see the evening to its close.

But anyone who looked closely would have seen a determined spark in Clara's eye and a slightly devious set to her faraway smile.

FOUR

PREPARING FOR THE SEASON

The next morning dawned as bright and blue as the previous day, and Clara woke with a renewed spirit. After splashing some cold water on her face, she tossed on her robe and hurried into her mother's room as that lady finished her morning chocolate.

"Clara, darling, how good to see you up so early. Are you recovered from last night's trial?"

"Yes, Mama. He is nothing but a nuisance to forget. I surely won't see him again at the Thompsons', and even if I did, I would just be the lady you raised me to be. Mama, I've decided to accept Aunt Sheila's offer to spend the Season with her in London." Clara's haste to finish her speech left her short of breath.

"What! Oh, darling, how wonderful! But what has made you change your mind so suddenly? Why, just last week you wouldn't listen to any of my pleadings or cajoling. And you know I tried to convince you of all the fun to be had during a Season."

Clara stopped short in her reply. She hadn't really

thought through her plan for a reason to give to her mother and aunt. She had just focused on her main objective and not given a thought to how her abrupt change of heart would appear to others. But if nothing else, Clara was a quick thinker.

"Why, Emma and I spent so much time discussing her come-out last night. She made it all sound so wonderful and exciting. Since you and Aunt Sheila are forever going on about the grand balls and wonderful musicales and delightful theater, it just seemed the right time to give it a try. And with someone to share it with, it just might be fun after all."

"Well, I certainly won't look twice to ask you why. We haven't a moment to lose to start your ensemble. Now we'll only order a few simple things here in town. Miss Martin is a wonderful seamstress but nothing like the modistes in London. We'll leave the bulk of your wardrobe to Sheila's capable hands. Oh good heavens! Sheila! My dear you must dispatch a note to her immediately so she'll know of your change of heart. Why she'll have a million things to do before you arrive to be sure. Please hand me the paper and pen from my table so I can start a list."

Clara sighed as she moved to do her mother's bidding. Another list. Mama was so organized it took all the fun and spontaneity out of doing anything. Now Clara remembered one of the many reasons she'd always said no to a Season the past three years. But, with all Clara had to plan, she thought she might do well to emulate her mother and start her own list to help her trap her prey.

"Thank you for the paper, dear. Now run along and write your note to Sheila. I know she will be thrilled when she receives it."

As Clara left, Mrs. Edwards began the first of many lists that would occupy her over the next fortnight. She did spend some time lost in thought as she tried to understand her usually predictable daughter's unpredictable turn. Even though the line about a Season with Emma made perfect sense, she knew there had to be more to this sudden change of heart. What could it be? The only disruption to their usually quiet lives was Harry's unexpected visit and Clara's contretemps with Lord Carruthers. Harry's visit had left her in the mopes, but it hardly seemed reason enough for her about-face on a Season. So that left Lord Carruthers. Could he be her reason for going up to town? It certainly didn't make sense when she wanted to avoid the man. And who even knew where he spent his time? It stood to reason, however, he'd be in London for the Season. What could her daughter be plotting?

Josie's entrance into the room to remove the chocolate tray interrupted Marie's train of thought, and by the time her maid left, she was back to her lists. With so much else to think about, Marie had little time for analyzing her daughter's motives.

In the meantime, Clara had returned to her room to dress for the day. Meg had laid out her gray morning dress, and Clara immediately threw open the wardrobe door for another selection. Nothing drab on this fine day! She spied one of her favorite morning dresses—the blue-flowered muslin with wide flounces—and grabbed it instantly. *Just the thing to face Mama's lists,* she giggled. She rang for Meg just as the girl brought in her morning chocolate.

"Oh, Meg, you're here. Thank you for the chocolate, but I think I'll dress now and have breakfast with Papa. Well, maybe just a sip while you do my hair."

"Yes, Miss." Meg set the tray near the dressing table.

"Meg, can you try a new hairstyle? Something dramatic and sophisticated?" asked a speculative Clara as she sat before the mirror.

"For the morning, Miss Clara? Whatever can you be thinking?"

"Oh you needn't be such a Puritan. Where else can I try out something new but at home? Mama will tell me if she thinks it looks well on me. I won't see anyone this morning. And Meg, we have to get ready for London, and you're coming with me!"

"London! Oh, Miss, don't ever say you've decided to go to town! And I am to go, too?"

"Well, of course, you silly goose! How else am I to get around without you to take care of me? You know I depend on you, Meg. Who else could care for my clothes and hair so well?"

"Oh, Miss," and the usually boisterous Meg blushed a tomato red at the compliment. "How you do go on."

"So, what will it be for my hair today? We have a fortnight 'til we leave, so you'll have plenty of mornings to create something new and exciting. Emma said she had tried something from *La Belle Assembly,* so I'll have to search out Mama's copy for us to look at this afternoon."

Meg soon went to work on creating a smooth and exotic twist with Clara's long blond tresses. She knew it wasn't appropriate for morning, but Miss Clara had said to try something sophisticated, and Meg knew that this style would cause a stir. As the hairstyle took shape, Clara clapped her hands in delight.

"Meg, you're amazing! How did you ever learn to do this . . . and why have you never done it before?"

"Well you never asked for it, Miss Clara. Since we're always in the country, it was never the right occasion. I used to do some real fancy hair for Lady Dawes before marrying my Jem and coming here five years ago. I guess I haven't forgotten."

As Clara stood up to go down to breakfast she leaned over and gave Meg a hug. With Meg's help she would surely catch that certain someone's eye when she arrived in London.

Clara did feel a little self-conscious as she walked downstairs to the dining room. She knew her hair was overdone for this early an hour, but it would be fun to try something new each morning. Meg could always change it back to a more acceptable style before luncheon and the arrival of any visitors. And with dinner times, too, she could try twice as many new styles. As she approached the open dining room door, Clara really did hope her father had finished his meal and retired to the estate room.

But Clara had to face both her parents. Apparently, styling her hair had taken more time than she realized, and her mother had preceded her downstairs. She stood now at the sideboard filling her plate, but her father had finished his meal, and sat reading the paper to keep his wife company. Clara wondered if her mother had mentioned her change in plans to her father.

"Well, good morning, slowpoke," came the affectionate greeting from Mr. Edwards as he folded the paper.

"Hello, Papa."

"My, my, what have we here? Is there a ball after breakfast that you forgot to tell me about, Marie? It seems that Clara is ready to go now! What are you up to, Missy?"

"Darling, it looks lovely, but isn't it a bit much for breakfast?" came Mrs. Edwards's bewildered reply.

"Do you really like it, Mama? I know it isn't the thing for this hour, but I couldn't resist trying something new. I felt like such a dowdy one last night next to Emma with my usual hairdo, and I plan on new styles each day before I leave."

"Leave? Where are you going?" Now Mr. Edwards's face shared the look of his wife's bewilderment.

"Mama didn't tell you?"

"No, I thought you might like to tell your father yourself, dear," her mother said.

"Tell me what! What are you two plotting behind my back?" But Clara knew he wasn't truly upset—she could hear the laughter in his voice.

"Well, Papa, I've decided to have my Season in London this year."

"Will wonders never cease! It's about time, young lady, though you might have decided earlier in the month to give your mother and aunt more time to plan. Though I suppose they'll be able to have you rigged out in record time. Well, Mother, she finally came to her senses, and you didn't have to enlist Harry's help to convince her."

"What does Harry have to do with this?" asked Clara.

"Oh, nothing. Your father is just trying my patience! I told him last night that I might write to Harry and ask him to write you about accepting a Season. It really is too bad of you, Harold, to be telling Clara something I told you in confidence." She had a delicate pout on her mouth that showed her words were not entirely in jest.

"Now, sweetheart," said a chagrined Mr. Edwards, "I didn't mean to speak out of turn—I guess I'm still a bit shocked at this surprising change of plans. Why the sudden turnabout, young lady?" His gaze fell sharply on his daughter. It wasn't like her to be a flighty miss.

Clara was prepared for the question this time.

"Oh, Papa, I guess I finally caught the society bug from Emma last night. We talked together after dinner, and I found myself envious of her excitement." *It isn't a complete lie,* she thought. She truly was finding country life a bit boring and predictable these past months, and an extended trip might be fun—even without her scheme to bring a certain someone to his knees. It was a small salve to her conscience, though.

"It certainly took you long enough to agree to the Season, though I expect having a close friend to share the balls and routs and goings-on can only make it more fun and a bit less daunting for a county girl."

"Papa! Just because we live in the country doesn't make me a simpleton!" Why did men equate county living with a lack of sophistication—just like that certain someone?

"Well, dear, no matter the reason, I for one am very happy you've decided to make the trip. Your mother and I do worry that you'll waste away here at the manor, and I know your Aunt Sheila has been disappointed each time you refused her invitation to come to town. She does enjoy that social whirl I find so tiresome." He rattled the newspaper as if to begin reading again now that he'd finished speaking on the subject.

"Oh, not so fast, my dear," said his cheery wife. "I fully intend to spend part of the season watching our beautiful daughter become the toast of the debutantes, and I do not plan to go to town unescorted. Now I'm sure Clara can ride with Emma in the Thompsons' coach for the trip to town, but you had better polish your dancing shoes for her come-out ball. Tiresome social whirl, indeed!"

Clara smiled at her parents as they continued their playful squabble and pushed aside that twinge of guilt for deceiving them. They were so happy for her, and her small plan seemed so insignificant right now.

Jeremy threw down his cards in disgust. He'd just played the third hand in a row where he was sure he'd had the better of his opponents only to lose. His mind hadn't been attending today, or for the past few days if he were to admit the truth.

"Ho! Another win for me," said Richard "Dickers" Smythe-Hattan as he pulled in the chips. "That makes seven tonight, Jeremy. I don't think I've ever had such good fortune from you since you taught me this blasted game." The smile he sent Jeremy's way showed pure glee at his turn of the cards.

"I say, you have had a rather bad run haven't you?" Edward Waters looked at his friend with speculation. "Not like you to lose to a flat such as Dickers."

Jeremy made a small grin as Dickers boasted loudly that it was his skill that gave him the wins. Edward was right, it wasn't like him to lose to anyone, let alone a player as poor as Dickers. He looked at his two good friends and decided he'd better end his gaming now before he went home with empty pockets.

"Gentleman, I bid you good night," Jeremy said as he pushed his chair back from the table.

"What, leaving just when I'm beginning to get the hang of this game? Not very sporting of you, man," Dickers gave him that hurt puppy dog look that made him such a favorite with the debutantes and their mamas.

"Care to come out to the Harleys' ball later with us?" asked Edward. "It might bring you out of the sulks."

"Ah, yes, you must see the Fair Incomparable! A fire of red hair that makes the others look pasty," Dickers added.

"Maybe another night. I'm not much in the mood for a party now. I'll see you at Tattersalls at noon tomorrow to look at that new pair of greys." He moved away from their table to the receding protests of Dickers.

Jeremy couldn't fathom his ill humor these days. He didn't keep his mind on the topic when conversing, gaming, riding, or even walking, it seemed, as he stumbled over his own feet. As he leaned against the card room wall to relax his bruised toes, he reflected that perhaps it was best that Colette was out of his life. God knows where a night with her would lead him right now, and he shuddered at the thought.

He thought back over his past few days here in town and couldn't find any event that might have triggered these new feelings. Since returning from that singularly strange country trip, he'd spent his days visiting his clubs, going to a race at the downs, and ordering some new clothes from Weston. His nights found him again at his clubs or at dinner with Edward and Dickers. *Nothing unusual there,* he thought.

He'd been at school with Edward, and they met the younger Dickers several years ago at an out-of-town race. The three spent much of their time together and found themselves in much of the same frame of mind concerning politics, women, and horses—and not necessarily in that order.

Edward was in a marriageable mood and had been frequenting the evening balls and routs. He'd even gone so far as to present himself at Almacks several times last season. Only the three of them knew of his search, and Dickers had been most amiable about accompanying his friend on his "evening rounds," as they'd started to call the season of parties.

Though the Season had barely started, Edward had again begun attending the parties. Jeremy only hoped his intentions could be kept from the mamas of the young girls while Edward took his time in the looking. He knew only too well what it was like to be pursued by encroaching mamas bent on finding the most advantageous matches for their darlings. While Edward's prospects did not include a title, his fortune and impeccable birth would make him a high prize indeed.

Jeremy didn't feel any strong urge to marry, even though he and Edward were of the same age at two and thirty. His three younger sisters were married, and happily, it seemed. And he had a basketful of nieces and nephews, ten at last count. His sisters seldom came to town for the Season any more, preferring their country estates and the family life. He did envy them that, he admitted ruefully to himself.

He knew that he would have had to pay more attention to the family estates if his father did not take such a strong interest in their management. Rather than speaking before Parliament or playing cards at his clubs, the Marquess of Sutherdown truly preferred traveling among their properties, seeing to the tenants' needs and meeting with the bailiffs to go over accounts, crop rotations, and repairs.

Jeremy had spent three years at it several years ago to make sure he could step into his father's shoes when the time came, hopefully some far distant date. He went home at least once a quarter and often found himself touring the estates with his father and calling on tenants with his mother. It would all be his someday, he mused with pride.

He found himself reflecting on life far too much lately. Was he missing something? Certainly not the fair Colette, but he would welcome some female companionship. Finding a replacement didn't interest him, though. The effort to find and woo and eventually lose another one left him stone cold, and that surprised him. Was it a wife he looked for, like his friend?

What an astonishing thought! He glanced around him in the club wondering if the others noticed. Silly of him, he grinned, as if they could read through his face. He saw Dickers and Edward rise from their table and head away from him toward the door. Maybe he would go with them to the Harleys' and see the red-headed Incomparable, though shining blond tresses sprung to mind. He moved away from the fireside and caught up with them as they ambled out the door.

The packing had begun in earnest two days before Clara would start for London. She never imagined there could be such a good deal of preparation for just one person.

Miss Martin had made up a few morning dresses for her, and her wardrobe wasn't as bad as Mama kept saying. Why, so many of her beautiful clothes would do just fine, she was sure. Certainly the evening clothes suitable for London's drawing rooms would have to be made after her arrival, but she felt Aunt Sheila would see that her wardrobe was more than suitable.

Clara held up one of those new dresses and pressed the soft muslin to her face. It was a beautiful shade of pale yellow with a delightful flounce at the hem and yards of lace to adorn the bodice and sleeves. She saw herself posing in Aunt Sheila's morning room looking over to see him standing in the doorway.

Nonsense! How ever would she make him take notice of her? He must know everyone and everything about London and the Season. How was she, a green girl, going to catch his practiced eye? Oh, how she hoped Aunt Sheila could work a miracle! A knock at her door brought Clara back from her daydream as her mother came into the room.

"A letter from Harry for you, dear, and another one from Aunt Sheila. Ah, I see that Meg has begun your packing. It is good to start early even if you are taking so few things from your own wardrobe closets." Her mother settled next to her on the large bed.

"What do you mean 'so few things,' Mama? I have mountains of clothing to take with me for the Season."

"Clara, honey, we discussed this before, and I'm sure your Aunt Sheila will echo what I've said. A country wardrobe will be a sure albatross to your success. Your new clothes and a few of your old wardrobe will see you through the first few days, but you mustn't think of attending *any* social function until your London clothes arrive."

"But Mama, it all seems like an exorbitant expense. Yes, I love a new dress now and again, but an entire wardrobe with evening gowns and a court dress is just too much."

"Well, you've only begun to describe the new clothes, dear. You'll have morning gowns, afternoon ensembles, at-home evening wear, the beautiful evening gowns that just can't be worn twice in a Season, new riding habits, carriage dresses, walking dresses, several capes, and cloaks. And then there are the fripperies to complete the outfits with: gloves, hats, shawls, and the unmentionables in the finest silks to smooth your skin."

"Mama, stop! I won't have you and Papa buying all that nonsense." Clara laughed in spite of herself. Her mother had been so earnest with her descriptions and now looked so sad at the abrupt end to the narration.

Mrs. Edwards did smile at her foolish goings-on but gave her daughter a thoughtful look.

"My dear, I don't want you to worry about the expense or feel you are too extravagant. A Season is a wonderful time in a young girl's life, and it should be enjoyed to its fullest and not cause you any guilt or misgivings."

Guilt, thought Clara. She was going to London for all the wrong reasons, and it was hard to forget that she had created such a lie. Her parents had always been everything that was wonderful to her.

Her silence only convinced Mrs. Edwards that her daughter was going to scrimp and save on her wardrobe and probably anything else that would hold down the cost. There was only one thing to do—she'd send a letter to dear Sheila to make sure she hid the cost from Clara!

"Mama, maybe this idea of a Season isn't such a good one."

"Now Clara, I'll have none of that talk unless I thought you truly had no interest in going. Why, Emma would be so disappointed if you did not share in all the fun with her. You must look to the time as an adventure where you'll meet people, see unimagined sights, and experience a whole new life. Why, you might even meet a man you could love as I met your Papa and Sheila met her Marcus."

Clara was sure the look of a guilty conscience must be all over her face, whatever guilt looked like.

"And don't feel as if you've failed if that special someone doesn't come along right away. Sheila ignored Marcus for two Seasons until she felt ready to settle down. I think she enjoyed herself too much during her come-out!" Mama laughed as she remembered several summers back.

Clara thought about what her mother had said. Only she and Harry knew about "the plan," and he certainly wouldn't tell anyone. Maybe she could have two purposes to this Season—have fun *and* bring a certain gentleman down a peg or two.

Clara reached over to give her mother a hug. "I suppose it won't be so bad to wear new clothes practically every day, attend the theater, see the sights of London with Emma, and dance the night away," she teased.

"That's the spirit!" With that, mother and daughter continued talking until they went downstairs to luncheon.

FIVE

LONDON AT LAST

The carriage ride had been long and bumpy and dusty even in the Thompsons' well-sprung and luxurious traveling coach. Clara longed to delicately rub her backside as she stepped down in front of Aunt Sheila's townhouse. Oh, but it was a lovely home situated so snugly in the square.

The doors burst open as her feet touched the ground, and she heard an indecorous shriek of delighted welcome from her aunt.

"Darling Clara, you're here at last," Lady Sheila Clifton cried as she swooped down on the arrivals. She enveloped Clara in an enthusiastic hug and then turned her face to greet the other two ladies in the traveling party.

"So wonderful to see you both again, Emily," she said warmly, and then included Emma in her greeting as she focused her beaming smile on the girl. "I know you probably want to hurry to your own home, but can I tempt you with a cold collation to give you a restorative?"

"Why that would be lovely, Sheila. It is still early in

the afternoon yet, but we haven't eaten anything but a bit of bread and cheese since breakfast at the White House Inn."

"Reilly will see that your staff have a rest and something to eat. Would you like your carriage brought 'round to your home so the town staff can begin the unpacking? Our Jeames can see to it for you."

"Oh, Sheila, you do think of everything," Emily replied, giving her a grateful and ever-so-tired smile as the party moved up the front steps into the house.

"Aunt Sheila, it is as beautiful as I remember it," breathed Clara. The house truly was a magnificent place and reflected Sheila's elegant style and taste. She had an indulgent and wealthy husband who also appreciated the beauty she created with the furnishings.

"You do flatter me," Sheila said with a smile. "I so enjoy the decorating that I've threatened Marcus with more here or at Cliftside if he doesn't purchase a hunting box. He just points me to the Dower House, but I've redone it twice since we married—it's hardly a challenge for me now." And they all laughed with her foolishness.

They entered the elegant drawing room where delicate sandwiches, biscuits, and tea awaited their pleasure. The girls exclaimed together that the "cold collation" had more the appearance of an early tea, but they were delighted with the treats.

"Now, Sheila, you must tell us all the news of town. We've felt somewhat isolated in the country and will depend on you to bring us *au courant,*" said Emily as she settled into a comfortable chair.

"The Season has barely begun, so we are rather thin of parties now. The next fortnight ought to see that change, though," Sheila replied, handing Emily a cup of tea. The girls had already filled their plates with treats before Sheila had the second cup poured.

"Millicent Farleigh arrived in town but two days ago," Sheila said. "She has her darling twins to launch, and the *on dit* is she will have them dress alike! Madame Villette told me yesterday at my fitting that she has the order for two identical ensembles." And both ladies shook their heads at the nonsense of it.

"Such a shame," said Emily sadly. "Has she no regard for how those poor girls will be treated? I suppose she only wants to live up to her image as an 'original,' and I can but hope the girls' sunny nature will carry the day for them. Fortunately, they will each have ten thousand as a dowry, and that will go a long way toward smoothing their path into society. Do you recommend Madame for Emma's wardrobe?"

"For a few of her more elaborate evening gowns, perhaps. Madame Villette tends to overdo herself in my opinion. I think you'd do much better with Mademoiselle Francoise. She makes most of my clothes and those for many of the new debutantes. She has a fine eye for fashion style and always has a wonderful array of exquisite to simple fabrics from which to choose. I have an appointment with her for Clara at eleven o'clock tomorrow, and you are welcome to join us. You can investigate her shop and see if she will meet yours and Emma's needs." Sheila always knew the fine line between suggestion and pushiness.

"Sheila, you are a dear. You'll make this Season so simple for us." Emily gave her a sincere smile with her look of thanks.

"Oh, tosh," said a slightly embarrassed Sheila. She didn't know any other way but to make people feel welcome and at ease. "Clara and I will appreciate your opinion, and Emma can get her first taste of shopping among the *ton*. I'll send a note to Mademoiselle to expect the extra custom on the morrow."

Clara had watched the way her aunt had skillfully maneuvered tomorrow's shopping trip and marveled at her ways. Why, Mrs. Thompson had no idea what had just occurred, and probably would not have cared if she did know. Aunt Sheila was a charmer with such a sincere and sunny disposition that it was no wonder she was a favorite among the *ton.*

Clara had a twinge of guilt for the underhanded trick she was about to play on her aunt—involving her without her knowledge in her scheme to bring the lofty Lord Carruthers to his very knees.

That very worthy gentleman was at that very moment closeted with Farrell, his man of business, going over his accounts. A dreary business, but a minor task compared to the work of his father. Why, the few hours Jeremy spent every quarter were merely what his father managed every day.

"Well, I think that will cover it, your Lordship," Farrell said, straightening the papers on the desk between them.

"Thank you for your excellent work, Farrell. As usual, everything was in order, and you've managed my holdings quite well. We realized a tidy profit this quarter."

Farrell permitted himself a small smile at the praise. He had handled this dealing well. "I'll send the final papers to you within a fortnight," he said.

"About that other matter I asked you to dispose of last month . . ." Jeremy's voice trailed away with a touch of discomfort.

"Ah, the cottage occupied by Miss Jollee. Yes, she has vacated the premises; they are cleaned and for let, sir. She presented no problems, and I believe she has found another pro—establishment," Farrell said delicately. He hardly wanted to let Lord Carruthers know how quickly she'd selected her new protector.

"I thank you again for your excellent work."

"That is why you employ me, sir," he replied with a false sigh of resignation as Jeremy chuckled. Lord Carruthers was a singularly honest and fair man, and Farrell counted himself fortunate to have been in his employ these past seven years.

"I will see you in a fortnight with the papers, your Lordship." Farrell took his leave.

After he left, Jeremy found himself wondering about Colette and their last evening together. He did not deceive himself that she mourned his loss— far from it, he was sure. If anything, he chided himself that he had not foreseen her defection earlier. He knew he'd slipped into a routine that was easier to continue than bring to an end. Only when he'd heard tales of her late nights with other men did he force himself to take action.

Oh, she had cried that last night and protested her love even when confronted with evidence of her unfaithfulness. But Farrell's investigations had proved too damning, and she crumpled at the accusations. He could only assume a new protector would shower her with more baubles and attention than he had of late.

Jeremy rose to take his afternoon ride. He wanted to clear his head of all memories of Colette Jollee and counted on his new stallion to turn the trick. Meeting Edward and Dickers would surely turn his mind from the past as well.

Jeremy walked from his office through to the front entry. He had lived the past three years in the family townhouse in Grovesnor Square and was glad for the familiar surroundings. He had spent many years in rooms, but after his youngest sister's come-out, he'd decided to keep the family home open. His parents rarely came to town for the Season, but his father made regular trips to take his seat in the House of Lords. Jeremy welcomed the company as often as it was possible.

His horse awaited him on the street. He made a few swift strides to the gate and mounted with ease. The feel of the magnificent beast at his control made him forget the past before he'd gone three lengths. He really did enjoy a brisk ride while in town. Fortunately, he had started out before the fashionable hour and faced a small risk of any modest censure with a gallop through the park.

As he made his way toward the park his mind wandered to last week's ball. The Harleys' squeeze had not surprised him in the least. The crowd had been small compared to what the Season would soon bring, but he had renewed a few acquaintances and seen the Fair Incomparable.

She had held court like a princess with several beaux crowded around her between sets. Edward had danced with her once and said she was quite charming, but Jeremy could not see himself joining the press of gallants. The last time he'd graced a dance floor was for his sister's ball. Now, it somehow seemed contrived and routine, and he'd found himself looking to the card room after watching a few dances. He had noticed several of the matrons watching him, trying to judge his intentions. He had felt their eyes and could almost hear their whispered comments behind elaborate fans. The whole charade just added to his indifference.

His jaded attitude bothered him as he cantered into the park. Why could he not see the fun and romance of courting a lovely young debutante? After all, that was the reason why he'd gone to these parties. He sighed and supposed romance played no part in today's marriage mart. What a terrible task Edward had set for himself.

He saw his friends in the distance at their favorite stretch of open grass. Truly, the park spread out ahead of him was a lovely bit of countryside in this large metropolis, and he silently praised the city planners of long ago.

"Ho there, Jeremy," yelled an enthusiastic Dickers, and the two men rode toward him quickly.

"You left so soon after supper last night—pining for the fair Collette?" joked Dickers.

Giving him a caustic look that spoke volumes, Jeremy said, "No, you old sot. The company held no interest for me. I don't know how the two of you can endure the start of another Season."

"It helps to have a purpose, I suppose," said Edward, "though that doesn't explain Dickers's fascination with the evenings."

"I'm your support, my man. Plus, I confounded the mamas with my every turn on the dance floor. They didn't know what to make of me when I danced twice with the Fair Incomparable."

"But it's so much the same every night and every soiree. Have you found the right girl yet, my friend?"

"No, not really. Oh, there are many lovely young girls, but none of them seems to appeal to me. 'Tis my third Season, but I haven't lost interest in the hunt. I'm actually looking forward to the Gearys' ball on Saturday to mark the beginning of the Season."

Jeremy pondered this statement with both amazement and a shudder as they rode on for their gallop. Three Seasons! Could *he* last that long?

The ladies hurried up the steps of Clifton House, hoping to dance between the raindrops. The day had dawned bright and cheery but had quickly turned to light sprinkles while they shopped through the early afternoon at Mademoiselle Francoise's.

Their third visit to the modiste's since arriving in town had seen to the completion of the girls' wardrobes with a proper flourish. Had it been almost a fortnight already? Sheila was very pleased with the stylish turnout she'd arranged for Clara and Emma. She smiled at Emily's easy capitulation when it had come to shopping for young girls. And Clara certainly seemed to enjoy the fripperies for one who'd taken so long to make her way to town for a Season.

"Are you girls ready for a warm and heartening tea?" she asked.

"Oh, please, do stay, Emma; we have to pick which of our heavenly creations we plan to wear tonight to the Gearys' ball."

"A bit of warm tea would help take away the dampness of the afternoon. I certainly have no passion to hurry back out into the rain, and talking about our ensembles would be a delight," she teased.

"Now that's doing it a bit too brown, my dear. A 'delight'—really!" Sheila laughed as she led the way to the drawing room. She gave a smile of approval to Reilly when she saw that he had already sent the maid for the teacart.

"Oh, Lady Clifton, I don't care how silly I sound!" Emma exclaimed. "This fortnight *has* been a delight, so everything we do must be just as wonderful. I know I act the schoolgirl, but if I don't let some of these giggles out of me now, I am liable to disgrace myself tonight. Our first ball!" Her eyes lit as she sighed out the words.

"Oh, please, my dear, I do wish you would call me Aunt Sheila. Lady Clifton is far too stuffy and formal for me."

"Thank you, ma'am, Aunt Sheila." Emma blushed a little at the kindness.

"Now girls, which of your pretty dresses do you plan to wear tonight?"

SIX

THE SEASON'S FIRST BALL

The press of carriages slowed once more as the Clifton barrouche pulled forward to the Geary townhouse. The three occupants were quiet during the final few minutes of their drive, and it gave Clara a chance to calm her nerves. Nerves! She never thought she'd feel such trepidation for a simple party. Well, if truth be told, she knew this night was no simple party. She would finally make her first appearance among the *ton* at a fashionable London address—a far cry from the country parties and dances around Waverly.

She knew she looked well in her new ballgown. The beautiful dress was everything she could have hoped for with its simple elegance and style. The green and gold trim reminded her of her favorite old riding habit, and she was thankful for the familiarity as she pondered the night ahead. And the beautiful new style of twists and curls in her blond hair gave her an ever-so-slight feeling of confidence.

Would she see him? Would he recognize her and

give her the cut direct? She really had no plan for tonight now that she'd realized the start of her grand scheme to bring him to his knees. How would she be able to flirt with him when she didn't even know him? It was all very well for her to think she could make a London lord fall in love with her when she had plotted this night weeks ago from her room at Waverly, but the reality was causing her stomach to turn somersaults.

"We've arrived." Aunt Sheila's voice broke into her thoughts.

Clara started out of her reverie with a slight jump and turned to look out the window. Oh, but it was lovely, with the lights and footmen surrounding the partygoers as they moved up the stairs into the house. The carriage door opened, and Marcus jumped down to help the ladies. She truly had arrived.

Dickers laughed as Jeremy ended another story about the hunt last week. The three men had met at Edward's townhouse for a light meal before going to the party and now lingered over the last of their brandies. Edward had wanted to arrive early to ensure he signed the cards of as many ladies as struck his fancy, but Dickers insisted they make a late entrance. Grand, he called it.

Dickers bounded from his chair in an unseemly show of haste. "Gentlemen, are we ready?" he asked.

"Good grief, man, slow down! We aren't going to a race, but a ball for pity's sake." Some of Edward's frustration at the delay came through in his voice.

"And you were the one nagging us to leave an hour ago!" said Dickers. "This ball is like all the others, and we never arrive before the third dance." He downed the rest of his brandy.

"I know you've styled yourself as the architect of my

betrothal, but I do have a say in this, my man. I do believe I will pick my own bride, and I'd like to arrive before the supper dance at the very least." Edward's frustration was replaced by amusing sarcasm.

"I do believe it is time for us to quit these close quarters! Yes, let us go and meet your lady at the ball," said Jeremy. And the gentlemen moved into the entry hall to gather their hats and gloves.

"Lord and Lady Clifton, Miss Clara Edwards," intoned the butler as the threesome entered the ballroom. It was everything that Clara had ever dreamed of—and dreaded. Her normal confidence and aplomb seemed to desert her this night, and she gave herself a small shake to focus her thoughts.

"Oh, you've finally arrived," gushed Emma as she came forward to greet the new arrivals. You look beautiful, Clara, and Aunt Sheila, you are positively stunning!"

"And you look lovely yourself, my dear," said Sheila as she hugged the girl. She surveyed the ballroom and saw a large crowd. "My, the party has already attracted so many people. The season has truly started."

"Emma, thank you, and it's wonderful to see you. You do look so lovely in the azure crepe; it was the perfect choice for tonight."

"The dancing will start in a few minutes, and I took the liberty of starting a card for you, Clara," Emma added. "I hope that's all right with you? And you'll never guess who is here? Annabelle Richards! She is home from traveling since her father has given up his diplomatic post, and she's to make her come-out with us. Isn't that marvelous? And she has the most charming brother who immediately signed my card for *two* dances! He put his name down for your second dance."

Sheila laughed at the young girl's enthusiasm. "Emma, stop! You must come up for air!"

"Why, I want to sign your cards too, ladies," said Marcus. "I must have a dance with each of the most beautiful debutantes in the room." And the girls giggled at his gallantry and happily gave him their cards.

"Come, you must say hello to Annabelle and her brother, Sir Richards." And Clara happily followed along beside Emma without even realizing that she had neglected to look for her prey.

The gentlemen stopped to greet friends as they left their coach in front of the Gearys' townhouse. The line of carriages heading to the mews spelled a veritable crush, and Jeremy let go an inaudible sigh. Perhaps the Fair Incomparable would hold court again and divert him some this night.

He thought back to the confidence he'd shared with Edward before Dickers had arrived. It had surprised him some at how easy it had been for him to admit, anxious almost it had seemed, that his attendance at tonight's party had a purpose for him as well. Edward had laughingly welcomed him to the fold and promised to cut him out of the prettiest and wittiest of the debutantes. That, of course, was after he'd almost spilled his wine in shock at Jeremy's announcement. All in all, it would be an interesting Season, and he was sure Dickers would cane him when he discovered Jeremy had held back this news.

"Annabelle, how lovely to see you again." Clara and Annabelle embraced with warm affection.

"Clara, you look beautiful tonight," Annabelle replied. "I was so delighted when Emma told me that you were making your come-out, too. We must get together tomorrow to catch up on the past few years!"

"Oh, I should like that immeasurably. Emma and I have seen some of the sights, but you are our first familiar face. I know there will be others, but it is especially delightful to see you."

"And Clara, I want you to meet my cousin Patricia—she's been wonderful in showing me around London and accompanying me to the balls and routes."

As the ladies exchanged greetings, a noticeable "ahem" interrupted their conversation. Clara turned and gazed into a pair of startling blue eyes. She heard a chuckle from Annabelle.

"And may I present my irrepressible brother to you, Clara? This is Sir Martin Richards. Martin, Miss Edwards."

"The pleasure is all mine, Miss Edwards. I am enchanted to meet you," Martin took her hand and bowed.

Clara was a bit dumbfounded at the intensity of his words, but his behavior was all that was correct. She found herself staring into those eyes and stumbled to find the polite words of greeting.

"It is n- nice to meet you, sir." Nice—what a simpleton word! Where was her mind going?

Martin added, "I believe I have signed your card for the second dance, but I now know I must have another. May I sign my name here?" He indicated the supper dance.

"Why, of course, you may," Clara replied, glancing shyly at this disarming man.

Annabelle's laugh bubbled through the small group. "Martin! You are too much the charming scapegrace! What must Clara think of us as you sweep her off her feet?"

Clara's Uncle Marcus arrived just then as the musicians signaled the beginning of the dancing. The party began to pair up for the first set, and Clara could hardly control her quickly beating heart. As she and Uncle Marcus twined through the steps of the dance, they managed to exchange but a few words. Clara realized that she would have to shake herself back to attention, or every handsome face would turn her heart upside down. And that would never do, as she once again gave thought to her real purpose here this evening.

The same fears she'd felt while in the carriage still held her in suspense. She couldn't help thinking that not knowing when she would see him would prove as unnerving as actually seeing him. Perhaps tonight would not be the most auspicious evening to start her plan—she really ought to formulate that plan first! But now she must dance the next dance with Sir Richards and manage to say something wittier than "nice"!

The men arrived too late to be announced and found a party in full sway. Supper would soon begin. Jeremy saw that a lively country dance brought many of this city crowd to the dance floor. A side room with several card tables already showed signs of deep play—perhaps a fortune would be lost or won tonight.

At the center of attention to the side of the dancers reigned the fair Incomparable. Her red hair blazed under the lights, and her laughter carried throughout the room. She looked to be enjoying her success without appearing to exult over it, and each of the men seemed to be enraptured. *No mean feat to juggle all those balls,* he thought.

She held no attraction for him, though he wasn't sure why. He certainly liked lively and interesting women—no shrinking miss for him. Perhaps it was her obvious enjoyment of her court and almost preening quality as she turned for another compliment. Or that red hair—he did, after all, prefer blonde flowing tresses.

"I'm off, men. The lady beckons, and I must beg a dance." Dickers headed off to join her court.

"Well, Edward, so how do I find the right one?" Jeremy asked.

"What! You think you can just walk into a ballroom and pick a wife?" Edward replied.

"Keep your voice down, man! The whole room will hear you, and my secret will be out. That's all I need, to have the mamas after me night and day."

"Oh, just being here will have them after you. A man of your prominence and fortune, not to mention your endless charms, will have them beating down your door this very night."

"Very amusing, sir. Endless charms or not, I cannot just stand here with you all night. I must mingle and let them come to me. Oh, blast, here comes that Farleigh woman! I'll leave you to her clutches." With that, Jeremy made a smooth turn to head in the opposite direction.

Little did he realize where his path led! He strolled around the edge of the dance floor and saw Dickers fawning at the feet of the Fair Incomparable. Dickers seemed to be enjoying himself, or at least gave a good impression of a man in raptures. Jeremy's eyes wandered to the dancers, and he watched as they moved through the intricate steps. They, too, seemed to enjoy themselves. So, why couldn't he?

His eyes slid to the end of the line and stopped suddenly. She was lovely, her smile a delighted gaze up at her partner. The blonde hair framed her face almost as a halo. He shook himself to break the spell—such poetics were hardly his style. But he was captivated and hardly drew a breath.

She stepped gracefully through the end of the

dance, and he felt entranced in watching her. The couple moved over to the chairs where he supposed her chaperone waited. He saw her talking with several others who'd also been part of the set. After a few minutes, the music began again, and the group laughed as they partnered for another dance.

He couldn't help but notice that both of her partners looked as captivated as he felt in watching. Graceful, vivacious, angelic, and a wonderful dancer. He knew he must meet her—and meet her now. But how? He could hardly just walk up and introduce himself. No, no, it just wasn't done. He had to find an introduction, and his eyes started scanning the chaperones for someone he knew, someone who would not read too much into his request.

Clara could hardly believe her eyes! He was here and almost close enough to touch. She spun through the rest of the dance with precision and some automation as her mind raced in a million directions. She had no plan and knew not what to do! As the musicians played towards the song's end, she knew she must think very quickly.

The dance came to an end, and Clara thanked her partner as he escorted her to her Aunt Sheila. Before they reached her though, Sir Richards intercepted the couple.

"It is our dance again, Miss Edwards. Servant, Burroughs."

She gazed again into his deep blue eyes, but this time had a better hold on her emotions.

"I've looked forward to it, sir. Thank you again for the lovely dance, Mr. Burroughs."

"'Twas my p-pleasure, ma'am," stammered a lovestruck young man. And William Burroughs turned to find the perfect vantage point from which he could stare at his new beloved.

"You seemed to have made a conquest of that young cub, Miss Edwards. I can surely understand his regard, but I must fear for his person." Sir Richards chuckled as Burroughs abruptly bumped into the wall with his shoulder.

Clara tried not to laugh aloud and did manage to get through with just a smile.

"Really, Sir Richards, you embarrass me with your comment. He merely stumbled—'twas nothing more."

"Ah, ma'am, you do not know—no, I do think you do not know." A contemplative Sir Richards took her hand and led her across the floor to begin the supper dance.

Clara could hardly think to hatch her plot with those blue eyes gazing down at her.

Jeremy watched the little scene from a distance and could not fathom his sudden anger. It was obvious the young Burroughs had fallen for the lovely woman, but Richards had no business making sport of it all. If he'd bothered to analyze his sudden righteousness, he would admit he had done much the same as Richards many a time. Why was tonight so different?

He must find someone who knew the chit or he would soon become obvious as he prowled the ballroom. Burroughs was certainly not the right person. He was loath to return to Edward in case the Farleigh woman still bent his ear, but he felt he must do something. He quickly scanned over the tops of many a head until he spotted Edward. Yes, the woman was still there, and one of her twins was now close to her side. *At least the Farleigh girl is pleasant enough to look at, if not a bit oddly dressed,* he thought.

He supposed Edward could do with a rescue as well. He doubted Edward had neither been on the dance floor nor signed a single card for the evening's later dances after supper. If he didn't move quickly, he was sure he'd miss Edward, since Edward would feel compelled to ask the Farleigh twin for the next dance. He didn't see Reggie Farleigh anywhere near his encroaching mama, but he could hardly blame the man for steering clear of her.

As Jeremy moved towards the small group, he realized that the twins' mother, Millicent Farleigh, could be of use to him. She certainly would know all the eligible young ladies making their come-outs this year with her twins—good to know the competition, as it were. Yes, this rescue of Edward might just work in his favor as well. But he must be discreet or the gossip would be dining out on the story of his matrimonial hopes for the next fortnight.

"Why, Lord Carruthers! What a pleasant surprise to see you here tonight," Millicent Farleigh said, gleaming at him.

"Delighted, ma'am, Miss Farleigh." Thank goodness convention dictated he could not address the Farleigh twin by her first name—damned if he could tell them apart. "How are you enjoying the Season's first ball, Miss Farleigh?"

"Oh, la, but 'tis a terrible squeeze, don't you think?" Miss Farleigh said. "I say the crush of people will certainly dirty this old dress." Her hand smoothed an imaginary wrinkle.

Angling for compliments, as well as a pretentious jade. Gad, was this a sample of today's debutante? Jeremy suppressed a sigh as he knew he must answer her very obvious ploy.

"Such a lovely gown to be sure." He tried to say it with some feeling.

"Gentlemen, supper is about to start. If you don't already have plans, won't you join us at our table for a bite to eat?" Millicent Farleigh asked.

Edward looked at Jeremy, and both knew they were caught. They could hardly claim a previous engagement when the crowd had already started to make its way into the supper room. So much for arriving late to make a grand entrance only to find yourself outmaneuvered by a champion.

"We'd be delighted, ma'am," said Edward, and he moved to offer his arm to Millicent.

Jeremy offered his arm to the twin and hoped he could manage a conversation with her until they joined the others at the table. Tonight was not going well at all—no, not at all!

"Now, Miss Edwards, what are your plans for the Season?" asked Sir Richards as they came together in the final steps of the dance.

"Why, I hadn't given it too much thought really. It's all so new right now, and we're here to just enjoy ourselves," said Clara. Dancing surely made for a difficult conversation!

"May I call on you tomorrow for a carriage ride?" he asked as the dance ended and they moved toward the supper room. He surprised himself at the quick invitation.

"Oh, that would be lovely, especially if tomorrow is as fair as today's weather."

They joined the throng heading into the supper room, and Clara could find no trace of "him." *He mustn't have left so soon!* she almost cried out loud. She wanted to turn her head away from Sir Richards to look toward the other side of the room but knew she couldn't be so rude. She didn't know why she was so worried he might leave, though, since it would give her some time to develop a plan before their next meeting.

They found the table close to full, with Annabelle, William Burroughs, Emma, and Reggie Farleigh. They had all started to eat, so Sir Richards seated Clara and made his way over to the supper table for two more plates.

The champagne flowed freely at the table, and laughter filled the air. Clara realized she really was enjoying herself and not just the intrigue of her plan. It was fun to dance, see friends, and even, she had to admit, turn a head or two—a new experience for her and one that made her feel strangely self-confident. Yes, she could hold her own among society's finest, and that small fear was laid to rest.

The Farleigh supper table had soon become a sad mistake for both Edward and Jeremy. While the outward appearances showed a happy crowd enjoying their repast, laughing at the day's stories and night's intrigue, the two friends at the table knew they were trapped. They could take solace in that it would not last beyond dessert's champagne ices.

And Millicent Farleigh was fast approaching apoplexy with her coup. Two such distinguished members of the *ton* at her very table at the Season's first ball! And she with two daughters to launch. She could not help but scan the nearby tables to see who would be taking notice of her triumph. Ah, several mamas with debutante daughters, so she knew she would be the talk of tomorrow's morning calls. She let slip a contented sigh as she brought her attention back to the gentlemen at her table.

What of the two Farleigh misses? Elisa, the elder twin, fully understood her mother's contented smile.

She had fairly waltzed to the table on Lord Carruthers's arm and knew her season was sure to be a success with such a start. She could only hope he would ask her for a dance after supper to make her night complete.

Melissa had barely managed more than two words of greeting to the young men. She had already been seated when her mother's party arrived. Her supper dance partner sat to her right, and for the life of her she could not remember his name. Oh, but it was all so overwhelming with the crowds of people, the heat, and the noise. She looked forward to the carriage ride home.

The merry laughter at Clara's table was both genuine and infectious as their meal came to an end. Several people turned their heads from nearby tables to first look in wonder and then envy at their obvious enjoyment. It was quite a happy table of young people who found themselves looking forward to the rest of the evening and more dancing.

"Such tasty ices," said Annabelle.

"Well, we could hardly fail to notice as you snagged that second cup from the waiter," said a laughing Sir Richards.

"Why Martin, you have no right to announce such a dastardly falsehood to everyone!" But, the two empty cups next to her champagne glass proved him true.

"Come, come, little sister. You've never been able to hide that sweet tooth from me. And I think this fine company couldn't care in the least."

"You're so right about that, Sir Richards," Clara added. "Why, even when we were at Miss Howard's, Annabelle found ways to sneak extra sweets." And Clara joined the table in more laughter at Annabelle's mock horror at her words.

"I do think we'd better end this delightful meal, or the dancing will start without us," said Reggie. The couples began to pair off for the next dance. Reggie Farleigh offered his hand to Clara, while Emma had her second dance with Sir Richards. That left a sparkling Annabelle with a stumbling but earnest William Burroughs. The six moved to join the forming sets and soon lost themselves in the music and the dance.

"Ladies, it has been a delightful meal, and we thank you for inviting us to share it with you," said Edward. Jeremy was quick to take the hint and offered his own proper words of thanks.

Millicent Farleigh worked at lightning speed to think of something to keep the gentlemen at her side until the first strains of music reached their ears. To have her daughters follow their triumph at supper with a dance would seal the evening. The men would surely ask the girls to dance if she could but stall them a mere minute or two.

"Gentlemen, it was our pleasure as well to have such distinguished escorts and company for dinner. But where are my manners? I have neglected to invite you to our little dinner party in a few nights' time." There, that was vague enough for her to plan "something." She bravely ignored the gasp from Melissa and coughed loudly to cover the sound.

Jeremy, too, was aware of the discordant strains of music as the orchestra settled in with their instruments for the second half of the night's dancing. He was in no mood to cap a tedious dinner with a tepid dance with either a mouse or a firebrand on his arm. It would be a poor show of manners to walk away from the table without asking them to dance, but he felt they'd both more than fulfilled society's expectations during the dinner.

"Mrs. Farliegh, that sounds delightful. Please send cards to Edward and myself, and we'll be sure to attend if we are in town. Now ladies, sir, we bid you good evening." Jeremy turned to make his leave and would have grabbed Edward's arm to ensure his escape had it been possible to maintain a semblance of good manners at the same time.

"I'm headed for the card room, sir," Jeremy declared. "I cannot take the chance of another hour such as this one. What was I thinking to come to such an affair!"

"Calm down, man, and lower your voice," said Edward in a very clipped manner.

The two men walked in silence toward the card room, each lost in his thoughts. Edward vowed to make an earlier appearance at the next ball to secure his choice for dancing and dining partners. Dickers could make the grand entrance at the eleventh hour. So far this evening had been a disappointment, and he didn't wonder at Jeremy's disgust with the whole affair.

Jeremy was angry with himself for the poor start to the evening. He didn't really intend to hide in the card room, but it at least gave him a chance to reconsider his plans. He had all but forgotten the blonde beauty, and he would hardly find her in this direction. He supposed he could watch a few hands of play, have a brandy, and then slip back into the ballroom to try for another introduction to the mystery lady.

"I'm not in the mood for cards tonight, my friend," Edward said. "I'll leave you here to go look for Dickers. He's sure to have some good cheer to put that meal from my mind."

"I don't blame you, Edward, and I'll probably join you in a short while. I need a bit of time to calm my nerves—Gad, what a supper." At least Jeremy could laugh at the picture in his mind.

Edward strolled around the ballroom looking for Dickers. It didn't take long to find him hanging at the edges of the throng surrounding the Fair Incomparable. Edward did see how a gentleman could be captivated by her presence, but her style did not appeal to him. A fresh face was more to his liking.

"Edward, my man! Where have you been all night?" Dickers asked.

"Don't ask, and consider yourself fortunate to have been in this happy company. We'll tell you about it some night over a few fine brews."

"Well, the company here may be a happy one, but there's just too damn much of it! Her card was full before the first dance, and I haven't been able to do more than gaze at the lovely Charlotte. Why even at supper I sat at the far side of her table."

"Perhaps we should arrive a bit earlier next time?" Edward's earlier frustrations came through in his tone.

"I say, what's eating at you?"

"I'm sorry for that, but it has been a less than satisfactory evening."

"It sounds like we've each had a long and trying night for the season's first outing. I think some morning calls to selected homes will serve us well for the coming evenings. Yes, securing a dance or two ahead of time will improve our fortunes."

"Just as long as la Farleigh is not on your list, I'm willing to try anything!" Edward clapped Dickers on the back in friendly camaraderie.

* * *

"Jeremy! Good to see you." Jeremy felt a friendly pat on the shoulder as he turned to the voice.

"Why, Marcus, what brings you to the Season's first ball? Is your lovely wife here as well?"

"Yes, Sheila is somewhere watching after her niece, who's making her come-out. 'Bout time, too—the girl must be two and twenty."

By the tone of his voice and its hint of disapproval, Jeremy judged the tardy niece to be something of an original not given to conventions. For Marcus's sake, he hoped she wasn't a blue stocking as well.

"Let me find her in this throng, and I'll direct you to her for a dance," Marcus added.

"Oh, I'm not much in the way of dancing this evening. Just here to take in the company and see old friends," Jeremy hedged. Good God! First that interminable supper and now this! He might be stuck with the niece when all he wanted was to meet a special blonde.

"Nonsense! We've been friends for many a year, and I've never known you willing to go to a ball with no purpose. Now a bawdy party, yes, but a ball with society's matrons hovering," Marcus's voice trailed off with a laugh.

"Actually, I am here with Edward Waters." Jeremy nodded in the general direction of the Fair Incomparable and her friends. Happily there was no sign of the Farleigh clan.

"I'm sure she's on the dance floor." Marcus continued to scan the crowd for Clara. "Aha! Found them. Let's move over to Sheila's side so you can meet her when they end the dance."

Jeremy felt a firm grasp on his arm—not unlike the metaphoric one he and Edward had experienced with la Farleigh. Oh, what had he done in coming here tonight? He could hardly refuse to meet the niece of his good friend. Why, Marcus was like an older brother to him and had helped him immensely in business dealings. Well, he supposed one dance wouldn't be his undoing.

When Clara's dance ended with Reggie Farleigh, she glanced across the crowded ballroom toward Aunt Sheila. Oh no! *He* was there. What would she do? She couldn't very well leave the room with no good reason, and besides, where to go? Reggie had offered his arm to escort her back to Aunt Sheila, and she had little choice but to link her arm in his and accompany him over to her aunt.

As Clara and Reggie began to thread across the dance floor, William Burroughs spurred himself to action. He had suffered through supper watching the lovely Clara across the table, and now she was heading away from him and back to her aunt. With unaccustomed purpose he moved onto the dance floor to intercept the couple.

"Servant, Burroughs," said a startled Reggie Farleigh. Why the man had fairly bumped into him and now blocked their path!

"Farleigh, Miss Edwards, a d-delight to see you."

"Why Mr. Burroughs, you surprised me," said Clara with a short gasp. She knew it was hardly proper to accost them in the middle of the ballroom.

"I'm s-sorry, ma'am. I did not mean to disturb you so abruptly. I merely w-wished for the next dance."

"I am sure Miss Edwards is already promised for this dance, so take yourself away, man," said Reggie in a gruff and commanding voice. He could easily see the young man's eagerness had caused him to forget convention and toss aside the normal way of things. But, one man's poor manners would be no excuse for him to do the same. He rather enjoyed this knight-in-shining-armor role thrust upon him.

"Oh, I had hoped there would be room for me," William replied. He could feel some of his nerve slipping away.

Clara felt for this shy, young man. She had noticed his staring during supper, and now his infatuation was quite obvious for all to see. She did not want them to become a spectacle on the floor now quickly thinning of couples. There would be a few minutes before the next set formed, and she thought quickly to remove them from the floor. All fear of who awaited her on the other side of the room flew from her head when faced with this minor melodrama in front of her eyes.

"Why, actually, no one has spoken for this next dance, Mr. Burroughs. Why don't we move over to the refreshment table for a cup of punch before the set forms? I would be pleased to have two such charming escorts."

Reggie bowed to her smooth handling of the cub. He could play the gentleman and see them both back to the punchbowl.

"Blast, she's moving in the other direction. That's odd—wouldn't she come back to you, my dear?"

Sheila had watched the threesome's maneuvers on the floor and now turned at the sound of Marcus's voice.

"I would expect her to, yes, dear. Perhaps they are in deep conversation. We'll introduce you later in the evening, Jeremy."

Jeremy breathed a silent sigh. This night would never end, but at least he had dodged one more tiresome chit, even if she were Marcus's niece. He knew he should repair posthaste to the card room and stay there for the duration of this abominable night. He would move more slowly in his quest to meet his own Fair Incomparable, but in the meantime he must not offend Sheila.

"I thank you for your kind offer, and I certainly look forward to the honor of meeting your niece later this evening. Your servant, until then." Jeremy bowed and took his leave.

"Seemed in a bit of a hurry, wouldn't you say?" observed a laughing Sheila.

"I don't think he's too interested in dancing this evening. He's headed in the direction of the card room and will probably disappear for the rest of the night," agreed Marcus.

"Hmm, I do approve of your pairing, though, my dear. I think he and Clara would make a delightful couple. I'll have to think this idea through, hmm."

"What are you plotting, Sheila?" said a very skeptical Marcus. "I never had any 'pairing' in mind—I just wanted to give Clara an introduction to my good friend. Don't you read any more into it than that very simple explanation."

"Yes dear, whatever you say," said a smiling and suddenly thoughtful Sheila.

As she sipped her punch, Clara scanned the party around Aunt Sheila and the other chaperones for a glimpse of *him*. She somehow felt cheated, even though his disappearance gave her the much-needed time to plan. Before the next party, she vowed to prepare herself on just how to approach him—no more hiding at the punchbowl for her! Despite her wonderful enjoyment in the evening and her growing confidence in society, Clara's frustration continued through the night, as she looked for him in vain at the end of each succeeding set.

SEVEN

WHO IS SHE?

"Up, you sleepyhead!" said Aunt Sheila as she opened the curtains in Clara's room. In came the bright sunshine of another glorious spring morning.

The tousled lump in the bed groaned ever so slightly as Clara awakened. The late night, the first of many to come, was out of character for the country miss.

"I have some delicious chocolate to warm you this morning, and the cook baked some of the bread you like so much. Now, will I have to feed you, too, young lady?" said a laughing Aunt Sheila as she put the tray on the bedside table.

Clara emerged from under the covers and slowly sat up in bed. Sheila plumped her pillows and laughed a little more at the sleepy face before her.

"I can see you'll need a nap this afternoon since we've the Mardsdens' ball tonight. However will you ever keep your eyes open during the late nights for the rest of the Season?"

"Oh, no, another ball tonight?" Clara almost wailed. "I had forgotten—I didn't think I'd have to make my plan so soon."

"Plan? What plan, my dear?"

"Oh, my—my wardrobe, you see. I haven't planned what to wear tonight," Clara improvised quickly.

"Oh, pish posh! That will take us but a minute or two after luncheon. Now you drink down your chocolate, and I'll ring for your Meg to help you dress for the morning. Come find me in the morning room when you're ready, and we can discuss the day and more about last night." Sheila gave her a kiss on the forehead before she rang for Meg.

As Sheila moved to the open door, she looked back at the charming picture of Clara sipping her chocolate amid the pillows and sighed. "I don't think I've told you enough, my dear, but I am so glad you finally decided to join us in London for your come-out. I've always delighted in the Season, but it is such a joy to have you to share it with and to see you so enjoy yourself as you did last night. Marcus and I are truly pleased that you are with us now."

Clara felt such a twinge of guilt at Sheila's sincere words. Since her purpose in coming to London had such a devious and underhanded beginning, it was hard for her to answer her aunt with the same purity and goodness of feeling. She was spared making any response as Meg bustled into the room.

"Such a slug-a-bed, Miss Clara. I've brought some warm water and towels for you to wash the sleep from your eyes."

"I'll see you downstairs shortly then," Aunt Sheila replied as she left the room.

"Thank you, Meg. I'll wear the blue flowered muslin with the ribbons today. And I think a simple style for my hair—I had plenty of finery last night." Clara moved over to the table and bowl to wash.

"Oooooh, Miss, how was your ball? You were too sleepy to say much last night."

"I never seemed to stop dancing, Meg, and the music was delightful. Plus the wonderful people, such beautiful clothes, and best of all, Lady Annabelle was there."

"I remember her from her visits to Waverly. Such a lovely young miss. But what of the men? Did anyone catch your fancy?"

"Now, Meg, I only spent one evening out! No one has 'caught my fancy,' as you say. There were several young men, to be sure, and one has asked to take me for a drive this afternoon."

"Oooooh, a drive, how romantic," Meg gushed. "I'll make sure your new carriage dress is pressed and ready for you." She finished laying out the light blue muslin and started to brush Clara's hair.

"Thank you, Meg. You make it so easy. I appreciate all your work."

"Oh, miss, I enjoy doing for you. Now step over here and slip on your dress. I'll take care of your hair in a trice."

As the two young women finished the morning's tasks, Clara turned silent. She thought about the night just past. It had been a delightful time seeing some old friends and making new ones. She surprised herself to admit the ball had truly been fun. She really had enjoyed herself and looked forward with much anticipation to tonight's ball.

Tonight! When would she have the time today to formulate her plan, what with receiving morning callers with Aunt Sheila and then driving in the park this afternoon with Sir Richards? That left her little time to herself before dressing for the ball. When would she be able to think?

"There you are, Miss Clara. You look lovely in this dress, with your hair threaded with the blue ribbons to match."

"Thank you, Meg. It does look very nice. Can you let Aunt Sheila know I'll be down in a few minutes?"

"Why, yes, Miss. Is there anything else you would like?"

"Not now, thank you. You've thought of everything as usual."

After Meg left the room, Clara turned to her task to devise a plan for their first meeting. It could come as early as this evening at the Mardsdens', and she must be ready!

If only there were some way she could draw attention to herself at the ball. In a good way, of course, so that he would notice her and want to meet her. As a modest and normally unassuming young woman, Clara had little realization of the "notice" she had already attracted at her first London party last night.

And then, if he wanted to meet her, she would have to find ways to avoid him without drawing attention to her maneuvers. He must be held at bay while she further piqued his interest. Such a difficult assignment she'd given herself!

Certainly, a bright dress was out of the question. She was quite sure Aunt Sheila would never countenance anything but pastels for her first Season. And she did want the attention to be for a good reason and not notoriety!

Could she and Emma affect a new fashion style and become the talk of the Season? Certainly Annabelle would enthusiastically join in such an effort. Why, the three of them could wear a new style of hats, or perhaps carry some unique fans. But the time it would take to order and make the garments might be days. She needed something for tonight!

Why not invite her growing group of friends on an outing? And they could plan it during tonight's ball.

Oh, but how would she bring him into the party when they hadn't yet been introduced here in London?

Could she include Emma in her planning? She was certainly more *au courant* than Clara was with the intrigues of society. But wouldn't that also involve telling Emma the reason why it was so important for Clara to attract the attention of a certain gentleman? Oh no, Clara was not ready to confess to anyone her reason for coming to London! How was she ever to think of something?

Well, what was the harm in his just meeting her at any old time during a ball? Did she have to have a plan to cause their meeting? *Why, no,* she told herself. She need only have her wits about her when the meeting did take place! Sparkling conversation to draw his attention was all she needed.

But then Clara remembered her "sparkling conversation" when she first met Annabelle's brother last night. Why, she'd been a veritable simpleton with her stuttering "n-nice to meet you" to Sir Richards! How could she expect herself to do any better than last night at this unknown meeting with Lord Carruthers?

Clara sighed in frustration at the task ahead of her. Perhaps she would not worry about her plan just now.

Sheila sipped her last cup of tea as Clara entered the morning room. She concentrated on the letter in her hand from the day's post, so she did not hear Clara's quiet tread.

"Not bad news, I hope?" asked Clara.

"Oh, no dear. It's just a note from Marcus's younger sister, Anne. I'd hoped she could join us for part of the Season, since she so enjoys dancing. But she is helping a neighbor through a spell of influenza. My, that dress looks lovely with the ribbons threaded through your hair."

"Why thank you, ma'am." Clara gave a twirl with a small giggle before she sat on the comfortable chair next to Sheila.

"I also have a short note from Emily Thompson. She and Emma plan to come by early this morning before other callers. They're on their way to a last-minute fitting with Mademoiselle Franciose, so they won't be here too long."

"Oh, it will be lovely to talk with Emma without a crowd of people. I do want to learn how she enjoyed herself last night."

"From where I stood, it looked like you both had a wonderful time, with nary a moment to catch your breath from the dancing."

"It *was* a wonderful time, and I surprised myself with how quickly the evening was over. I had always thought parties so frivolous and, well, unnecessary in life. But, there is value in fun, too."

Sheila tried valiantly to hide her smile at such a profound statement from her darling niece. "Did you find anyone particularly interesting?"

"Seeing Annabelle again was such an unexpected delight, and her brother, Sir Richards, was quite charming."

"Charming, was he? And he invited you for a ride in the park later today?"

"Yes, he did, though I hope I'm not so tongue-tied today as I was last night. I felt like such a green girl when we met, and I actually heard myself stutter as I said hello!"

"My, is he so imposing?"

"Well, no, but he has the most spectacular blue eyes, and I found myself just staring in the most ill-mannered way."

Sheila let out a delighted trill of laughter at this statement but hastened to assure Clara that she was no different from any other girl at her first London ball.

"I have several more invitations in this morning's post that we can discuss after luncheon. I'd like you to become familiar with the hostesses in town for the Season; plus, it's simply not possible for us to attend them all. We'll have to send our regrets to some, and I'd appreciate your help in making those decisions."

"My help, Aunt Sheila? Why, thank you for the honor, but I don't really know anyone yet, so how can I be of any help to you?"

"Well, you'll get to know people as we make our decisions. Some of the parties will be tedious but necessary affairs, others will attract an older crowd rather than your younger set, and yet more will be perfect avenues for you girls to dance your slippers through. We need to balance our evenings and also allow you some nights at home for rest and reflection. The season does involve some planning to make sure you enjoy yourself."

"But what about you and Uncle Marcus? I want you both to enjoy this time, too."

"Oh, don't you worry about us! Marcus makes a fine escort and is happy to drift between the parties and the card rooms. He claims to conduct more business during the Season's parties than on the House floor! I am so enjoying seeing the Season through your eyes, and it's a wonderful dress rehearsal for me for when our Sarah has her come-out in a few years."

"But Sarah's only ten! You have quite a few years yet for her."

"Well, then, I must confess I just love the fun and excitement of the Season. You give me an excuse to attend more parties than I normally do. So please don't think that any of your time here is a chore or unpleasant for me."

Reilly entered the room just then to announce the Thompson ladies. They spilled into the morning room with a flutter of lace and greeted their hostess with wide smiles.

"Good morning, ladies. Such a cozy room you have here, Sheila, and the fire is especially nice on this cool morning," Emily said as she sat on the couch next to Sheila.

"And welcome to the both of you. You must have strong constitutions to brave the morning chill after such a late night." Sheila smiled at both her guests.

"I'm not sure if it's our constitutions or just a love of fashion," said a laughing Emma as she sat gracefully in the chair Reilly moved next to Clara. Sheila nodded her thanks to the butler. She knew he would refresh the tea and tray of morning treats without her having to ask.

"So, Emma, Clara has been telling me how much she enjoyed the Gearys' ball, and your smiling face must mean you concur?" asked Sheila.

"Oh, yes, but it was wonderful!" replied Emma. "I know we're supposed to be quite worldly about the Season's events, but I found it much too much fun for a blasé attitude. It's nothing at all like the assembly in Colverton back home!"

"She's been gushing like this all morning—I think we've launched a storm into society, Sheila!"

"Now, Emily, I can see by your laughter that you're joking. Why, these girls have begun a delightful time in their lives, and I'm so happy we can all enjoy it together." And the two ladies continued to discuss the Season and the mutual friends they'd seen the previous night.

"Oh, Clara, wasn't it a wonderful night! And to think that we can continue with more parties every night this week." Emma's eyes were round as saucers.

"Emma, you're such a silly girl. You'll drop from exhaustion by the end of the week if you don't consider slowing down a bit," Clara replied.

"But I'm not tired at all, and we stayed for the very last dance. I know that I can't do everything at every turn, but it certainly is fun to consider all the possibilities."

"Tell me what you liked best," asked Clara.

"The lively atmosphere and delightful people. Why, we've always enjoyed the local assemblies at home, but they were never in such a grand scale as the Gearys' ball. What about you, though? I couldn't help but notice you never sat down at a single dance!"

"I agree, it was a delightful time. Seeing Annabelle was a treat, plus all the invitations for dancing fairly made my head spin. So many charming men," smiled Clara.

"Any particular person?" Emma held her breath in case Clara echoed the name on her mind.

"Well, no, not really. Annabelle's brother, Sir Richards, certainly seems interesting, but no one I danced with caught my fancy." Clara felt like crossing her fingers at the small fib she told. *But I hadn't danced with* him, she told herself.

"I'm glad you didn't develop a particular fondness for Reggie Farleigh, for I found him so charming."

"Yes, he was a delightful partner, and he told a wonderful story at dinner about last Season's hunt at Farleigh Park."

"Wasn't it fun? He made the park sound just lovely," Emma said. "He asked me for the first dance this evening, plus he wants to sign my card for the supper dance." Clara saw a glowing look in Emma's eyes.

"My, but he does seem determined."

"But no more than Sir Richards inviting you for a drive in the park this afternoon," said a playful Emma.

"We both seem to have made conquests at our first ball."

"Now, I wouldn't call Sir Richards a conquest, Emma!"

"Oh, don't worry yourself. I just enjoy teasing you, and you know I won't say these things around anyone else but us. Have you decided what you'll wear tonight?"

"No. Aunt Sheila mentioned choosing a gown together after luncheon, though."

"I just love your new green one. The color does wonderful things for your eyes."

"Why, thank you, Emma. It's so nice of you to say so. I'll have to put it in front of the armoire so Aunt Sheila sees it first this afternoon." The girls laughed together in their good friendship.

Confound the man, thought Jeremy! They were to meet twenty minutes ago to look over the new stallion Dickers wanted to buy. Jeremy had been waiting more than half an hour and was more than ready to leave this horse farm for an early lunch. His stomach had loudly announced to everyone nearby, or so it seemed, that he'd breakfasted long ago.

"Enough!" he muttered and turned to walk back to his curricle.

He saw Dickers riding up the lane and stopped walking with a sigh. It just didn't pay to be on time with the man.

"Ho, there Jeremy. Splendid day for a ride." Dickers handed the reigns to a groom and walked the short distance over to Jeremy.

"And good morning to you. Is your watch broken by chance?"

"I know I'm late! You needn't rub it in with your not-so-subtle question. When you see this horse, you'll know it was worth the wait."

"It had better be, but even so, you're buying lunch."

"Yes, yes, whatever you say. Good, Wilkens is bringing Blackie out for us."

"I couldn't help but notice that you rode over here. How do you plan to ride home on two horses if you buy this Blackie?"

"Well, I was kind of hoping you'd tie my other horse to your curricle and bring him home for me. That way I can ride Blackie home."

"You *what?*"

"Now, Jeremy, it's not a long drive back to town, and—"

"Don't even think that I might enjoy parading through town with your nag tied to the back of my rig! Have you gone daft, man?"

"Oh, all right. I'm sure Wilkens can stable him here for a night or two, and I'll have my man come over for him. Never knew you to be quite so puffed up with your own consequence, though." Dickers laughed as he ducked the idle throw from Jeremy's fisted hand.

The men turned to look as Wilkens walked the horse out of the stable and began leading him through the jumps in the ring. Jeremy did have to admit the stallion had fine lines and jumped quite well. If he looked as well up close, and they wanted a fair price, he'd give Dickers credit for an excellent mount.

"He looks like a prime goer from here, Dickers. I'd say you have found yourself a winner. How does he ride?"

"Capital, just capital. I rode him for an hour two days ago, and it was as if we were made for each other."

"Well then, what's stopping you from buying him?"

"Nothing now. I do appreciate your opinion, you

know." Dickers motioned for Wilkens to bring the horse over to their side of the ring.

"What say we go for a ride in the park this afternoon? I think you need to show off your new acquisition."

"Great idea! I'll tell Wilkens it's a deal, and then we'll get you that lunch."

"Do you remember my telling you about my good friend from school named Charlotte?" asked Emma, and Clara nodded. "I'm sure I saw her last night towards the end of the ball."

"Why, Emma, that's wonderful. We'll have to look for her tonight and perhaps ask Aunt Sheila if she knows of her."

"Oh, that's a splendid idea, Clara." Emma turned to speak to the women.

Just then Sheila looked over at the girls to see if they needed more tea and saw the expectant look on Emma's face.

"Ma'am, are you acquainted with Charlotte March?" Emma asked. "I think I saw her at the Gearys' last evening, and she's a dear friend of mine from school."

"I do know of her, Emma, but I've not made her acquaintance," Sheila said. "Her aunt is acting as her chaperone and is a good friend of mine. She had a very successful Season last year and is back in town. As I recall, she had two fine offers but did not accept either of them."

"My, she was always quite a fun girl in school, but two offers!"

The ladies all laughed at Emma's astonishment as Emily gathered her gloves to leave for their appointment with the dressmaker. The Thompson ladies thanked Sheila for her hospitality and Reilly showed them out the front door.

"What a nice surprise about Emma's school friend, Charlotte," said Clara.

"Yes, you girls will have a nice circle of friends here in town to enjoy the parties and morning calls."

"I hope we're able to find her easily tonight."

"Oh, I shouldn't think that will be a problem," laughed Sheila. "Just look for the girl with stunning red hair surrounded by her many beaux."

"Not the Fair Incomparable! My goodness, but Emma is in for a surprise. Annabelle was telling us about her last night. She said she's ever so nice, even with all those silly men falling all over her."

"Then I imagine she'll enjoy the company of you girls. Plus, some of 'those silly men' might fall your way," smiled Sheila.

Reilly entered the room then to announce the arrival of the Farleighs, mother and daughters. Happily, thought Sheila, the girls were not dressed in like ensembles for their morning calls.

"Sheila, so delightful to see you again, and we so wanted to meet your niece," Millicent Farleigh said. "I am so sorry we didn't have a moment to talk together last night, but there was such a sad crush, and we were so busy at supper with two such delightful men. My, that Edward Waters and Lord Carruthers are such pets of mine."

Clara, busy greeting the Farleigh girls, did not hear Millicent Farleigh's name-dropping—and of a name that meant much to her.

Sheila, though, felt certain Jeremy would take a strong objection to Millicent's label of "pet." She knew Marcus would have a good laugh at the story when she told him of it later today. *My, but morning calls can be a trial at times,* she sighed to herself.

"So nice to see you again, Millicent. And, I'm glad you brought your girls with you so you all could meet my niece, Clara. Clara, this is Mrs. Farleigh, but I must beg your pardon, girls, and ask you to introduce yourselves. I would hate to make the mistake of mixing up your names when you look so alike." Everyone laughed at Sheila's honest appeal.

Melissa Farleigh spoke first. "I am Melissa, and Elisa is my sister. You can usually tell us apart by our hairstyles, since Elisa wears hers with more curls than I do."

"Why, thank you, dear, that information will be a help to me in the future. Now, please, everyone do sit down and have some tea. Are you girls enjoying your first season?" asked Sheila.

"Oh, 'tis such a routine of parties that I'm fair to wilting with all the dancing and late nights," Elisa replied affecting a yawn behind her hand to further display her boredom.

"Now, Elisa dear, not everyone is as accustomed as you girls to such exalted company as we shared at dinner last night with dear Jeremy and Edward," gushed Millicent. She turned to Sheila to add, "They'll be joining us at our little dinner party Tuesday next. Oh ladies, you too must attend. I'll be sure to send you cards."

Sheila nodded her thanks and couldn't help but wonder if Millicent's purpose in this morning call had less to do with meeting Clara and all to do with simply boasting to all who would listen. She fervently hoped they'd already accepted another invitation for Tuesday next.

Jeremy and Dickers lunched at a nearby inn and agreed to meet later in the day for their ride in the park. They parted company back at the horse farm where Dickers completed his purchase and made arrangements to stable his other horse for a few nights.

Jeremy drove back to town at a leisurely pace and contemplated his evening at the Gearys' ball.

He really was at a loss as to how he might make the acquaintance of that lovely girl. Short of admitting his interest to someone like Marcus's wife, Sheila, and then having her introduce him, he didn't see how he could make it happen easily. And that plan presumed that Sheila already knew the girl, too.

He knew he could not endure another evening such as last night! That supper had been enough to sour him on mamas and their matchmaking ways, but what choice did he have? Society dictated that its members meet in prescribed settings such as the ball, Almacks or perhaps a house party. *Kidnapping is certainly out of the question,* he laughed to himself. For a man who had led troops into battle and won the day, the frustration of this crusade was a unique experience.

But of course! He needed to prepare a campaign. Put it into military terms, which he had managed for years, and he could certainly accomplish the task. Arriving at the ball last night with no plans had been his mistake. Admittedly, he'd only realized yesterday afternoon that the prospect of marriage appealed to him, so it had been quite a surprise to find such a charming and entrancing girl a few hours later.

As much as it might grate on his nerves to be dependent on the man, he would stop by his club this afternoon and strike up a conversation with Richards. He knew the girl—why he'd danced and supped with her. Chances were he'd spoken for a dance tonight as well, and Jeremy could engineer a meeting when he saw them together. Plus that yearling, Burroughs, could provide much-needed information, too. Knowing her name might be nice, he muttered.

Yes, he could already feel his spirits lighten. He had several hours before meeting Dickers in the park, and he planned to put the time to good use on this campaign.

"What a beautiful day for a ride in the park, Sir Richards," said Clara.

"Oh, yes, I ordered it 'specially for you," he laughed as he led the carriage through the streets from the Clifton townhouse.

"I spent most of the day indoors, so it feels wonderful to have the sun on my face and feel the breeze."

"Do you ride at home much, Miss Edwards?"

"Oh yes, it's one of my great pleasures. I've not spent much time in the city, so it's taken some adjustment these past few weeks being out of the country."

"Did you bring a mount with you?"

"No, but Uncle Marcus assures me he has a beautiful mare named Cocoa that I may ride anytime. I just haven't had the time with all the preparations for the Season."

"Wonderful! If I may be so bold as to ask you, I'd be delighted to meet you one morning for a brisk ride in the park. No galloping, though, if your aunt hasn't already told you. Not at all the thing here in town, and I wouldn't want to see you make a misstep."

He spoke with such an earnest and kind voice that Clara could not at all take offense at his words.

"Why, thank you for the invitation. Aunt Sheila did tell me no country riding here in town, but it is nice to have someone else to guide me."

He covered his quick intake of breath by focusing his attention on the horses. She couldn't realize what a tangle she'd made of his heart just then. He found it an odd sensation to have someone's welfare in his hands. *A nice sensation,* he amended.

They turned into the park, and Clara was surprised

at the number of carriages and riders she saw. While they had arrived at the fashionable hour, it seemed all of London had decided to join them. Sir Richards drove them expertly through the crowds at the gate and was happy when the press of carriages thinned some as he drove further.

"My, look at everyone! Is it always this crowded?" Clara asked.

"The Season has just started, so company is actually a bit thin here in the park. In another fortnight, you won't be able to turn a carriage around at this hour."

"Is that Annabelle with Reggie Farleigh?" asked Clara, and she wondered if Emma knew about this meeting.

"I believe it is. I don't recall her mentioning a ride today when I saw her at breakfast this morning, but I did spend the afternoon in my club. I'll drive over so we can say hello."

Annabelle saw them as they approached and waved her hand. Reggie slowed his carriage to wait for them to draw close.

"Hello, Clara," Annabelle said. "I am sorry my cousin and I didn't come to call on you this morning. She had a touch of the headache after our late night at the Gearys'. And, if I do confess, I was happy to stay home and relax myself. I just can't be out so late and dance through my slippers."

"My sister, the inexhaustible dancer," drawled Sir Richards.

"Oh, quiet you!" Annabelle affected a delightful pout.

"Well, I think both of you ladies look splendid this afternoon. Why you'd never know you had danced away the evening," said a gallant Reggie Farleigh.

"And a good bit of the morning," added Clara, and they all laughed.

"Don't tell me a little fatigue will stop you from attending the Mardsdens' affair this evening?" asked Sir Richards of his sister.

"'Twould be a crime!" teased Reggie.

"Now you two must stop your silliness!" laughed Annabelle. "We'll be there certainly, but I for one will head home a bit sooner."

"We'd best move on so we don't completely block the lane here. Your servant, Farleigh," Sir Richards replied, expertly turning his carriage.

From the opposite direction came Dickers and Jeremy. They'd finished a bit of riding on the open green and were now content with a slow trot through the park. Jeremy could see that Dickers was close to bursting with his excitement over the new horse and the fun of showing it to the several friends they'd met this afternoon.

"What a mount!" said Dickers with enthusiasm.

"Yes, you've chosen a prime goer there. Edward will be most envious and impressed."

"Too bad he was promised to his aunt this afternoon, or he could have joined us for our ride."

"You'll have plenty of time to show off Blackie to Edward."

"Too bad I can't ride him to the ball tonight!" laughed Dickers.

"So, what time are we to arrive tonight?"

"Oh, late again. Don't want to appear too eager with my Fair Incomparable."

"Since when is she 'your' Fair Incomparable? Seemed to me she was pretty unattached at the Gearys'," Jeremy said dryly. "Perhaps you'll want to rethink that late arrival plan and be there first to greet her with sweet compliments when she arrives."

"Do you think so? I hadn't considered the advantages of being first. I could put my name down on her card for the supper dance rather than just hanging about the table. Capital idea!"

"It might be a novel experience for you to be announced and greet the hostess, too," offered Jeremy.

"Oh, no, too much ceremony for me," laughed Dickers.

"Well I know Edward will be happy for the earlier start."

"Still on his campaign, is he?"

"Don't call it a campaign, man!" That reference was too close to home for Jeremy.

"Well, all right then, his quest. Is that better for you? My, my, never knew you to be so touchy."

Jeremy let the barb go and continued their ride. He'd had little success this afternoon in starting his own "campaign," and it bothered him. Burroughs had never shown his face at the club, and he'd learned precious little from Richards. Oh, they'd talked some and even discussed the ball last night, but he'd not learned a spec of information about the lovely blonde.

He'd had a nice talk with Marcus about the politics of the day, and the time had calmed his mind some. He had even gone so far as to mention wanting to meet someone, and Marcus had promised to mention it to Sheila for the introduction. He knew he could count on their help and discretion, so the day was not a complete loss.

Perhaps he'd been foolish to think he could extract information from Richards, since Richards was so clearly interested in her as well. He wasn't used to having his plans proven so fruitless, and he sighed again in frustration. Would he see her here in the park? He could only hope so.

* * *

Clara saw him as soon as their carriage returned to the lane. She felt calm, but her heart started beating wildly, or so it seemed. My, but he looked magnificent seated on that stallion.

"Well, Miss Edwards?"

"Oh, I'm sorry, I guess I was lost in this wonderful view," improvised Clara.

"I'd wondered if you, too, planned to cut short your time at the ball tonight?" asked Sir Richards.

"I think it a good idea. Why I slept past nine o'clock this morning!" said a shocked Clara. She kept *him* in view under the cover of the brim of her hat.

"That's hardly scandalous." Sir Richards let out a hearty laugh—a laugh that attracted attention from many of those near their carriage. Clara turned towards him and joined in the laughter.

Jeremy heard it and looked across the lane. Damn! Richards again, and she looked as lovely as he remembered from last night. *What a stunning shade of blue in her carriage dress,* he thought. He looked away to avoid Dickers' following his stare.

Will he notice me? Clara thought? What if he approached the carriage? Did he know Sir Richards? So many questions, and no opportunity to find the answers in the middle of a crowd in the middle of the park!

"We're almost though the park, Miss Edwards. Shall we turn for home or ride back through again?"

"Oh, I don't mean to keep you driving all afternoon, Sir Richards. Perhaps we'd best head home so your horses won't tire." She knew her words sounded a little stilted and forced. Fortunately, she thought, her escort was too much the gentleman to make any comment.

Jeremy watched as the carriage exited the gate and was glad for it. He knew he wouldn't have approached her today in the park. He wanted a more comfortable setting than one seated on a horse looking into another man's carriage, with that man watching!

EIGHT

A FATEFUL MEETING

The room fairly glistened with stars, or so it seemed to Clara upon entering the Mardsdens' brightly lit ballroom. She knew she looked her best in the beautiful gown of shimmering ivory and lace. Even though Aunt Sheila had told her that debutantes were to wear white, her aunt had felt that her maturity allowed her to carry subtle shades of color. Clara couldn't help giving a silent prayer to her aunt for her good judgement in her Season.

Clara had rested after her carriage ride in the park and taken the time for some reflection. Even though the rest had made her arrive late and miss the first few dances, she valued the time to craft her plan. She had realized the futility of trying to engineer a meeting between them—it was just too hard to plan without enlisting the aid of others. And she was not prepared to reveal her mission to anyone, even Emma.

As she thought back to the previous night's party and counted the number of people she'd met and now considered as friends, she felt confident that their paths would soon cross. Why, with all of Aunt Sheila's popularity and Uncle Marcus's connections, they must know most everyone in London. And if they didn't meet soon, she would just have to call on her aunt or uncle to introduce her to such a fine specimen!

Instead, she had steered her thoughts towards how she might act at their first meeting here in town. Should she be affronted at seeing him again, or feign not knowing him? She decided for honesty and that it would be best to acknowledge a prior meeting and appear pleasant and refined, perhaps even a bit aloof or mysterious. Now that thought had made her giggle—mysterious, indeed!

So, she would toss him a sunny smile and say . . . what? "Pleasure to see you again"—no, that would imply she'd forgotten or didn't care about his actions when they'd met. What about the simple "How do you do?" Bah! What a plain response—she'd never capture his attention with words such as these!

She would offer a smile and move into a question about him, such as "Have you been back in town long?" Yes, that would imply that she'd not noticed him until then and also let him know that she hadn't forgotten their roadside meeting.

Would it be enough of a "hint," she thought? It might not serve to be *too* subtle. She hardly wanted to make reference to that meeting with the first words out of her mouth—no, much too forward! She might follow up with a reference to the countryside or their small village to jog his memory.

And what if he didn't remember her? Well, all the better. Then she could give him that mysterious smile and make him a bit uncomfortable. No gentleman would ever admit to forgetting a meeting with a lady. She would even laugh about that interminable dinner together at the Thompsons'. He couldn't have forgotten that scene!

So Clara surveyed the ballroom with an oddly expectant feeling and a confident square to her shoulders. Little did she realize the eyes trained on her from each of the other corners of the ballroom! William Burroughs looked longingly at her party and hoped he'd find the nerve to sign his name to her dance card. Sir Martin Richards moved immediately toward the entry to greet the charming girl. And, lastly, Lord Jeremy Carruthers shook himself to relieve the tension he'd felt while waiting for her to arrive.

By gad! Could *she* be Marcus's niece? Jeremy was stunned—it was the only word to describe his heart-stopping surprise. Why, she must be the niece, since they'd all arrived together. He couldn't imagine a young woman such as she arriving unescorted. He found himself smiling broadly and just barely caught the laugh that rumbled in this chest. What a wonderful coincidence!

His tension all but gone, he saw his "campaign" falling into place so smoothly. Rather than biding his time tonight as he'd planned, he'd find Marcus posthaste for that introduction. Or, better still, he'd find Sheila. She wouldn't delay acquainting her niece with her husband's good friend. And he'd best move quickly before her dance card filled with the names of other men.

Clara now chatted comfortably with Annabelle as the musicians started another set. Emma hadn't yet arrived, and Reggie Farleigh was the third in their trio. Clara faced the windows with her back to the room, so she failed to see the approach.

"Ladies, you look lovely. Farleigh, good to see you," Sir Richards said.

"Why hello, Martin. What a pleasant greeting, and from my own brother!" smiled Annabelle.

Clara smiled her own greeting and laughed aloud as Sir Richards simply held out his hand.

"What, no pretty request for a dance?"

Everyone laughed at Clara's affected pout, and then laughed again when she obligingly handed over the dance card. Sir Richards signed his name to the supper dance and one later in the evening. He knew he'd enjoy her time between the dances leading up to supper.

"I believe this dance is mine," Reggie added, holding his arm for Clara to lead her out into the set. Sir Richards and Lady Annabelle soon followed.

"Jeremy, good to see you again. I see you're heading my way into the card room. Can I challenge you to a game?" Marcus asked.

"Hello, Marcus," Jeremy replied. "Yes, I was coming over to see you, but not for cards just yet. I only arrived a few minutes ago and thought I would enjoy the ball first. Perhaps even a set or two before supper."

"Splendid! Sheila can't be too far away even in this crowd, and she can present you to her niece. Fine girl, and quite pretty, too." Marcus gave a conspiratorial wink to Jeremy as they headed towards Sheila. "Sorry. I forgot to mention to her about introducing you to the gel you wanted to meet. Might be a bit awkward now with her niece at her side. We'll see what we can do another night."

Jeremy smiled at that wink, and couldn't help but wonder if any of his friends would comment on his decided good humor this evening. Far from the rarely social persona he often presented at *ton* affairs, this smiling and affable squire to green debutantes could hardly go unnoticed!

"Jeremy, it's nice to see you again so soon." Sheila held out her hand for the proffered kiss.

"I'm here with several friends, but I sought out Marcus, knowing he'd lead me to his beautiful wife."

"Such a compliment, but don't waste your folderol on a married woman!" laughed Sheila.

"I thought he meant to accompany me to the card room, but he'd have none of it."

"Well, you men must be kept from that card room at all costs. There are far too many lovely young ladies here this evening." And Sheila caught Clara's eye and silently signaled her to join her aunt when the set ended. *Best not to say anything about Clara to Jeremy until the girl is right at hand,* thought Sheila. She'd not let him out of her grasp so quickly tonight.

"You said you're here with friends, Jeremy?" asked Marcus.

"Yes, Dickers Smythe-Hattan and Edward Waters. They're here somewhere, though I'm sure we'll spot Dickers at the feet of the Fair Incomparable." Jeremy turned towards the dancers to see if the entourage was nearby.

"Ah, caught in her web, is he?" smiled Sheila.

"He has Edward and me coming and going from these affairs at just the precisely right time to make 'an entrance,' but it all seems a bit ridiculous to me," laughed Jeremy, and he turned back to face Sheila and Marcus.

Clara and Reggie finished their set, and Clara nodded in Sheila's direction when Reggie asked if she wanted some refreshment.

"My aunt signaled to me earlier in the set—I think she wants to talk with me now. I see that Uncle Marcus is with her, too," she said.

"Perhaps she has some news of Miss Thompson and her party," Reggie mentioned slyly.

Clara smiled at this bit of information. She knew Emma would be in transports to learn that Reggie was looking for her tonight. And they soon covered the short distance to the side of the ballroom.

"Seems your aunt is busy with some people," Reggie said.

"Ah, here she is," said Marcus.

Jeremy turned toward the dance floor and could have sworn he felt his heart lurch. She looked lovelier than ever he remembered from last night, and he had to consciously exhale lest he embarrass himself gasping for air!

Clara barely caught herself from tripping when she saw him at her aunt's side. How had she missed seeing him standing there! Could she ever put her plan into action now? Oh, what *had* she decided to say first?

"Clara, dear, may I present Marcus's good friend, Lord Carruthers. Jeremy, this is my niece, Miss Edwards," Sheila said.

Jeremy said, "My pleasure to meet you, Miss Edwards." At last, he knew her name!

"Hello, Lord Carruthers." He did not seem to remember her!

"And are you acquainted with Reggie Farleigh, Jeremy?" asked Sheila.

"Yes, good to see you again, Farleigh," said Jeremy.

"Great guns to see you, Carruthers," Reggie replied.

Clara asked, "Have you been back in town long, Lord Carruthers?" There, she'd collected her thoughts and remembered her opening remark while the men exchanged greetings. But how could one such as he be a good friend to Uncle Marcus?

"Well, yes, a fortnight or more," Jeremy said, a bit puzzled.

"I've certainly found London a far cry from the countryside," she said with a smile, but her tone implied that he, too, should make the same comparison.

"Yes, I must agree with you there." What was going on here? It was as if she expected him to know her. As if he could forget such a face and figure!

"Have you recently been in the countryside, Jeremy?" asked Marcus.

"I had a short trip before the Season started, but I plan to be here in town for some time now."

"Clara's just up from the country herself," added Marcus.

"Miss Edwards, may I have the pleasure of this next dance?" asked Jeremy as he tried to steer the conversation in a direction he preferred.

"Why thank you, Lord Carruthers, but I am already promised for the supper dance. Perhaps something after supper?"

"That would be delightful, if I might sign your card for the dance following supper?"

Clara extended her dance card to him and found herself holding her breath as their hands briefly touched. *It is a very good thing Emma was late in getting here this evening,* she thought. Why had it never occurred to her that Emma might have been a problem had she witnessed this "first" meeting?

Jeremy was glad for the short break in conversation as he penned his name on her card. This must be the strangest introduction on record!

"I look forward to our dance later." Jeremy gave her a charming smile as he returned the card.

Sheila had watched this entire exchange with a puzzled frown at her brow. There seemed an undercurrent to their meeting, but she couldn't put a name to it. She planned to have a word or two with Clara at the first opportunity.

"Lord and Lady Clifton, so good to see you tonight," said Sir Richards as he joined their party. He nodded greetings to the two men and turned to speak to Clara. "Miss Edwards, you do remember our dance?"

"Why of course, Sir Richards. I hear the music starting." She turned to take his arm.

"Pardon me for taking her away from you gentlemen and Lady Clifton."

"Enjoy your dance," smiled Sheila as the pair headed onto the floor.

"Your niece is lovely, Sheila. This Season is her first?" Jeremy asked.

"Thank you, Jeremy, and yes, Clara makes her bows this year. I've tried for the last two years to entice her up to town, but she's always professed a true love of the country. She seems to be enjoying herself here, though, so perhaps it was just a case of finding the right time. She does have two good friends making their debuts this season, and I'm sure the company of girlhood friends makes the rounds of parties more fun."

"We are all grateful you found the words to bring her to London now, ma'am," smiled Jeremy.

"I'll certainly second that, Lady Clifton. Miss Edwards and her friend Miss Thompson are truly lovely additions to our Season," said a gallant Reggie Farleigh.

Jeremy looked quickly at Farleigh. What was nagging at the back of his mind? Surely he had missed a vital piece of information—something was just below the surface, and he couldn't see it.

"I'm not sure what's keeping the Thompson party tonight. They gave no indication this morning that they might arrive after supper," said Sheila.

"Perhaps they just got a late start and are now caught in the press of carriages as they neared the Mardsdens' townhouse," offered Jeremy.

"Yes, that's undoubtedly the answer. All of London

seems to be here, but I still see more people coming through the doors even though the receiving line has long dispersed. I'm sure they will arrive soon." Sheila felt it was a plausible explanation.

"Come to think of it, I don't see Dickers with his Fair Incomparable tonight—the whole group seems to be missing," said Jeremy.

"Another party, perhaps?" suggested Marcus.

"Oh, but who would slight the Mardsdens' by arriving here second?" said a slightly scandalized Sheila.

"I'm sorry I mentioned it, my dear. Forgive me my churlish and inconsiderate tongue," smiled Marcus.

"Now you're making fun of me! I've a good mind to send you packing to that card room now!" laughed Sheila along with the gentlemen.

"Why don't we start for the supper room now before this set ends? I must confess I feel a strong twinge of hunger, and the Mardsdens' do set a sumptuous table. And we can hold a few places for the Thompson party," said Marcus.

"Why, I'll be the envy of all the women here with three such handsome dinner partners," laughed Sheila.

"The envy will all be with the men, dear lady, when they see us with you," Reggie said smoothly.

Clara did her best to pay attention to her partner as she turned her way through the patterns of the country dance. Fortunately, she knew her steps well and could afford a glance to the edge of the dance floor more than once. Sir Richards did not seem to notice her inattention, or perhaps he was just too much the gentleman to remark on it.

What a surprise that he knew her aunt and uncle! Nothing could have shocked her more in the introduction from Aunt Sheila than those words about Lord Carruthers. Did that fact change anything in her plan? Wasn't she now under an obligation to abandon all thought of teaching him a lesson, given his friendship with her uncle? Even honor-bound to give him a second chance? Oh, what a coil!

She'd best think about her predicament later and make a decision in the morning. For tonight, there would be no harm in simply treating him as she would any friend of her uncle's. Why yes, she could be the polite debutante as expected, and it would even further her plan should she decide to continue it on the morrow. What better way to "catch" him than to charm him during their first dance? And even if she'd admit it to no one but herself, she really didn't have anything in mind for what she would have done differently had she put "the plan" into action now.

Surprisingly, she hadn't given a thought to the startling blue eyes of her partner during the entire dance. They came together in the last figure, and she smiled at him with just a twinge of guilt. Little did she realize that the smile gave her a demure look of attractiveness noticed by Sir Richards *and* Lord Carruthers.

"Shall we find our table for dinner, Miss Edwards?"

"Yes, thank you, and I hope we can join your sister, too. I saw her across the dance floor as we ended the set, so we may have trouble finding her in this crush."

"Never fear! Annabelle, champagne, and sweetmeats will find us, I'm sure," laughed Sir Richards. He held out his arm for her and led her toward the supper room.

Emma and her mother had finally appeared at the ballroom door. Mrs. Thompson quickly surveyed the room while Emma turned back to the entrance to acknowledge the greeting from her good friend, Charlotte March.

"Charlotte, it is wonderful to see you again," Emma said, and the girls embraced warmly.

"Emma, I'm so pleased to see you, too. The Season will be so much better sharing it with you," replied Charlotte." May I present to you my aunt, Lady Maria Snow? Auntie, this is Emma Thompson, my good friend from school."

Mrs. Thompson turned around just then to greet the young lady and meet her chaperone. "Ladies, please join us for supper," she said. "I'm sure that our friends have room for us at their table, and they would be pleased to meet you and have you join us as well."

"Why, thank you, Mrs. Thompson. We do appreciate your kindness. We were late in arriving tonight and hadn't made any arrangements for supper," said Lady Snow.

"Oh, please do call me Emily."

"And I am Maria," Lady Snow replied. The ladies linked arms, just as the girls did before them, and headed into the supper room.

NINE

MYSTERY SOLVED

Sir Richards ably steered Clara toward the supper room, where they met Annabelle and her cousin, Patricia Withers, who were just sitting down at a cozy table.

"What, no partner for the supper dance, dear Sis?" he asked.

"Oh, you beast! Of course I had a partner—I enjoyed a lovely reminisce with Papa's former aide, Colonel Clarkston. He's procuring the most delicious of treats for us now. Clara, how do you put up with this incorrigible man?" laughed Annabelle.

"Sometimes I think you two are sworn enemies, with all your bickering and teasing," said Patricia affectionatly.

Sir Richards stopped short in his signal to a passing footman to bring them two plates, just as Annabelle's dinner partner arrived with a footman laden with food. The colonel had brought enough for two tables, and the small group began a delicious and filling repast.

At another table, Emma and her mother had joined Sheila, Marcus and the two gentlemen. Charlotte and her aunt were made known to the group, and Sheila delighted in seeing her good friend, Lady Snow.

Reggie Farleigh, counting himself most fortunate to have Miss Thompson seated at his side during supper, might have been accused of incivility with nary a second glance to the rest of the company. While certainly noticing Miss March and her beauty, his eyes and heart belonged to Miss Thompson. He wished the meal would last the whole night, if he could only spend the time with Miss Thompson!

Miss March, on the other hand, caught herself several times as her eyes leapt across the table to Mr. Farleigh. He seemed so animated and full of life—and certainly did not act the fool at her feet like many of the other boys. *Yes,* she thought, *I'd like to learn more about this Mr. Farleigh.* She would have to ask her aunt if they might pay a morning call on Lady Clifton on the morrow.

Miss Thompson found herself enraptured to be seated next to Mr. Farleigh, but her eyes kept straying to the unknown man at the end of the table. Who was this mysterious lord, where had she seen him before, and why did Mama seem as if she knew him already? So many questions! Once she'd seen Reggie holding a chair for her, she'd paid scant attention to the man and their introduction. Perhaps after supper she'd ask Mama how she knew him—that would surely clear up the mystery for her.

For Lord Carruthers, his mystery would soon make sense. Mrs. Thompson had greeted him like a friend, and he couldn't attribute it to her natural demeanor. She did not seem an overly effusive woman, such as La Farleigh, so her kindness and consideration for his person could only come from prior acquaintance. And where could that meeting have taken place? Well, he'd bide his time at supper and try to draw her out without asking too many prying questions. He'd have his answer before the ices, he vowed.

Sheila glanced around the table and saw a lively group of friends and newcomers enjoying the fine meal and company. Thoughts of hosting a dinner party jumped into her head. It would be a wonderful way to bring Jeremy and Clara together without seeming to push them toward one another. And a little dancing afterwards or a carriage ride to the opera could bring them even closer. Yes, she'd start planning tomorrow and enlist Clara's help with the guest list so that all her new friends were included. She supposed, with a sigh, that the whole Farleigh clan would have to be invited if she wanted to have that darling Reggie for Emma.

"Oh, Colonel Clarkston, stop! I can't keep laughing like this and hope to finish this delicious food on my plate. Please stop telling such wild stories!" cried Annabelle.

"A life in the Diplomatic Corps gives me some hilarious tales, I must admit," said the colonel.

"Did you always want to be a diplomat?" asked Mrs. Withers.

"Heavens, no!" exclaimed the colonel. "Had my heart set on riding into battle. But during my first campaign as a brash lieutenant, I ran afoul of my horse and found him on top of my leg."

At the ladies' gasps, he hurriedly explained that he had recovered quite nicely but his hard riding days were over. The life of a diplomat allowed him to stay in the military and serve his country from a carriage rather than astride a horse.

"Been a wonderful life, and I do feel fortunate to have traveled the Continent and even to the Americas for a time," Colonel Clarkson said. "Serving with your father these past seven years has brought my foreign service to a satisfying end. I've returned to London now to work and perhaps do some writing about military strategy. Even though I barely saw a battle, I feel I can tell these young officers a thing or two."

"Excellent idea, sir. Our father speaks highly of you in his letters, and I'm sure you will find much to keep you busy here in town," said Sir Richards.

"Thank you, my boy. I feel as if I know you two young people as well as my own children. And having Annabelle with us in Vienna for the last few years certainly made your father happy. I understand you're to join your father soon, Martin?"

"Yes, in the autumn. I've enjoyed these two years here in town assisting you and Father, but it's time I gained some field experience. I'm rather looking forward to the new assignment."

"Just be careful of those horses!" warned the Colonel with a wink, and the others joined in with laughter at his joke.

"What could have happened to your friends this evening, Jeremy?" Marcus asked.

"I do know we walked into the ballroom together, but beyond that fact I haven't the slightest notion," smiled Jeremy.

"You young men often disappear into the card rooms, much to the despair of the ladies looking for dancing partners," said Emily.

"I'm sure they've found their own pretty ladies to dine with," offered a gallant Marcus.

"Undoubtedly, and I'll hear about it tomorrow at the club when most likely they'll accuse me of deserting them," said Jeremy.

"I think we should entreat our hostesses to do away

with the card tables," exclaimed Sheila with a teasing smile.

"Well that's all well and good, my dear, but I rather think it's the hosts you'll need to speak to about the card tables," laughed Marcus.

"Just think how many matches might occur if you gentlemen had no cards to retreat to during the evenings! Why, Westminster would be reserved years in advance!"

"Sheila, you are so true," said Emily as she joined in the spirit of teasing the gentlemen. "I vow it would be a capital idea."

"I fear you would start a riot rather than a rush of weddings. I for one have no interest in leaving you lovely ladies for a hand of cards," said Marcus.

"Hear, hear," exclaimed Jeremy. "And to prove our point, we'll just have to sign the dance cards of each of the ladies at this table."

Sheila and Emily laughed at this bit of silliness, but it appeared Jeremy was serious. Marcus gave him a stare of mock horror, and Sheila fairly whooped at his discomfort.

"I declare, young man, I don't remember you being such a trickster when you visited us at Hadley Abbey last month," Emily said fondly.

"You've visited the Thompsons?" Sheila asked Jeremy with surprise.

"Oh, not a visit precisely," offered Emily. "More like an unexpected drop-in when his curricle broke down. Roger found him in town and entreated him to stay the night while he waited for the repairs."

Jeremy was very glad of his poker face at that moment. He finally had the answer to the question that had nagged at him throughout the meal. It wouldn't have done to exclaim about his sudden insight, so he merely nodded his agreement with Emily Thompson's story to Sheila. Fast thinking of that Roger to simply attribute his arrival to just the broken curricle!

"Yes, I'd planned to attend a mill in the area, but I found the Thompsons' company far more enjoyable," he said.

"Now aren't you the sweet talker? I'll let Roger know that we met you again in town when I next write to him."

As they continued their conversation, Emma and Charlotte found much to say to each other. Though it had been little more than two years since they'd left Lady Henrietta's Conservatory for Young Ladies, Charlotte had spent last Season in town while Emma had had a quiet time at home after her grandfather's passing.

"I'm truly enjoying my time in London," said Emma.

"Oh, yes," agreed Charlotte. "I've found this Season to be so wonderful. When I debuted last year, it was a bit nerve wracking with so many new people to meet. I feel a bit more confident today."

"But weren't there any other girls from school with you last year?"

"Why, yes. I spent much time with Mary and Elizabeth from Lady Hen's, but they both barely stayed in town for half the Season. Mary met Lord Clayton-Griggs at her very first rout, and they announced their engagement not a month later. And I'm sure you heard the sad story about Elizabeth?" At Emma's blank stare, Charlotte continued.

"Two men actually fought a duel over her! She was mortified and wanted nothing to do with either man when the awful affair ended. We attended a few more balls together, but she returned home a short while later. The stares and whispers were just too much for her. She wrote me at Christmas that she planned to stay at home this Season, but I am hopeful she'll return. In my last letter I told her that the *ton* has forgotten last year's gossip and she need not have any fear."

"I remember Elizabeth as a very sensitive girl, though, and I'm sure she took it all very hard," said Emma.

"Oh, yes, it was wrenching for her! I'm not even sure why the men dueled, since she had no partiality for either one of them," mused Charlotte.

"I often thought they fancied themselves in love with her," offered Lady Snow. "Perhaps one of them felt the other was gaining the upper hand, as it were, and challenged him. Men can be quite daft when they've had too much to drink."

Charlotte and Emma nodded their agreement, and Reggie squirmed a bit uncomfortably. He had watched the two young women during their conversation, and he greatly admired Miss Thompson's feelings for the missing Elizabeth. *She is an angel,* he sighed to himself.

"Please, let us talk of something else," said Emma. "It makes me sad to think of the pain she must have gone through."

"Yes, you're right, and I'm sorry to have mentioned it here," Charlotte replied.

"Oh tosh, don't give it another thought! I'm so glad that we met tonight. It is lovely to see you again after a whole year. And Lady Clifton tells me *you've* made quite a splash yourself!" giggled Emma.

"It is quite a whirl, I must admit," Charlotte said with a blush. "I do despair of the attention sometimes, and this lovely supper with all of you tonight has been delightful."

"Let us make plans to meet tomorrow morning. I should love to have a long talk and truly catch up on the past year."

"Yes, Emma, that sounds perfect. Supper here is almost ending, and I want to hear about you."

"Well my time has been quiet, but I know you have so much more to tell," teased Emma.

At the lull in their conversation Reggie jumped in. "Miss March, may I sign your card for later this evening?"

"Why, thank you Mr. Farleigh. I look forward to a dance with you." She fished her card from her reticule.

"And your card, Miss Thompson? Might I find an open space for my name?" Reggie asked.

"You silly! Every space is open, since we just arrived." Emma happily handed her card to Mr. Farleigh.

"Keep those cards out, ladies! Marcus and I would beg the favor of a dance with you, too," Jeremy said, turning his attention toward the foursome.

"We'd be honored, Lord Carruthers," said Charlotte.

Emma turned to hand her card to the gentlemen and chanced a look at this mysterious lord. He did look familiar, and what was that name Charlotte called him? Lord Carruthers?

Sheila smiled as Marcus signed his name to each of the girls' cards. It would do him a bit of good to dance with them and certainly wouldn't harm the cachet of the young ladies either. Not that Miss March needed any more conquests—no, the Fair Incomparable was managing just fine.

Jeremy signed Emma's card and smiled his thanks to her as he returned it. He noticed a familiarity about her and imagined he must have met her when he stayed that night at the Thompsons'.

"Are you enjoying your stay in town, Miss Thompson?"

"Oh it's been wonderful, though I think my friends have tired of hearing me say so," smiled Emma in return.

"I'm sure you've been told that a bored, indifferent manner is much more the thing among debutantes.

But, I must admit I find your appreciation of the Season's events most refreshing."

"Thank you, sir."

"Are your other friends here this evening?" asked Jeremy.

"Oh, to be sure they arrived long before Mama and I did. We'll see each other on the dance floor. I have two good friends here tonight—one from school and another from home for her first Season, too. Oh, my, no!" Emma delicately clapped her hand to her mouth in shock—no, horror! This man was Clara's nemesis from the curricle on the road back home!

"Miss Thompson, what is it?" Jeremy asked with concern.

"Oh, nothing, sir. I just remembered—no, I just realized, oh heavens!"

Jeremy could not begin to understand her discomfort and felt at a loss as to what he should do to assist her.

"I believe we have this dance, Miss Thompson," said a smiling Reggie as he turned from Miss March and held his arm for her.

"Oh, yes, Mr. Farleigh." She breathed a sigh of relief and gratefully placed her hand on his arm as they moved toward the dance floor.

Jeremy still couldn't fathom their last exchange, but he saw Marcus walking over to assist Miss March from her chair for their dance. He knew he must find Miss Edwards, but one more conversation delayed him. Mrs. Thompson joined him just as he started to move away from their table.

"Sheila tells me you're to have the next dance with her niece?"

"Yes, and I am looking forward to it very much."

"Oh, I am so glad that you're not refining too much

on that little incident during dinner at our home." Emily both asked and stated.

"Little incident? I don't quite follow you, ma'am?"

"What a gentleman you are, sir, to so gallantly deny remembering it. I imagine Clara is sure to have forgotten it as well."

"Clara? Do you mean Miss Edwards?"

"Oh, you truly have forgotten, or perhaps you haven't connected Sheila's niece with your dinner partner at our home?"

But, of course! Jeremy thought. How could he have missed the resemblance, even though the Miss Edwards at this ball was a far cry from the woman he had met that day in the country? Now, her cryptic comment before supper fell into place, and he began to make sense of it all.

"I assure you, Mrs. Thompson, that your dinner was the furthest thing from my mind tonight. I look forward to this dance with Miss Edwards with the greatest of anticipation and enjoyment. Now, if you'll excuse me, I'd best find the young lady before she thinks I've deserted her!"

He nodded a goodbye to Sheila and headed himself into the fray. What a revelation, and to think the little minx had been testing him with her comment earlier: "Have you been back in town long, Lord Carruthers?" She wasn't sure if he remembered her! He couldn't decide if he should roast her with the innocence of his supposed forgetfulness or tease her about that interminable dinner. What a lovely coil!

"I do hope your next partner hasn't forgotten your dance together, Miss Edwards," said Mrs. Withers. She had stayed with Clara at their supper table when the others paired off with their partners for the dance.

"Oh, I expect he'll be here soon. The orchestra is still settling itself, so we have some time," Clara said, but her outward calm hid a heart full of doubt. Had he truly forgotten? Or perhaps he'd remembered her and couldn't countenance the idea of a dance? Would it be much too forward to simply stand up and look for him?

Clara took several deep breaths to help her relax. This dance was *only* a dance after all, and she truly did not think he'd embarrass them both in front of her aunt and uncle. No, she had nothing to fear tonight, and she held the advantage with knowledge of their previous meeting. She had vowed to act the perfect lady at this meeting, if only to please her aunt. She felt better now after reasoning through this muddle and smiled as she realized it might even be fun!

He spotted her at a table not far across the supper room. His task was really quite easy with most of the dancers now drifting toward the strains of tuning instruments. He found himself holding his breath at the sight of her and such a beautiful smile. She was a lovely girl, but her smile was radiant. He reached the table in a few strides.

"I believe this dance is ours, Miss Edwards."

"Yes, Lord Carruthers." She rose gracefully to her feet. "May I present Mrs. Withers, sir? And ma'am, this is Lord Carruthers."

"A pleasure to meet you, my lord," Mrs. Withers said.

"The honor is all mine, ma'am. I knew and admired your husband, and I was very sorry to hear of his passing last year," Jeremy replied.

"Thank you very much, sir. Even now I find myself realizing anew what we lost. Time has made it easier for me, though." She shook her shoulders ever so slightly and gave them both a wide smile. "Now, you two run off for your dance, and I will join the other ladies."

They were silent at first as they walked to the floor.

Clara had lightly placed her hand on his arm as they began the stroll.

"I had no idea her husband had passed away. She was so gracious just now in trying to make us feel better. I felt so inadequate, somehow."

"You needn't refine too much on it," he said gently. "He once told me they knew for several years that he was not well, but he had months at a time of good health. I met him at school, and we kept in touch over the years when we saw each other in town."

"Thank you. I appreciate your kind comments." She looked up at him with another smile.

As they joined the set, Jeremy found himself quite surprised with how well he felt in helping her in so small a way. He was certainly no stranger to playing the gallant, but it was anything but playing tonight. He felt neither artifice nor need for society's polite conversations in her company.

He watched her as the figures of the dance separated them. She moved quite gracefully and even had a kind word for that cub Burroughs when he stammered out his hello. It seemed she attracted all manner of men, and somehow that realization both rankled and pleased him. Damn!

It was obvious to him now how he must approach her tonight—teasing was out of the question. He would tell her he remembered their meeting on the road plus the dinner and all its frightful silence. But, perhaps the teasing would come later when they had established a friendlier footing?

"Miss Edwards, I must confess to you that at supper this evening Mrs. Thompson reminded me of our dinner at her home." He saw her eyes widen in surprise, and he hurried on with his words. "I say 'confess' since it is hardly the gentlemanly thing for me to admit forgetting a lady. I do hope you can have forgiven me my churlish behavior on the road that day?"

"Oh, my. I, well, I don't know what to say, Lord Carruthers." She stopped abruptly, true to her words.

He smiled to himself at her confusion and found he liked her all the more. He decided to confess the whole of it to her and right now.

"I think I am correct in saying that you hadn't forgotten our charming introduction on the road or the lively conversation we shared at dinner that night?" His smile now filled his face at these bald exaggerations.

She dimpled at his words and gently nodded her head.

"As I walked over to your table for our dance I found myself in an argument, and with myself of all people! After my talk with Mrs. Thompson after supper, I realized that you had remembered me—probably couldn't have forgotten such a boor. But I didn't know how I should present myself to you now. I wanted to simply wipe away the past and meet you as if for the first time, but a small part of me also wanted to roast you for your evasive comments when your aunt introduced us earlier."

The words were out of her mouth before she could stop them: "Roast me! But, that's what I'd planned to do to you until I found out you were such a good friend of Uncle Marcus."

He let out a chuckle that soon turned into laughter heard by everyone nearby. He could tell by the stunned look on her face that she truly hadn't meant to tell him so much about her plans, and it was all he could do to stop his laughter before his sides began to ache. Clara couldn't help but see the humor in their twin purposes and began to laugh with him.

"What a fine pair of connivers we are," he sighed. "I'd say we deserve a good set-down, but who's to do it? We're both the guilty parties here."

"I have an idea."

"Please, do tell, Miss Edwards."

"Why don't we begin with your original thought of wiping away the past? That day never happened. I'm having my first dance with my uncle's good friend, and you've met his niece for the first time tonight."

"What a delightful plan. We begin anew from this point forward. A pleasure to make your acquaintance, Miss Edwards." He bowed ever so slightly in his greeting.

"I thank you, sir, and I am happy to know you." She smiled her greeting back at his grinning face.

"Whatever are those two up to?" asked Sheila of no one in particular.

"What do you mean, dear?" said Lady Snow.

"My niece and Jeremy. Before supper, they were as stiff as boards when I introduced them, and now they're about to cause a scene with their foolish grinning. What *are* they talking about?"

"Who knows what young people talk about these days?" replied Emily Thompson. But she followed Sheila's look and glanced on the dance floor to find the couple. She saw what certainly appeared to be a romance from her point of view. Sheila had stumbled onto something, but it was easily apparent for all to see. And judging by the whispers around her, many of the matrons and their daughters had noticed the lively couple.

"I do think they look lovely together," said Lady Snow.

"Yes, but how could it have happened so quickly?"

"Well, they have known each other for more than a month, my dear. Didn't Clara tell you about their meeting at a dinner at our home, Hadley Abbey?"

"No, she never mentioned it to me."

"Well it wasn't the most auspicious of beginnings—they appeared at cross purposes all through dinner. But they seemed to have worked out their differences now don't you think?"

"The dance is nearly ending. I only hope they can remember me and join us here. I've never seen anything like it—from cool politeness to warmth and gaiety in a single dance," mused Sheila, mostly to herself. She'd certainly be having a talk with Clara at home after this evening's entertainment came to an end!

Jeremy and Clara walked toward Sheila with no notion of the commotion they'd caused or the notice they'd received. With heads close together, they talked quietly of the party and their enjoyment of the evening.

"Lady Clifton, I return your niece to you after our enjoyable dance together. And thank you, ma'am, for our introduction and my chance to know her better."

"You're most welcome, Jeremy," Sheila replied.

"And thank you, too, Miss Edwards. I had a delightful time and look forward to seeing you again soon."

"You're most welcome, Lord Carruthers, but I must thank you for being such a wonderful partner this evening," added Clara.

He bowed over her hand and smiled his goodbyes to the other ladies as he made his exit from the group.

Colonel Clarkston quickly claimed Clara for a stroll in lieu of the next dance before Sheila had a chance to ask a single question. Jeremy was soon dancing with Miss March, so she was left alone to ponder the amazing dance between two of her favorite people.

TEN

THE AFFAIR PROGRESSES

"What do you mean, dancing with my lady this evening?" exclaimed Dickers.

"Well someone had to, my man," Jeremy replied. "You were nowhere in sight, and I couldn't very well let the lady dance alone. Wouldn't you rather it be me than a rival for her hand?"

"No!" growled Dickers, but with a smile twinkling in his eyes behind the frown.

Jeremy smiled, too, as he sipped a delightful brandy and remembered thinking earlier in the night that Dickers would certainly threaten to call him out for dancing with "his" Fair Incomparable. Wouldn't he be surprised to learn the dance was only intended to distract others from his time with Miss Edwards?

"Where did you two disappear to?" asked Jeremy.

"La Farleigh was our nemesis. She cornered us just after we left you at the door, and we found ourselves trapped," Dickers complained.

"Twice in two nights—that must be inhumane,"

laughed Edward. "We were able to escape after signing her daughter's dance cards, but by then we'd lost you in the crowd. Later, we retreated to the card room to avoid her at supper, and I only spotted you again just as Romeo here was about to disgrace us all by lunging at you on the dance floor."

"Never say I'd be so lost as all that!" exclaimed Dickers, and the other gentlemen laughed at his shocked face.

"Now admit it—you spend more time pining for your lady than you actually spend with her," said Jeremy.

"My suit is honorable and true, and you are the last one to lecture *me* on courting a lady. Why you've hardly danced a jig with anyone until tonight!"

"Well, how could I refuse to sign her card when we sat at the same supper table?" Jeremy offered in his own defense.

"You had supper at her table?" asked an amazed Dickers. "However did you . . . ? I was right! You are trying to take her from me!"

"Cut line, you fool! I'm no more courting her than Edward is." Just a trace of edginess crept into Jeremy's voice.

"The distinguished company here at White's is beginning to look at the two of you with marked attention," said a grinning Edward. "I fear your somewhat heated conversation has caught their interest. Perhaps we should end our night now and head for our respective corners, er, I mean, homes?"

"Yes, you are right. I'll call for our coach and meet you both at the curb. I could do with a bit of fresh air," muttered Jeremy, and he jumped up before the other two men had settled their glasses on the table.

"Well what's gotten into him tonight?" wondered Dickers. "He seemed a bit short with us."

"Perhaps he's just tired," offered Edward, and he

rose from the comfortable chair to make his leave. What would Dickers think if he knew that Jeremy was also looking for a wife? *Probably take on the task of managing his search as well as mine,* Edward thought with amusement.

"Clara, dear, do join me in the salon for a few minutes," said Sheila. Clara barely heard her aunt's invitation, let alone noticed the calculating tone in her voice. She knew she just wanted to be alone to sort out her thoughts from the amazing ball that night.

"Can I be excused, ma'am? I'm frightfully tired after these two late nights."

"I think you both should be in bed," said Marcus. "Your girlish chitchat about the ball can wait until breakfast tomorrow—well breakfast later today." He steered his wife toward the stairs.

"But, Marcus, there's something I particularly wanted to talk about with Clara," said a protesting Sheila.

"Unless it's the color of your nightgown, it will have to wait. Neither of you, nor myself for that matter, is capable of intelligent conversation at this hour. Now, off to bed!"

Clara giggled at her uncle's military tone. All he lacked was a sword and the order to his petticoat troops to march.

She bid them both good night and hurried on to her room to change for bed. She was glad she'd told Meg not to wait for her, since the quiet gave her a chance to think through such an unexpected turn of events.

Why, he was so nice! The thought amazed her and somewhat frightened her, too. How could she ever follow through with her plan when he had turned out to be a gentleman? And a friend of her uncle's, too. But it had been such a wonderful plan, and she really wasn't ready to give it up now. What was she to do?

It was hardly fair of her to trick her uncle's good friend into falling in love with her! And after meeting him again tonight, she really didn't think she had a ghost of a chance to actually make that happen.

Fall in love with her? What had she been thinking? Why, he could have any girl on that dance floor, and what made her think she would be the one to catch his eye in such a way? Now that she'd been in town a few short weeks, she really had to laugh at her simple schoolgirl notions. But she kept coming back to the fact that she didn't want to give up her plan. Now why was that?

There really was no glory in making someone look foolish, and that was what she'd intended for him. As she considered it more objectively, staring past her reflection in the mirror, her hand paused as she brushed her hair. It had certainly become obvious that she'd have to devise a new plan.

The next morning found Sheila slumbering in bed long past her usual hour. Two late nights out with her niece, while hardly unusual for her during the Season, had taken their toll. She yawned with a delicate stretch and then sat up ramrod straight in bed. *Clara!*

What had that girl been doing last night? If she'd known Jeremy for an entire month, why hadn't she mentioned it when Sheila first introduced them last night? She was determined to get her answers, and get them this morning! She gave a decisive tug to the bellpull to summon Lizzie with her morning chocolate and then sat back in bed to think through the night's uncommon events.

At first meeting, Clara and Jeremy appeared to her

as complete strangers. Clara had seemed a bit odd with her questions, but Sheila couldn't quite point to any one remark as out of fashion or even close to rude. As she reflected more on that meeting, Clara's stiffness spoke volumes about how uncomfortable she must have felt. Yes, stiffness was the right word, and Clara had always seemed at ease among the *ton.*

She next saw them together after supper on the dance floor, and they were as two different people—laughing, smiling, heads close together in conversation as if they were intimates. When contrasted to their earlier reserve, the turnaround became even more shocking to Sheila.

She knew they could have had no conversations during supper—not with Jeremy seated at her table and Clara off with her friends. So, that left the amazing transformation for the dance floor. Hardly a place conducive to convivial conversations or mending fences!

Mending fences, she mused. Perhaps something unfortunate had occurred at the Thompsons' dinner at Hadley Abbey. Could the short time on the dance floor have afforded them an opportunity to find common ground for reconciliation? It would appear so, and their newfound friendship hadn't escaped notice from the gossips either.

Perhaps she was a bit hasty in trying to confront Clara with the events of the party. It wouldn't do to direct unwanted attention to their budding relationship. No, she would have to be subtler in drawing out the details from Clara.

She found herself remembering her thought from last night to hold a party to bring the two of them together. Enlisting Clara's help to plan the party would give her ample opportunity to learn more about the pair. Perhaps she was already too late to bring them together, but she could certainly give them a gentle push forward to whatever the future held!

Sheila fairly jumped from the bed to start her day.

Jeremy slowed as he approached Edward's lodgings. He wanted to talk about the night's events with his good friend, but he didn't know what to say. He'd fallen asleep with no thought beyond his pillow, but the morning had brought forth all the questions with no answers. He found Edward at his breakfast and joined him for a cup of coffee.

"I thought you'd come by this morning," said Edward.

Jeremy smiled and said, "Was my temper at White's not quite so vile that you can still manage to see me?"

"I have no notion what has caused you to become so touchy, but I am at your disposal for consultation and correction."

"Very amusing, I'm sure," Jeremy sighed. "I wish I knew how a dance with one woman could cause me such a tangle."

"What! Never tell me you've met someone in just one dance where it has consumed me into my third blasted Season with no luck!" Edward fairly yelled at his friend. Jeremy's smile was all the answer he needed. "So, you have met someone."

"What makes you think that, my friend?" Jeremy asked in all seriousness.

"Oh, it's worse than I assumed. You don't even realize you've fallen for her—you're still in the mystified stage."

"The mystified stage? Whatever are you talking about?"

"Something I overheard my mother tell my older sister years ago about men falling in love. She said before we even realize it, we're in an euphoric state of bliss—her words, so don't give me that battle face! She called it the mystified stage, and any challenge for any reason, such as Dickers lashing out at you about his Fair Incomparable last night, is met head on with scorn and then anger. And now with that silly grin on your face, it fits you perfectly." Edward was surprised when Jeremy let the "silly grin" remark go by with no rebuke!

"Well, what's next?"

"Do you mean the next stage? Don't know—when I sneezed, they found me behind the couch listening and shooed me from the room."

"So, I should write to your mother for guidance?" asked Jeremy, now laughing.

"I don't think the advice was meant for men to hear. I'm convinced they prefer it if we're in the dark and they have all the answers."

The men sat in a companionable silence for several minutes, each lost in his thoughts, each hoping to find the answers, somehow. Jeremy abruptly broke into their reverie.

"She's just lovely, and not only her looks. Behind her eyes there's a kindness, and she has a wonderful sense of humor, too. She cares about people and how they feel, and she dances like an angel."

"All of this from just a dance?" Edward asked dryly.

"Well, there's more to us than the one dance."

"'Us' you say. You have my full attention, and I can't help telling you I am quite intrigued."

So Jeremy told him the tale of the events on the road and their unexpected dinner at the Thompsons'. He didn't hold back on his later impressions from his first glimpses of her on the dance floor followed by his less-than-enthusiastic agreement to meet the niece of his friend and mentor. Nor did he try to hide his excitement at the enchanting surprise in finally getting to know her some when they danced last night. The men's coffee had long gone cold by the end of the story.

"Congratulations, my friend. I will soon dance at your wedding and be the happiest of men to see you so well settled," Edward said with a fierce sincerity.

"My w-wedding?" asked a surprised Jeremy. And after a thoughtful pause, he added, "Yes, my wedding."

"I must meet this woman, and meet her now! We're dressed for morning calls, and I for one intend on dropping in on the Clifton household. She is staying with her aunt, isn't she?"

"Yes, I presume so. If not, I'm sure we can wrest her direction from Sheila."

"We'd best keep this all from Dickers until you're ready for his onslaught of advice."

They headed for the door laughing, with Jeremy feeling a sense of purpose and wonderful anticipation. He now knew what it had all meant—his feelings of concern, contentment, and longing for this woman would lead them to a lifetime of happiness.

"Emily, so good to see you this morning. And Emma, you look lovely in that shade of yellow with your dark hair," said Sheila to her guests. "Please come in and join us for some warming tea and help us plan our dinner party."

"A party? What a delightful idea," offered Emily Thompson as she sat on the sofa opposite Sheila. Emma sat in a low chair near to Clara so they might talk softly while the ladies planned.

"I thought we'd hold a small supper later this week and then go to the opera," Sheila explained. "I hear there's a superb performance, and our box will hold a large group. I've enlisted Clara's help in making up the guest list for her friends, and we'll pen the invitations after luncheon. I do hope you and Emma can join us."

"Of course, and I don't hesitate in answering for both of us," though she needn't have worried about Emma's acceptance. The two girls had become even closer friends since their trip to town.

"Clara mentioned to include the Farleigh ladies, since we're to have that darling Reggie—plus they have invited us to their home tomorrow. The girls seem well enough, though we'll find out more at their dinner." The ladies continued their party discussions on menus and decorations.

"Your Aunt Sheila is a dear to have a dinner party on such short notice," said Emma.

"But she loves to entertain," Clara replied. "With Uncle Marcus's government work, plus all their social friends, they have guests over quite often. Her letters to Mama are always filled with stories of this diplomat or that minister seated at their table."

"I was glad to hear that Mr. Farleigh will be invited," Emma said shyly.

"You are such a goose, Emma Thompson! As if I would leave off his name knowing of your feelings. Oh, I did not tell you of his marked interest in you last night! He asked about you while we danced and seemed most concerned that you had not arrived before supper."

"Oh how thrilling to think he spoke about me to you! Perhaps our late start last night was a good thing if our absence caused such pleasant notice."

"You will be at the Farleighs' tomorrow night?" Clara asked with a smile.

Emma giggled and then nodded. "But what about you, Clara? How does your romance progress with Sir Richards?"

"Emma! It's hardly a romance, and please don't call

it that," Clara said a little sharply. "We're simply friends, and I wouldn't want anyone to think more of it."

"My goodness, but I did not mean to cause you an upset! I was only teasing you, and you must admit his attentions are marked—two dances most evenings."

"I don't want to show favor to anyone yet—I'm just enjoying my time right now."

"All right, I won't mention it again until you do. I hope that makes you feel better."

"I'm sorry, Emma; I do feel a bit touchy about all this."

"Is there a problem, Clara? Did something happen last night? Oh, my heavens, of course it did—you saw *him*. I can't tell you how shocked I was when I saw him at our supper table when we joined your aunt and uncle. Did you see him?"

Before Clara could answer, Reilly opened the doors to announce two more visitors, "Lord Jeremy Carruthers and Mr. Edward Waters, my lady." The gentlemen entered and walked over to Sheila to greet her and her guests.

"Jeremy, how lovely to see you again so soon. You met my niece, Clara, last night, of course, and I understand you already know Emily Thompson and her daughter, Emma."

"Thank you, Sheila, and it is delightful to see all you ladies. May I present my friend, Edward Waters?"

The gentlemen bowed to all the ladies and did not delay in joining them. Jeremy, however, did hesitate to sit on the small sofa with Clara, so he chose a seat near Sheila. Edward, on the other hand, had no compunction settling right next to Clara to better meet the young woman.

"I was just telling the Thompsons of our plans to hold a small dinner party this week. I do hope you gentlemen can find time in your schedules to join us as well?" asked Sheila.

"We would be delighted, Lady Clifton," Edward said swiftly.

"Didn't you say last night that you had another friend with you, Jeremy?"

"Yes, our friend Dickers—or, more properly, Richard Smythe-Hattan," said Jeremy with a smile.

"We'll certainly include him amongst the guests then. Clara and I will pen the invitations after luncheon, and I'll send a footman to deliver them tomorrow morning. I haven't decided whether we should roll up the carpets for some informal dancing, or would you prefer an outing to the opera?"

"Oh, if I may be so bold, ma'am, but dancing would be my preference," said a smiling Emma.

"Yes, dancing to be sure," echoed Jeremy, and much to his own surprise.

"Well, I should say your votes settle the question, and we'll dance. I shall contact that lovely trio we heard last Season to offer music for the dancers."

"May I ask how you are enjoying your Season, ladies?" asked Edward.

"Oh, but it's lovely," said Emma. "I'm simply entranced by the wonderful people we've met and the entertainments we've attended, too."

"Be careful, sir," said Emily Thompson with a smile. "You've no idea how enthused my daughter has become since arriving in London. Why, our preparations while at home brought excitement to be sure, but they've paled when compared to her joy at finally being here."

"There should be no shame in pure enjoyment of a Season in London," said Sheila.

"I agree completely," offered Edward. "I can't tell you the damper I feel on my own spirits when companions at a ball or soiree profess boredom or ennui with their surroundings."

"It is a fashion that some affect, or for others perhaps they've just attended a few too many of the Season's events. I feel both Emma and Clara are truly enjoying their time here," said Sheila.

"Oh my, yes!" said an enthusiastic Clara. She then sat back a bit to hide her small embarrassment at her outspoken agreement.

Mrs. Thompson laughed and said, "I fear Emma's exuberance has reached to Clara as well. After all your protestations about not wanting a Season these past years, I'm certainly glad you've found it so enjoyable."

"But I thought every young woman wanted a Season," stated Edward.

"I've always found much pleasure in visiting town over the years," said Clara, "but all the parties seemed like so much frivolity with little purpose. I've realized, though, that while there is a great deal of merriment, it has been a wonderful way to renew old acquaintances and meet new friends."

"You'll also find quite a bit of business takes place at these social gatherings," offered Jeremy. "I've seen trade deals finalized, ships chartered for the Americas and even a plumed hat become all the fashion rage."

While everyone laughed at this last bit of nonsense, Edward looked at Jeremy with just the slightest of smiles. He admired him for trying to put Miss Edwards at her ease, and he admired her for stating an opinion that might not find favor in some circles. And Miss Thompson also intrigued him as well. He quite looked forward to the next ball when he might ask her for a dance.

Reilly opened the doors just then to bring in a large bouquet of flowers. He set them down on the table between the ladies and silently offered the card to Clara.

"My, my, young lady. Such lovely flowers. Now, who might they be from?" asked Mrs. Thompson.

"To be sure, I have no idea," said a surprised Clara.

"I can think of one name," offered Emma.

"Well, do open the card and let us know," said Mrs. Thompson.

Jeremy threw a glance at Edward and thought he had a fairly good guess. Much too grand for young Burroughs, but right in line with that infernal Richards. And since he wasn't here, it would make sense to send the flowers so he would be remembered.

"It is from Sir Richards. He apologizes that he cannot stop by this morning since he will be at the Diplomatic House today. My, what beautiful flowers."

To cover the palpable quiet in the room, Jeremy strove valiantly to think of an innocuous question. "What are your plans for this evening, Miss Edwards?"

"I believe we attend the theater tonight?" Clara said with a question in her voice as she turned to her aunt for confirmation.

"Yes, dear. We're all to see the new comedy, though I'm not sure I can convince Marcus to join us. He's not much of a fan of the theater."

Edward and Jeremy made the quickest of eye contact with a raised eyebrow from one and a slight nod from the other.

"If we may be so bold then, Jeremy and I would be honored to escort you ladies to the theater."

"Well isn't that charming of you," said Emily Thompson with a smile for each of them. "You gentlemen are so kind to offer."

"We happily accept your offer," said Sheila. "I don't mind telling you that I am very glad for your attendance. I really did not have much hope of convincing Marcus to accompany us, and I so dislike going to the theater without a male escort. It's rather vain, I know, but I feel so conspicuous arriving alone, not to mention 'on view' in our box. Well, enough of my silliness! Shall we see you here at eight o'clock this evening?"

"Eight o'clock it is," said Jeremy. "We'll bring my larger town carriage for all of us to ride together, or would you prefer that we go in two groups?"

"I think one carriage, if you feel we should be comfortable—then we can enjoy the entire night together," said Sheila.

Clara listened to this exchange with trepidation bordering on a mild panic. At least she would not be alone with Lord Carruthers during the evening, but she quickly realized that she needed to spend some time on her plan. Thankfully, she had no engagements for the afternoon, since Sir Richards would be in meetings all day and could not ride with her in the park. Yes, when their company left she would tell Aunt Sheila she wished to rest a short while after working on the invitations. A few quiet moments to herself would give her time to decide how to proceed tonight.

Clara brought her attention back to the guests as she heard Aunt Sheila offer her good-byes to the Thompson ladies. Clara also smiled a gracious good day and breathed a silent sigh of relief as she saw that the gentlemen would take their leave as well.

ELEVEN

A PLAY WITHIN A PLAY

Clara's quiet time later in the day lasted no more than a few minutes—she actually fell asleep! The late nights had taken their toll, and she awoke refreshed but quite mad at herself for sleeping away the afternoon.

A splash of cold water on her face washed away the last of her sleepiness, and she snuggled in a comfortable chair wrapped in a quilt by the waning fire to ponder her options. She might have done better to ponder her motives in continuing to find ways to spend time with Lord Carruthers.

Clearly her original plan could not succeed, and, to be honest with herself, she did not particularly want to see Lord Carruthers embarrassed or humiliated before the *ton*. Well, what did she want?

Would it be enough if he were to simply realize how he'd embarrassed and humiliated her? Enough what, though? She didn't really want revenge, and he had apologized very nicely several times. And quite sincerely, too, she thought. If one of her school friends had tried so hard to make amends, she'd have long ago forgiven and forgotten the incident. So, what was different about this situation?

He was different. There, she'd said it if only in silence to herself. From the moment of their inglorious meeting on the road, she'd hardly been able to stop thinking about him. And now with their formal introduction from her aunt, it appeared she'd hardly be able to stop seeing him, too.

Could she have feelings for Lord Carruthers? How silly to ask such a question—it surely was impossible to go from plotting his social downfall to tender feelings so quickly. Wasn't it? Or were her feelings just a normal result of getting to know such a dashing man?

Perhaps she should speak with her aunt about Lord Carruthers and find out more about the gentleman. *Best to know one's enemies,* she thought with a smile. Hardly an enemy, though, more like a conspirator with their conversation during their dance last night. He had seemed to go out of his way to be nice, but maybe that was just his way. Was his attention to her something to remark upon or not? It was hard not knowing much about the man. Yes, Aunt Sheila it was, and she'd seek her out now for a comfortable coze.

Clara found her aunt in her sitting room finishing some preparations for the dinner party. Sheila looked up with a smile for Clara, which helped put her at ease with her task.

"May I join you, Aunt Sheila?"

"But, of course, my dear. Anytime you want to talk, please come find me. Just make sure your uncle doesn't shoo us off to bed though!" And both ladies laughed, remembering his "commanding" presence the night before. "Did you have a good rest?"

"Yes, thank you. I actually slept for over an hour,

though it hadn't really been my plan. I guess I needed to regain some energy before we go out again this evening."

"What plan besides sleep did you have for your rest?" Aunt Sheila asked.

"Well, I'd wanted to think some."

"Perhaps about those lovely flowers that arrived this morning?"

"The flowers? Oh no, not those."

"My, but you sound like a young lady who receives flowers every day!" Sheila exclaimed with a wide smile.

"I did not mean to sound ungrateful, it's just that Sir Richards is not my problem."

"And who or what may be your problem?" Sheila asked with a barely concealed smile this time.

Clara sighed, opened her mouth to speak and sighed again. Where could she begin?

"It's always best to start at the beginning," Sheila said softly, as if she were a mind reader.

Clara began at the end instead. "Tell me about Lord Carruthers," she blurted.

"Well, would you like to hear that he's charming, dashing, a favorite among his friends? Or that your Uncle Marcus finds him intelligent and witty, that I find him quite the most attractive of the eligible bachelors and, until this week, he's rarely attended social functions these past three years since his youngest sister's come-out? Or perhaps his manners intrigue you and you wish to know if his attentions to you are simply duty to the niece of his good friend, or . . ."

"Please, stop! You're making me dizzy!" laughed Clara. "I hadn't realized I was so transparent."

"Forgive me, dear, it's just that you were so serious just now, and I couldn't resist having some fun with you. Unfortunately, everything I said is true about Jeremy. Or perhaps, fortunately—you tell me."

"I hadn't realized he was such an outstanding figure in the *ton,* not to mention such a good friend to Uncle Marcus."

"He and Marcus met just after we married. We knew his parents, of course, and Jeremy came right to town as many a young man does when he finishes school. He and Marcus just seemed to have an affinity, despite their age difference—I think they became the brother each of them never had. Marcus sponsored Jeremy in the clubs and mentored him early on in his career, though they are equals now. Why, he's godfather to our Evan, and I wouldn't be surprised if the two of you didn't meet at Evan's christening seven years ago!"

"My, what a recommendation," Clara breathed softly.

"Yes, he's quite eligible and many a girl or her mama has tried to catch his interest. I don't believe he's formed a serious attachment with anyone in the many years I've know him."

"So, his attentions to me should not be remarked upon since he's so much a part of society?" Clara asked with a strangely heavy heart.

"On the contrary, dear, his attentions beyond an occasional dance are quite out of his norm," Sheila said gently. "While he may know how to go about in polite society, he rarely frequents the balls and routs. His coming here this morning was quite the surprise to me, and then the offer to escort us tonight will certainly have every eye upon us at the theater. I can only surmise that you are the object of his attentions, dear. Does that surprise you, or perhaps upset you?"

"I don't know—er, I don't think so. No, no, it does not," stammered Clara.

"Tell me how you came to know him. Emily Thompson mentioned you met at her home in the country, but there seemed to be some mystery surrounding it that she couldn't quite describe."

Clara couldn't bring herself to reveal the whole of that disastrous day to her aunt. She had only just now realized what a fool she must have seemed to the dashing, if inebriated, lord. It would be too hard to hear Aunt Sheila echo those same opinions.

"There is no mystery. We sat next to each other for dinner at the Thompsons' and then met again last night. I don't know that I can really believe what you say about his showing attention for me, since I'm just a country miss and he's quite fashionable around town. Perhaps you read too much into his actions in coming here. I think he's just being kind for Uncle Marcus's sake and nothing more."

"Well, you can think what you will about Jeremy, but I don't want to hear another word from you about being 'just a country miss.' Of all the silly schoolgirl notions! I know that you have more gumption than that, Clara Edwards."

Clara smiled halfheartedly at her aunt and realized she did not want to be in her company any longer. She tried to make her smile a bit stronger to show that she was worthy of her aunt's praise, but she felt so low now with her realization that Lord Carruthers was so far above her touch. It had come as a shock just now to see that Lord Carruthers did hold a special place in her heart.

"Now, it is almost time to dress for dinner," Sheila continued. "So, put on one of your prettiest dresses, and we'll have a wonderful time this evening. You'll see that Jeremy is a delightful man as you get to know him better."

Clara made her departure from her aunt and returned to her room with foreboding. How could she even face Lord Carruthers for the theater party tonight? Her plan was in a shambles, and it was so clear to her now that she could have no replacement. Why did that fact bother her so much?

The tears began to slide down her cheeks at will. She admitted there was no point in even staying in town, except for the dishonor it would be to her kind aunt and uncle if she left so soon. Not to mention the expense of her wardrobe! No, she would stay in town for the fortnight, but then she would hurry home to the comfort and safety of Waverly Manor.

"Gentlemen, right on time," said Sheila as Jeremy and Edward joined the ladies in the Clifton drawing room. They looked splendid in their black evening dress and provided a perfect complement to the colors in the ladies' ensembles.

"How could we be late when such beauty awaited us?" said Jeremy as he gracefully placed a kiss on the back of Sheila's hand.

"I'd best warn Marcus that you are acting the fool, young man," laughed Sheila.

"Ah, but such a charming fool," Edward offered with a grin.

"I can see this party will surely compete for laughter with tonight's performance. Shall we gather our wraps and make our departure?" asked Emily Thompson.

"Please let me help you with your wrap, Miss Thompson," said Edward.

Emma nodded and handed the cloak to Edward with a smile.

As the party made their way to the entry hall, Jeremy noticed that Miss Edwards looked tired. No, that was not the right word. She looked sad—yes, that was it. Now, what could have caused such a change from the laughing and vibrant woman at last night's ball?

He moved to her side and offered to help her with

her velvet cape. She kept her eyes downcast as he held his arms with her wrap, so he gently placed it on her shoulders with his hands lingering on the material for just an extra second.

"Is everything all right, Miss Edwards? You seem a bit quiet tonight," he asked, himself quiet.

"Oh, yes, I am fine Lord Carruthers," she said without meeting his eyes.

"If I can be of any service, ma'am, please call on me immediately. I wouldn't want you to suffer in any way." The strength of his sincerity caused Clara to raise her eyes to his.

She saw kindness and compassion there and felt the beginnings of a tear well up in her eye. He saw the tear too, and could only wonder at her sorrow. He raised a hand and gently rubbed it away.

"Please let me be of help if I can," he whispered.

A gust of wind from Reilly's opening the front door broke the mood and brought them back into the realization of their surroundings. He vowed to himself to watch over her tonight but to keep his regard close to his chest. He did not want to arouse anyone's suspicions, least of all Miss Edwards's.

Clara found herself shaking under her wrap and glad for its camouflage. He couldn't come so near to her again if she were to survive the night. As Clara ascended into the carriage, she carefully sat on the far side of Mrs. Thompson to offer herself some small amount of privacy.

Much to her surprise, Clara found a great deal of comfort in the delightful comedy performance. At first she just sat in the front of the box, barely concentrating on the players. Gradually, though, the twists and unexpected turns of the plot had her full attention, and she found herself laughing and applauding with the audience. They were now well into the final act, and she felt somehow happier and perhaps even carefree.

At each of the intervals when the party had gathered in the back of the box to greet friends and enjoy refreshments, Clara was purposefully slow to leave her seat. She would glance at the gathering as she arose from her chair and then make her way toward the spot furthest from Lord Carruthers. In this manner, she'd carefully managed to avoid any private conversations with him and even kept away from him completely. She felt certain she could continue with this plan when they left the box.

Jeremy easily read through her careful dance as she diligently avoided his company. It would have amused him if it hadn't rankled so. Obviously, *he* was the problem that had caused the upset he'd noticed in her at Clifton House. He wouldn't press her tonight, but he was certain he would find many an opportunity during the Season to be at her side unexpectedly. Let's just see how she reacted when she had no theater box to keep them apart!

Sheila also noticed something amiss at the theater, but she hadn't detected the reason. She could only wonder at the sudden transformation of last night's intimate couple into tonight's merely nodding acquaintances. Perhaps her talk with Clara that afternoon had hurt the situation rather than helped? Had her glowing endorsement of Lord Carruthers somehow frightened Clara?

Edward found himself drawn to both young women in his company tonight. Miss Edwards presented an intelligent and demure lady who held herself with pride and reserve. Miss Thompson, on the other hand, was vivacious and vibrant. She intrigued him beyond words, and he felt himself fairly tremble in her presence as he sat next to her this night. He would pursue her with purposeful abandon!

"Was the play all that you'd hoped for, my dear?" asked Marcus as he and Sheila dressed for bed.

"Oh, yes, it was charming and quite as good, as your mother said. I'm not so sure about the company, though."

"Whatever was wrong?"

"Oh, nothing *wrong*, so to speak. But, there were undercurrents that I can't quite put in their place. Take Jeremy, for example. He seemed to hang off to the side and not really take part in the conversations. His friend, Edward, was all that could be charming and treated us lavishly. Clara, too, enjoyed the play, and the company but seemed distracted throughout the performance. Emma was a dear and, poor thing, seemed to carry many a conversation when Clara or Jeremy paid the party no heed."

"My, but you had a play within a play," laughed Marcus.

"Yes, you've quite hit on it, I think. I felt like I was watching a small production in our own box at some of the intervals. It bothered me so that I penned a short note to Marie before you came in tonight. I asked her to come to town soon to be with Clara. Perhaps her mother's practiced eye will see what I have missed."

"Don't treat yourself so harshly, my love. It was certainly unnoticed by the *ton*."

"But you are right there—all they saw were our escorts. Jeremy and Edward were magnificent in their attendance on us, and we did turn many a head."

"Oh, that reminds me of something Jeremy mentioned at the club yesterday. He's interested in obtaining an introduction to a certain young woman."

"My goodness, but what a surprise. Which young lady?"

"Don't know, and he didn't say. I got the impression he does not know her name and will simply point her out on the dance floor for you to effect the introduction. He seemed to be almost shy in his request, too. Perhaps he is smitten at last."

"Well, that devious boy! I don't quite know what to make of this information. We'll attend the Woodleys' ball in a few days, and I'll be sure to discover the object of his interest." After a moment, she murmured to herself, "But I thought I knew the answer to that question."

TWELVE

FARLEIGH FESTIVITIES

"Edward, my man, we must try a new tactic to find a lady for you," Dickers said.

"And how might you accomplish this feat?" asked Edward.

"I think it is a bit early in the game—er, Season—to go to Almack's, but let us attend some afternoon al fresco parties where you'll have more time to talk with the ladies. These balls seem to be singularly difficult to capture much of a lady's attention or time."

"Hmm, who's going to benefit from this change in tactic? Perhaps a man who already knows which Incomparable he wants to capture?" laughed Jeremy.

"Well, now, you don't think I suggest this idea for myself, do you?" Dickers asked with a wide grin. "I must admit that I do see an advantage for me, but I'd certainly do something for your cause which did not help mine."

"I guess I can believe that, but only because you are such a fine fellow," Edward said with a smile.

"Take this evening as a 'for instance.' We leave in mere minutes for what we can only expect to be a more than tedious evening. All to find you a wife, and I go willingly as a lamb to the proverbial slaughter with just the vision of La Farleigh and her chicks in our future."

"You know they'll offer more amiable company than the picture you present. If nothing else we can watch Jeremy evade the clutches of the oldest Farleigh daughter—never could remember their names," Edward said.

"Don't remind me," Jeremy said dryly. "I rue the night I dined with her and put notions into her head."

"Dining with her! Just speaking with her—no, glancing at her across the crowded dance floor, puts notions into her head, not to mention her mother's. I guess every Season has its challenges that we must endure, if not elude," Edward exclaimed.

"Dinners are too intimate an affair with too few people. The al fresco it must be for our future," championed Dickers.

"All right, the al fresco it is if it will make you happy. Now finish your drinks, lambs, and we'll be off to our slaughter," Jeremy joked.

The Thompson ladies arrived at the Farleighs' at the appointed hour with no such trepidations. Emma could think of nothing but the delightful prospect of an entire night with "her" Reggie. And while Mrs. Thompson approved of the match, she certainly hoped her darling would not be too hasty in her decision—the joys of a first Season happened only once in a young girl's life, after all!

They met Lady Clifton and Clara in the foyer as they gave their wraps to the footman. The girls exchanged compliments on each other's ensembles while the ladies shared raised eyebrows about their surroundings. The striped wall hangings were lovely, but not when paired with the elaborate coverings on the furniture. If possible, their eyebrows rose higher as they ascended the stairs to the drawing room.

"My dear Lady Clifton, so good to see you. And Mrs. Thompson, we are so pleased you could also join us this evening," gushed Millicent Farleigh.

"Thank you, Millicent. It was kind of you to invite us," said Sheila.

"I do so want to give my girls a chance to be with their friends, and they've made such charming acquaintances so early in the Season. I'm sure you know that Lord Carruthers will join us tonight, as well as his delightful friends."

"Yes, I do believe you had mentioned their attendance," smiled Sheila.

"Melissa, dear, please come forward and greet our guests," Millicent said somewhat crossly to her younger daughter, who hung back amongst the draperies.

"You look lovely, my dear, and it is so nice to see you again," Sheila said sincerely. The girl was dressed in charming ivory muslin with little adornment, and Sheila felt she'd never seen her look better.

"Thank you, my lady, and it is my pleasure to see you and Mrs. Thompson tonight," Melissa replied.

"Elisa will be down shortly—she's putting the finishing touches on her coiffure," Millicent added. "I'm sure she'd offer her greetings as well to you ladies. Please enjoy our refreshments while we await our other guests and the start of our dinner." Millicent turned rather hastily to the door at the sound of a masculine voice.

"We are so pleased you could join us tonight, ladies," said Reggie Farleigh. "I think Elisa has convinced Mama that a bit of dancing after our meal would be fun. She so wants everything to go perfectly tonight."

"I'm sure it will be all that is delightful and entertaining for us and a lovely way to mingle for you young people. And don't you look splendid tonight in your evening clothes?" said Emily Thompson.

"Thank you, ma'am." Reggie swept her an exaggerated bow and doffed an imaginary hat, much to the ladies' delight.

"I do hope Lady Annabelle and her party have no problems arriving here tonight. The weather looked so inclement this afternoon," Melissa offered quietly. She certainly hoped Lady Annabelle's party included her dashing brother, Sir Martin Richards!

"If anyone will find her way to a party, it is Annabelle," laughed Clara. "She's always enjoyed getting together with friends, ever since we met at school. She told me her last few years with her father on the Continent were wonderful fun, since she acted as his hostess at so many affairs."

"I imagine she quite enjoys the Season then," stated Sheila.

"Oh yes, she told me yesterday that she almost hopes not to form any attachment too soon so that she can continue attending all the parties! She said her father finds it all very frivolous," laughed Clara.

"Well I can surely attest to the practice of carrying on one's social obligations for many, many Seasons," Sheila replied. "You just tell her to let me put a word into her father's ear if he wants her to curtail her social activities." She fairly sniffed at the audacity of the man.

They were interrupted in their banter by the arrival of the lady in question, and she did appear on her brother's arm. The group widened their circle to include the new arrivals, and the girls soon broke into a smaller group for more intimate conversation.

"Annabelle, you look breathtaking in your dress," said Emma.

"Why thank you so very much. I was a bit apprehensive in wearing so daring a color—I am a debutante, after all, and such a shimmering pastel may be too much for some people in society," Annabelle said with some hesitation.

"Well it is lovely, and you've nothing to feel uncomfortable about in this convivial company. I daresay you'll start a trend for the Season," Clara added.

"I only wish my mother would allow me to wear something so stylish," breathed Melissa with just a touch of envy in her voice.

"Oh, please stop! I can feel my cheeks blush with all your compliments," giggled Annabelle with a combination of both pleasure and modesty.

More voices were heard at the drawing room entrance as Lord Carruthers and his friends arrived. Millicent was near to bursting with joy at the sight of the men as they greeted their hostess. The quiet entrance of William Burroughs largely went unnoticed by the lady as she focused her gushing on the three other men.

She made much of announcing their arrival, even though the butler had already performed the task. Just saying their names made her fairly swoon with delight.

As if on cue, Elisa made her own entrance into the ballroom. And, if truth were told, her maid had stood at the top of the stairs waiting to hear of the arrival of three specific gentlemen to report back to her mistress.

With the ease of a well-choreographed dance, Millicent effortlessly turned to greet the last arrival and announce her to the assembled company. Naturally, the three men stood near to the door, and she had made sure of their proximity with a light hand to Lord Carruthers's arm.

"Elisa, my dear, you look a picture tonight," Millicent

said. "Come greet our guests. I have Lord Carruthers here waiting for you."

And that worthy gentleman suppressed yet another sigh and executed a small bow over the hand of the elder daughter. At least they were dressed quite differently tonight, so he'd have no difficulty distinguishing the girls. Elisa looked a positive fright in that plumage seemingly coming out of her left ear. *Gad, what women do in the name of fashion!* he wondered.

"My pleasure to see you, Miss Farleigh. I trust you are doing well this evening?" asked Jeremy. It was a pedestrian comment, but it was all he could say and remain truthful. He refused to compliment her on her looks when they were so lacking in style or sense.

"How droll you are, Lord Carruthers. Yes, I am doing well, as you say." She playfully slapped his wrist with her fan.

So, she wasn't quite the ninny he'd thought her to be. She could recognize his slight censure even when it might have escaped her mother.

Elisa moved on to greet the rest of the assembled company as if they had expressly come tonight to see only her. She carried it off quite well, and the time before dinner passed with lively conversations.

"Dinner is served," intoned the Farleigh butler. The gentlemen paired with the ladies to enter the dining room, and Millicent was most touched when Lord Carruthers offered his arm to her. She would also have been satisfied to see her Reggie had remembered his manners to escort Lady Clifton.

The seating arrangements were artful if not obvious, and Jeremy had to smile as he found himself in the honored position to the right of his hostess. Dickers owed him a fiver. He had not expected to have Miss

Farleigh on his other side, though, since it bordered on poor *ton* to have mother and daughter so close together at the table. *So, I have to return that fiver,* he thought with a smile.

Sheila, too, thought the table an interesting combination of couples. Reggie sat at the opposite end from his mama, while she sat across from Jeremy on Millicent's left side. And that placement of Sheila across from Jeremy started a trend throughout most of the table where male sat opposite female.

While it was a small enough group that they might dispense with the usual convention of speaking only to those guests at one's sides, flouting convention was almost guaranteed by the seating plan. It was just too interesting for some to have a new face across the way and for others to gaze at a face they'd only dreamt and desired.

William Burroughs fell into the latter group as he quietly watched Miss Edwards through the soups, fowls, meats and sweetbreads. Fortunately for him, Millicent Farleigh felt she knew the secret to a successful dinner—more and more food in successive courses. Though he barely noticed the treats on his plate, during the lengthy meal he turned his eyes more than once with fond and entreating looks to Miss Edwards.

Dickers saw a new face across from him, and from the first morsel of food he was captivated. She was enchanting and lovely but barely paid him scant attention. His food had no flavor and the evening no time as he thought of little else but her. What a strange sensation!

Clara found herself a bit uncomfortable as she tried to avoid the smitten Mr. Burroughs. Emma to her left was of small help, since she only seemed to notice Reggie at her other side. She said a small prayer for Mrs. Thompson seated on Mr. Burroughs's right as she occupied some of his time during the meal. And Mr. Smythe-Hattan on her other side barely seemed to talk with Clara—it seemed as if he could only look at Annabelle across the table.

Edward found himself across the table and at the opposite end from Miss Thompson. It afforded him little opportunity to see let alone speak with the lady. He valiantly tried to draw the elder Farleigh away from Jeremy every other course, but she failed to notice him beyond common civility. He'd heard mention of dancing after dinner and so took heart that he might see more of Miss Thompson then.

And what of the two daughters of the house? Each young woman found herself sitting next to the object of her affections—one with confidence but the other with trepidation. Elisa was happy in the misguided knowledge that Lord Carruthers had come to her mother's party expressly to be with her. She knew herself to be in fine looks tonight and was sure Jeremy would find a way to let her know of his feelings.

Melissa, however, found it difficult to talk with the man to her right. Sir Martin Richards was all that was kind and correct in his conversations with her, but she felt her usual tongue-tied qualms when trying to answer him or speak on her own. She only hoped he would not take offense with her and find her an unacceptable dance partner later in the evening.

Sir Martin, for his part, was strangely drawn to the young woman. She was quite lovely this evening, and he found her obvious shyness triggered a protective feeling. She was so unlike his vivacious sister, and it surprised him how her quiet demeanor appealed to him. He had fancied himself quite content with a pursuit of Miss Edwards, but now he found that putting the younger Miss Farleigh at her ease interested him even more.

And Sir Martin's vivacious sister? Annabelle found herself across from an intriguing new man. They had not been introduced before dinner, so she could only madly speculate at who he might be. She caught him several times glancing her way as she turned her head between the two men at her sides.

It was truly a unique dinner!

THIRTEEN

DICKERS' DOWNFALL

Millicent graciously stood and signaled that the meal had ended. The ladies moved slowly toward the drawing room, looking forward to small private conversations about the men at this evening's table. While there might be dancing in their future, the next hour would hold time only for talk.

"My dear, that was a delicious meal, and you've truly outdone yourself," Sheila said appreciatively as they stepped toward the warming fire. She was quite sincere in her praise—Millicent certainly knew how to set a table and select just the right complement of dishes.

"Thank you so much, Lady Clifton. It was quite enjoyable to have all of you in our home, and I'm so glad you found favor with the meal."

"You are much too modest," said Emily. "It was more than favorable—simply exquisite!" she gushed.

Annabelle found herself drawn to her old friend Clara in hopes of finding some information about the mysterious man across from her at dinner. He seemed likable and fun, and she was definitely intrigued by his presence. She found Clara near the piano on a cozy settee.

"Are you enjoying yourself tonight?" Annabelle asked.

"Yes, I truly am. The dinner was quite good, but as always, too much food. I really have to restrain myself from eating all the delicious treats," Clara replied.

"Let us meet for a brisk ride in the park tomorrow morning! It will certainly dust away any remains from tonight's meal."

"That sounds like a wonderful idea. I haven't had a good ride for several weeks, and it will do me good to be outdoors in the park. I think I need to dust away more than food—riding always calms me and allows me to think."

"Oh, and what might you want to think about, Clara?"

"You were always too perceptive! Thinking to myself at this point," Clara said with a quiet sigh.

Melissa walked over to join the young ladies and sat on the chair near the settee at their smiles of inclusion.

"What a lovely dinner party, Melissa. You and your mother have given us a wonderful evening," said Clara.

"Why, thank you. This night meant so much to Mama and Elisa. They will be so happy to hear of your enjoyment."

"Aren't you enjoying yourself, Melissa?" asked Annabelle.

"Well, yes, I do find it an interesting night, and I'm not as tongue-tied as usual in company. Dinner was especially nice." Melissa's voice trailed away as her eyes gazed past the two girls in front of her.

Annabelle and Clara exchanged smiles and thought back to the table's seating arrangement—now, who had sat on each side of Melissa?

With a small start, Annabelle realized that one of

Melissa's companions was the mystery man occupying her thoughts. What a devilish pickle if they both had an eye to the same man! Now, how could she raise the subject with Clara to discover his identity?

Clara immediately thought of Sir Martin on Melissa's side at dinner, and was strangely glad that he might have another admirer. She hated to disappoint her good friend's brother, and Melissa seemed a sweet and sensible girl.

Before the girls could continue their conversation, they heard a small commotion from the other side of the room.

"But, Mama, I didn't prepare anything to play," said Elisa with a slight frown.

"Nonsense, dear. You always play a lovely tune. Now entertain our guests with a selection from your repertoire," insisted her mother with a demanding and quite uncompromising tone.

Melissa knew that tone well and whispered an "Oh, dear" under her breath as she hurriedly moved to her sister's side to offer support.

With a deepening frown, Elisa sat at the piano. "Yes, Mama." Her fingers hit the keyboard with a crash. Despite the disagreement, Elisa quickly lightened her hand and began a charming trill from the recent musicale. The ladies were delighted and roundly applauded at its conclusion. Elisa raised her head and smiled with delight—the furrowed brow now smooth.

"Please play another, my dear. That was charming," said Emily Thompson.

"Yes, it was a pleasure to hear," echoed Sheila.

"This song is one of my favorites from childhood. Our papa used to sing it to us in the garden in the summertime." And Elisa began a folk tune with a lilting melody.

As the applause ended after the song, Elisa looked

up from her music to ask if she could accompany anyone who might wish to sing.

The room grew quiet with modesty keeping the young ladies silent. After a moment, though, Clara spoke. "I'm sure we could persuade Annabelle to sing! She has a lovely voice and always starred in our school musicales."

Polite applause from the ladies drew Annabelle from her seat next to Clara. She bent her head to whisper a song title to Elisa and turned to face her audience with a smile.

"Clara knows how I love to sing, so I am happy for the opportunity to perform for you."

In the middle of her second song, the doors opened to admit the gentlemen. She waved a hello and continued her song as they quietly found their way to seats with the ladies. William Burroughs saw Clara sitting by herself and moved quickly to her side.

Clara felt a bit trapped on the settee with Mr. Burroughs. He was such a sweet boy, but it had become a cloying sweetness that she longed to see depart. Fortunately, with Annabelle's singing, she was spared having to draw him into conversation.

The room burst into applause at the end of the song. Annabelle had a beautiful voice that had captivated many a diplomat on the Continent. This group felt honored to hear her sing.

"Might we impose on you for another selection, Annabelle?" asked Sheila.

"Just one more, and then I think it is time to give Elisa's fingers a rest!" Annabelle replied. They all laughed.

Dickers stood transfixed by the door, listening to her lovely voice. She had held him enthralled during dinner, and now hearing her voice intrigued him even more. He must meet her!

Millicent thought that her daughters had been out of the spotlight quite long enough. Lovely as the chit's voice may be, she was competition for her girls and getting far too much attention. As the last song drew to a close, Millicent rose from her chair and approached the piano.

"Thank you, my dear. What a magnificent performance you gave us."

"Bravo!" shouted Dickers, and he bowed to the lady as she turned to the sound of his voice.

Sheila noticed Clara sitting a bit stiffly next to William Burroughs, and her heart went out to her. She could tell Clara was trying so hard to be polite. And that was odd in itself—Clara must be preoccupied with something quite extraordinary if she were unable to hide her discomfort during something so simple as a social conversation.

"Emily, did you notice something peculiar at last night's theater party?" asked Sheila.

"Peculiar? With the performance, you mean?"

"No no, with our party. It seemed to me that Clara was subdued during the evening, especially when I contrast it to the lively time she had at the Mardsdens' ball the night before."

"I did notice her reticence, but I attributed it to tiredness from our late nights. Is there something else wrong?" Emily asked concernedly.

"I don't know, and it bothered me so much I wrote to Marie last night to ask her to come to town. Clara is all that is proper, but she seems to be missing a sparkle."

"Perhaps a bit of dancing will cheer her. Millicent asked me to play a few sets tonight so the young people could enjoy themselves."

"I hope you are right and Clara is back to her old self when Marie arrives later this week."

"Don't worry yourself, my dear. These young girls go through such moods. Now, I'd best check with Millicent on the start of the dancing."

Annabelle had also noticed Clara as she sang. Mr. Burroughs could certainly be a pest, and she would have to find another girl to attach his interest. Yes, she would think on that subject later.

Annabelle had moved slowly through the room accepting the praise and accolades of the audience for her singing, but she now found herself at her quarry.

"Mr. Burroughs, sir, might you be so kind as to ask a footman to bring me some water? I find my throat is sadly parched from the singing."

"Why, yes, Lady Richards, I should be honored." Quickly he moved away to do her bidding.

"Sadly parched, Annabelle? What kind of silliness are you talking now?" Clara quietly asked her with a light laugh.

"Well, I just had to send him away from you—you seemed trapped on the settee. Now, stand up and let us go around the room. There's a particular gentleman I should like you to introduce to me, if you would be so kind." Annabelle turned to give her an entreating smile.

"Why, yes, Lady Richards, I should be honored," Clara replied, and both girls found themselves dissolving into giggles as they began their stroll around the room.

Dickers, the gentleman in question, had not taken his eyes from this new lady since the song ended. He had joined a group mingling after the entertainment, and he simply hovered on the fringes, not wanting to break his mood to join in their conversation. What had happened to him?

He saw the ladies stand and heard their accompanying giggles. Such a lovely sound as it filtered to him. He decided to stay his ground and see if they came toward him. Blast, they headed in the other direction!

Jeremy had completely missed the interesting dilemma for Dickers. In fact, he'd seen nothing of the company these last twenty minutes. Once the singing ended, Elisa had hopped up from the piano and attached herself to his side. He somehow found himself maneuvered with his back to the center of the room as Miss Farleigh chatted on about the season's paucity of parties—her words exactly. Would no one join his tête-à-tête?

"Miss Farleigh, this has been a delightful evening and dinner was most delicious," said Annabelle from behind Lord Carruthers's right elbow. He gratefully moved aside to widen the circle to include the two ladies.

"Thank you, Miss Richards. I am happy to hear you are enjoying yourself. Mama ought to start the dancing soon since I see she and Mrs. Thompson have put their heads together," replied Elisa.

"Dancing would be most fun, and we have more than enough people for a set," said Annabelle.

"A few too many, I fear," offered Jeremy. "Some of us will have to sit out a dance or two."

"Well, it will just be a chance to catch our breaths. I do hope Mrs. Thompson will play a country dance first—the steps are so lively. I do suppose it would be scandalous to play a waltz, even at a small house party, since we've yet to be approved by a patroness." Annabelle gave a small sigh as she made the statement.

"I believe scandal would hardly describe the furor such an event might cause," said Jeremy with a wide grin.

"Oh, you tease me, Lord Carruthers!" laughed a delighted Annabelle, but much to the distaste of Miss

Farleigh. How had this conversation moved from her control?

Clara watched this bantering with a nervous eye in case Lord Carruthers attempted to speak with her. As tiresome as Mr. Burroughs might be, at least he was quite harmless in affecting her fluttering heart. She stood across from him in their little group and was glad for the small amount of distance.

Dickers had seen the mystery woman approach Jeremy, and he quickly turned to join their party. Nothing better than an introduction from his good friend! He arrived at Jeremy's left elbow with what he hoped appeared as nonchalance.

Jeremy said, "Ah, Dickers, I don't believe you've met these two ladies? Lady Richards and Miss Edwards, may I present my good friend, Richard Smythe-Hattan. We affectionately call him 'Dickers', though I can't remember how that name came about."

"Just a childhood nickname from my sister who couldn't pronounce my name at first," Dickers replied with a disarming smile as he bowed in their direction. "I am delighted to meet you ladies, and I must say your singing was quite lovely, Lady Richards."

"Why thank you, sir. I do so enjoy it, and everyone has been most generous with their compliments. But, I must truly thank you, Miss Farleigh, for your delightful accompaniment."

Clara and Jeremy both echoed their praise at the same time, and the group laughed at the coincidence. Clara chanced a quick look at him, and found him smiling at her in such a way as to take her breath away.

"Your water, Lady Richards," interrupted Mr. Burroughs as he joined the group.

"You are most kind, Mr. Burroughs," Annabelle replied. She did find the drink cooled her some, but she suspected the warmth might be due more to the closeness of this new man than the earlier singing.

A crescendo from the pianoforte drew their attention to Mrs. Farleigh standing with her hands raised.

"Ladies and gentlemen! Mrs. Thompson has graciously consented to play for us so we might have a little dancing tonight. We're clearing an area here and we'll even roll up the carpets since I'm told it must be done for a proper setting. We'll be quite informal—the ladies have no dance cards, so you gentlemen had best be hasty with your invitations."

At the announcement, a few in the audience could be heard clapping while others murmured their assent. Many looked forward to a dance with a certain partner.

FOURTEEN

TERRACE TRIANGLE

"Miss Edwards, might I have the pleasure of this first dance?"

"And, please say you'll be my partner, Lady Richards?"

"I should be delighted, Miss Farleigh."

One of the couples moved to the dance floor with anticipation and pleasure. Dickers finally had this lovely young woman at his side. Annabelle smiled widely at her good fortune to have been standing near this attractive man.

A second couple could not have been happier, though their partners each thought of another. Mr. Burroughs counted himself fortunate to have Miss Edwards for the first dance, and Elisa gleefully accepted the hand held out to her by Lord Carruthers. Jeremy knew he could bide his time to ask for Miss Edwards to be his partner this evening, but Clara anticipated their dance with a mixture of longing and dismay.

Melissa Farleigh and Sir Martin Richards completed

the set, and the dancing began! The steps of the country dance kept them all busy, though it was not as lively as Annabelle had wished. The onlookers also found much enjoyment in watching the dancers and planning who might be their next partner.

Clara found she could plead concentration on the figures of the dance as an excuse for just the most minimal of conversations with her partner. Truly she could move her feet through the steps in her sleep, she knew them so well. She kept a polite smile on her otherwise expressionless face and hoped Mrs. Thompson planned a short selection.

Annabelle and Dickers provided an animated contrast to Clara and William, for they found much to say as the dance brought them together. They even flew in the face of propriety by talking to each other even when separated in the set! But at such an informal and friendly gathering, no one even thought to reprimand them for their actions.

Dickers could hardly believe his good fortune in dancing with Annabelle, and she seemed to be interested in his every word. He felt a tightness in his chest that he was at a loss to explain. He hoped he wasn't developing a disease just when he so wanted to be out in company.

For her part, Annabelle knew she'd found a special man. She would make discreet inquiries tomorrow to learn more about him, but she really didn't care what news the day brought. What a delicious feeling!

Sir Richards found more enjoyment than he expected in his dance with Melissa Farleigh. While she was a bit shy, he took it upon himself to set her at ease. Her frequent smiles and occasional laughter gratified him more than he'd felt before with shy debutantes. He did not even realize his thoughts never strayed to Miss Edwards.

Anyone looking at Melissa could immediately see the happiness of the young woman. She fairly glowed with excitement and felt so comfortable in Sir Richards's presence. How could she make it last longer?

Jeremy caught sight of Clara's face and his heart went out to her. Burroughs could hardly be considered a dashing partner, and his dogged pursuit of Miss Edwards was now bordering on the ludicrous. She so clearly felt no partiality toward her partner, or so it seemed to him as he hoped to recapture their friendship. He would ask her for the next dance.

Elisa could sense a preoccupation in her partner as they stepped through the dance. Oh, he was all that was polite, but he did seem more rote than rapt. Strangely that fact didn't bother her as much as she would have expected.

As the music ended, the dancers applauded Mrs. Thompson's charming song. She smiled at the young people and encouraged them to form another set. It should have been awkward with no dance cards to direct the order, but the dancers seemed to reassemble with little effort on anyone's part.

Sir Richards found himself opposite Miss Edwards as the music ended for the first set, and he graciously asked her for the next dance. She smiled her acceptance as she turned away from Mr. Burroughs and so missed the expectant look on Lord Carruthers's face. He glanced to his other side and found the set had formed around him with nary a space for him. He covered his somewhat sheepish smile with a cough and headed for the fireplace to plan for a better outcome in the next set. He'd be on his toes next time!

Planning his move carefully during the first set, Edward had joined a small group in conversation that included Miss Thompson. They all reviewed the news of the day, and Edward made sure he was near to Miss

Thompson as the music died down. He quickly asked her for the next dance, and she readily agreed. He was glad to spend a bit of time with her now to pursue her ever so casually. While he might have made a life-changing decision in a matter of moments, he didn't expect this lovely young woman to do the same.

The other two couples in the set happened by chance rather than design. Mr. Burroughs had not wanted to dance again after his blissful time with Miss Edwards, but Elisa had no intention of sitting out a single dance tonight. She fairly blocked his exit from their makeshift dance floor, and so he felt compelled to ask her to be his partner. Melissa, ending her dance in a delighted haze, had stumbled across Dickers's feet. He caught her with a swift arm and then twirled her into the set, much to the amusement of the other dancers.

"This evening has been quite pleasant," Edward said.

"Oh, yes, I agree, Mr. Waters. I have so enjoyed the small gathering of friends in such a cordial atmosphere," Emma replied.

"I hope your sentiments don't mean you'll give up your attendance at the Woodleys' ball tomorrow?"

"Oh, don't tease me!" laughed Emma. "Liking one type of party certainly doesn't prevent me from the joys of all the others."

Edward laughed at her determined enjoyment of all things about the Season. He watched her as the dance separated them and admired her graceful steps. Even if she slipped as Miss Farleigh, he was sure it would be done with style!

"Have you attended many a Season, Mr. Waters?"

"Oh, several I should say. When I came to town after school, I found it all very fussy and formal. I was horse-mad, race-mad and generally much too carefree to remember whose ball to attend," he said, laughing a bit sheepishly.

"What changed?"

"A bit of responsibility. My uncle died unexpectedly, and I was his only heir. Suddenly I had estates to worry about, tenants to see to and lives depending on my not staying out until the wee hours of the morning."

"What a shock for you," she said sympathetically.

"I hadn't expected such duty for years to come, since my father is quite well, so I immersed myself in the task. I found I had no time for parties, let alone coming into town. The estates were in excellent shape, fortunately, but I had so much to learn. A fine staff made my apprenticeship gó smoothly, and I have much to thank in them for the success of my work."

Emma admired the way he complimented his staff as well as his own efforts to manage his inheritance. He seemed to be a man who was quite pleased with his life and made sure it ran efficiently.

"But now you are back in town," she said.

"Well, as I said, it's all running quite smoothly now. I found I didn't have enough to keep me busy. I came to town for the Season a few years ago and found I liked the company. I renewed acquaintances, made many new friends, and simply felt at ease. My mother says I grew up in those years learning the estates."

"Your mother sounds like a very perceptive woman," she said with a smile.

"Yes, and she loves to tell me what a wastrel I was in my younger days," he laughed.

"I hardly think I'd use that term. Let's just say 'carefree'," she replied, laughing with him as they continued their dance in a comfortable ease.

Jeremy watched the dancers as they progressed in their steps and calculated where Miss Edwards and Sir Richards would finish. He left his companions near the fireplace as the song ended and thus had a perfect position to intercept Miss Edwards. He hadn't given a thought to how he might look to others, but Sheila thoughtfully watched his movements as he left the fireplace. He did seem to move with deliberate step to her Clara.

Elisa commanded her brother for the third dance while Edward and Annabelle met them on the dance floor. Sheila spotted Dickers and pulled him into the set as her partner—she wanted to be close by to watch Clara and Jeremy!

Jeremy succeeded in claiming Clara for this dance before she even realized her hand was on his arm. She was glad the first steps of the dance took them apart so she had a moment to collect her thoughts.

"We haven't had any time to talk this evening, Miss Edwards. I'm glad now for a chance to at least say hello and compliment you on your beautiful gown," Jeremy said.

"Thank you, Lord Carruthers. It has been a full evening."

Jeremy found himself straining for something to say. "Your friend has a lovely singing voice."

"Yes, Annabelle has always enjoyed singing, and she told me her father arranged for a private tutor the last few years. I really had not heard her perform since school, and I was amazed at how accomplished she'd become. I'd already thought she had a charming voice, but now it's wonderful." Why was she babbling on so?

He could sense the tension in her as they moved through the dance. Perhaps if she spoke about her friend and their time together at school, she might relax in his company. He kept his eyes on her as the dance led them through the set and eventually back together.

"Did you also enjoy singing at school?"

"Only as a listener, I'm afraid," she laughed. "My

singing voice is not something I'd want to share in public!"

"Far be it from me to contradict a lady," he said with a smile. "If not a singer, then you must be an artist?"

"I do enjoy painting with watercolors. I find it very quieting and peaceful to be outside on a sunny day in the garden or beside a lake with canvas and paints at hand."

"Do you find much occasion for painting?"

"Not since coming to town, I'm afraid. But, I also haven't missed it, since Aunt Sheila and I have attended so many wonderful parties and events. The Season has been so much more than I imagined." Her voice trailed away as she thought of how her plan had fallen apart so quickly and completely.

"I can only hope the 'more' is from the good times you've experienced with new friends and evenings such as these where we meet in smaller settings?"

She chanced to look up to his face upon hearing these words and saw only integrity and sympathy in the eyes gazing down at her.

As the dance separated them for the last time, Clara realized again the kindness of this man. That thought both calmed her and terrified her—what would he think had he known her true reason for coming to London? She experienced a most unsettling lurch in the bottom of her stomach.

For his part, Jeremy felt hopeful again in their relationship. She had grown more comfortable as they'd talked during the set, and perhaps he would call on her tomorrow morning to see if she would open up to him some more.

The dance came to an end with a loud crescendo from the piano. Mrs. Thompson loved a bit of flair and flourish, and the group rewarded her with their enthusiastic applause. Clara found herself at the edge of the dance floor near her Aunt Sheila as Lord Carruthers bowed politely to her and smiled at her aunt.

"I fear we've lost our chance to dance now," said Sheila. "The next set has already formed as we simply caught our breath when the music ended."

"I should enjoy watching the dancers and relaxing some during this set. It has grown a bit warm tonight," said Clara.

"I'll be happy to bring you some cool punch, ladies," Jeremy replied, turning toward the side parlor to the refreshments.

"Are you enjoying the evening, my dear?" Sheila asked.

"Yes, it is very nice and so much more casual than the balls we attend," Clara replied.

"I hope you have not found anything amiss with the lack of formality?"

"Oh, no! I did not mean to imply anything of the sort!"

"How was your dance with Lord Carruthers?"

"Why, it was fine."

"He seems most attentive."

"Attentive? To me?"

"Yes, to you. He does not normally attend the Season's parties, make morning calls, or dance with the debutantes. Yet with you, he has done all these things."

"I am sure you must be m-mistaken, Aunt Sheila," Clara said in a whisper.

"I do not mean to alarm you with my words. I just wanted you to be aware of the high regard that I feel he holds for you. Does that upset you?"

"No, I suppose I should be honored and find it most flattering."

"How do you feel about him, Clara?" Sheila asked gently.

"Your punch, ladies."

"Thank you, Jeremy. You are so kind to bring it to us," Sheila replied.

"It is but a small service, ma'am." He offered her a short bow with a wide smile.

"I see Mrs. Farleigh motioning to me. If you would excuse me," Clara fairly ran across the room to a most surprised hostess.

"What were you two just talking about so intently?" asked Jeremy.

"Now, we ladies can have our secrets," Sheila said playfully. "Are you enjoying yourself tonight, Jeremy?" She had decided to continue the questioning with the other half of this surprising twosome.

"Yes, it is most entertaining."

"Very diplomatically said, sir. Marcus mentioned to me the other day that you were interested in meeting a certain woman this Season. Would you like me to introduce you?"

Jeremy came close to spilling his punch with the surprising abruptness of her question. He had completely forgotten that conversation with Marcus at the club.

"Thank you for the offer, but I have had the pleasure now of meeting her."

"Is she everything you hoped?"

"Yes, she is a lovely lady."

"Might she be my niece?"

Fortunately his glass was now empty, but his poker face had deserted him at this new question that hit so closely to his secret. How had she read him so easily?

"You might as well tell me since you are so plainly pursuing her. I have been watching you since the Marsdens' Ball, and tonight you maneuvered very clearly to have this last dance."

"You amaze me, ma'am, and I should not like to face you across a battlefield or chess table!"

"You have not answered my question," she pursued with a slight smile.

"I find your niece both charming and delightful, and she is the object of my pursuit."

"Quite a statement. Might I ask if the pursuit will become a suit?"

"Ah, now you ask a question which I cannot answer. I do not begin to speak for the lady. So far, my pursuit has not faired as well as I would have hoped."

"Do come by for a call tomorrow morning, sir. You know you will be most welcome."

He lifted her hand for a light kiss of thanks and took the opportunity to survey the room to find the lady in question. He did not see her, and more disturbing was the glimpse of Burroughs going out a side door to the terrace. Could he have followed Miss Edwards?

Jeremy excused himself to Sheila and slowly made his way to the same door. He took care to move as unobtrusively as possible. He stopped to talk with the guests and even complimented La Farleigh on the evening. At last he found himself at the door, and his first glance outside made his heart lurch.

Burroughs had Miss Edwards' hand in his and was raising it to his lips for a kiss. He could have cheered when he saw her hand leap from his grasp and make sharp contact with his left cheek. *Whack!*

Burroughs seemed to list to his right with the unexpected blow, but he quickly moved closer to Miss Edwards. Jeremy's feet moved with lightning speed across the terrace to stop the man's impending embrace. William Burroughs had his arms around a struggling Miss Edwards with his face perilously close to hers when Jeremy reached her side.

"Take yourself off, man!" he hissed and then suited his actions to his words as he pulled the younger man away from his Clara. "The lady clearly does not welcome your attentions, or did you think that slap was meant to encourage you? Now, march!"

Burroughs moved himself with surprising speed across the terrace with a nary a glance behind him. Perhaps Miss Edwards did not welcome his suit.

"Are you hurt, Miss Edwards? I am so sorry that oaf put a hand on you." Jeremy stood near her to offer his assistance and support.

"T-thank you, Lord Carruthers. He did me no harm other than to my dignity," she said with a small smile.

"I must say you have a bruising right, ma'am!"

She smiled in earnest at his teasing and breathed a heavy sigh. Clara just now realized she was alone on the terrace with this intriguing man.

He moved a half step closer to brush a lock of hair away from her face. The slight movement gave her a start, and she looked up expectantly into his face bathed in moonlight. He tilted his head down to hers and gently, so gently touched his lips to hers. His arms seemed to find their way around her shoulders, and she shivered at his touch.

Could this man truly have feelings for her, as her aunt had said? She felt warm and safe in his tender embrace.

With her trembling his good sense fought forward, and he dropped his arms.

"You're chilled, Miss Edwards. Perhaps we should return inside to the company. I apologize to you as well—it appears I am no better than the man I sent packing just moments ago."

The chill in his voice far surpassed the night air, and she felt as if she too had been slapped. Didn't the man realize how she felt? She turned away from him and walked with haste toward the side entrance of the home.

He watched her walk into the house and could have

kicked himself for his own oafish behavior. What could she possibly think of him and his actions coming so quickly on the heels of Burroughs's churlish conduct? He would wait a bit longer on the terrace so as not to cause comment if they had entered the side door together. He had no interest in more dancing tonight.

Clara came into the room to find the fifth set in progress and was quite surprised to see Annabelle with Dickers for a second dance. *So this man must be the one Annabelle had alluded to earlier tonight,* mused Clara. Her eyes fairly flew open to see Elisa with William Burroughs for their second dance! My, what a surprising evening!

She moved to join Melissa and Sir Richards in their conversation near the pianoforte. They seemed surprised at her arrival—almost embarrassed, Clara thought. They very politely included her in their small circle, so perhaps she had not interrupted another budding couple.

She would have preferred to talk with Aunt Sheila, but Clara saw her dancing with Lord Carruthers's friend, Mr. Waters. Perhaps they would be able to talk tonight when they returned home? Emma finally had her dance with Mr. Farleigh, and her smile showed her delight.

As the piano notes came to an end, Mrs. Farleigh clapped for their attention.

"This dance will be our last. We must let Mrs. Thompson rest her weary hands after playing such delightful music for us." She led them in a round of applause for the blushing lady.

Annabelle had appeared at her side, and Mr. Smythe-Hattan executed a formal bow as he asked for Clara to partner him in this last dance. They joined a full set on the floor, and Clara couldn't help but notice Elisa opposite them for her *sixth* dance of the night with Mr. Waters as her final partner. Mr. Burroughs looked close to popping as he escorted Mrs. Farleigh while Melissa and Sir Richards completed their set. Hmmm, another couple for a second dance!

Clara gave her full attention to her partner and tried valiantly to avoid letting her eyes drift to the edges of the room. She neither wanted to see him nor know what he might be doing. She still felt quite humiliated by his abrupt behavior on the terrace even if a small part of her knew he had acted correctly to end their amorous plunge.

It actually proved easier than she expected to attend to her partner. Mr. Smythe-Hattan was a charmer and quickly put her at her ease. She really owed it to Annabelle to learn all she could from this new man so the two girls could have a comfortable coze with Emma on the morrow. Clara found herself laughing each time they came together in the dance, and she could only hope Annabelle did not think *she* might be interested in this engaging man!

As the music came to an end, the party seemed to ebb as well. The Thompson ladies were the first to call for their wraps after thanking their hostess for a delightful evening.

Jeremy appeared at Sheila's side to be near her when Miss Edwards joined her aunt. He knew it was a bit forward of him, but he simply did not care. He needed to know if he had ruined his chances with Miss Edwards by his behavior on the terrace. Little did he realize the behavior he worried about—their kiss—had but stirred her interest; his abrupt ending to their embrace should have concerned him more.

Clara hung back from joining her aunt once she saw him standing there. She knew it was a bit odd to simply cling to her partner's arm so long after the dancing ended, but she simply did not care. She could only hope Lord Carruthers would take his leave, and soon!

Dickers for his part was at a loss for how to remove the girl without attracting attention. He so wanted to speak with Lady Richards and secure a dance for the next ball. Well, he would rightly return his partner to her aunt, and no one would think him remiss in his duties.

As he turned to take Miss Edwards to Lady Clifton, he saw that the object of his interest had also joined that worthy lady. What delightful chance that she would be in just the place he needed her to be!

Annabelle was nothing if not an accomplished schemer. She appeared at Lady Clifton's side with the logical expectation of Clara's return. That Clara's escort would accompany her was all she could hope for to crown a glorious night.

Sheila signaled to Clara to join her. She was quite anxious to see how her two actors performed at evening's end. Her comfortable bed could wait.

"Thank you, Miss Edwards, for a delightful dance." Dickers bowed to Lady Clifton as he let go of Miss Edwards's arm and maneuvered himself to stand next to Lady Richards.

"Oh, it has been a lovely party, Clara." Annabelle gave her hand a conspiratorial grasp. Annabelle had much to say to her when they met in the morning.

"You ladies made the night wonderful," Dickers said diplomatically.

"I must agree with you—it was the company that made the evening enchanting," added Jeremy with a gaze at Clara.

"Tosh! You must stop this silliness. It was merely a dinner party after all, though the pheasant was divine," Sheila replied, laughing at her own enthusiasm.

"What, no accolades from you, Clara? Are you the

only one among us who did not enjoy the party?" asked Annabelle.

With all the faces turned to her, Clara was overwhelmed at the attention. But what could she say—that she'd been near to miserable all night long?

Jeremy replied, "I am sure she had as wonderful a time as the rest of us—can't you see she is so tired from the dancing that she can't even speak?" He watched her closely as the others laughed at his comment.

He could tell she had not enjoyed her evening, but not for a minute did he attribute it to too much dancing. Miss Edwards was unhappy, and that fact troubled him. Could it be his brutish behavior on the terrace? He recalled a reticence about her tonight that mirrored last night's theater party, so perhaps there was another cause. He would certainly not have any success drawing her out in this group tonight, though.

Perhaps he would stop by the club to talk with Marcus after his ride in the park tomorrow. He needed some advice, but he wasn't really sure what questions he would ask his good friend.

Sheila couldn't help but notice the kind look on Jeremy's face as he'd tried to protect Clara. He was certainly growing quite fond of her, and Sheila felt sure the feelings were reciprocated. Clara had been a lively and carefree young woman at the Marsdens' ball just two nights ago, and now she barely spoke two words if she could avoid it.

It was time to bid their goodnights so she and Clara could have that private talk. She was convinced these two just needed a delicate helping hand, and that hand would come from her.

"Perhaps it is time we gathered our wraps and left. I must say I am a bit tired myself," said Sheila.

"Please let me call your carriage for you ladies," said

Jeremy, and he turned toward the door to make good on his words.

"Did you ride with your brother, Lady Richards?" asked Dickers.

"Yes, and I just saw him leave the room, so I'd best find my wrap as well. Clara, I'll come by after breakfast, or did you want an early ride?"

"Oh, yes, an early ride tomorrow would be quite refreshing. We've missed the last few mornings," Clara replied.

"Then, I'll be at your doorstep before breakfast," she said with a smile. "Now I must say my goodbye and thank-you to our hostess."

"Please let me escort you over to the lady," Dickers added, offering his arm for the short journey.

With the two women left alone, Sheila took the opportunity to grasp Clara's hand. The abrupt behavior brought her eyes up to look at her aunt in surprise.

"I think you are too tired or perhaps unsettled to talk with me tonight, but I would like us to spend some time together after your ride with Annabelle tomorrow."

"Yes, ma'am," Clara said a bit shyly.

"Now put a smile on your face, and we'll make our goodbyes and thank-yous to the Farleighs."

FIFTEEN

THE PLAN IS OVER

"Oh, what a delightful morning we've had for our ride," exclaimed Annabelle as the girls turned their horses toward home. "The day is positively glowing with the radiance from the sun and flowers."

"My heavens! When did you take up poetry?" asked Clara with her eyebrows raised in mock horror.

"But it is such a lovely day, and the wonderful glow from last night is still with me. You did think he was wonderful, didn't you?"

"Yes, you wild goose. We've completely exhausted the subject of Mr. Smythe-Hattan and his wonderful sense of humor, his wonderful smile, his wonderful eyes, his wonderful dancing, his wonderful . . ."

"Oh, stop!" interrupted Annabelle with a giggle. "I have been a bit of a boring boor this morning, haven't I, Clara? I promise to stop monopolizing the conversation."

"You know I don't mind. It's actually quite fun to see you turn positively silly with the mere mention of his name. Actually, not even the mention of his name, since you quickly lose yourself in thought if I don't keep talking to you. I must confess I fear for your safety as you ride these treacherous city streets."

"Now you are making fun of me," said Annabelle with a pout. "But, I love it, and I love you, my good friend for bringing me into such wonderful company. Oh, there I go again with that 'wonderful' word. Do you attend the Woodley ball tonight?"

"Yes, and my new ball gown should arrive this morning. Not that I need anything new with all the clothes Aunt Sheila has already purchased for me."

"It does give one pause to think of the expense of a Season. We're fortunate to have your aunt and my cousin Patricia to guide us through the maze of events."

"Speaking of guidance, how many dances did you promise to Mr. Smythe-Hattan for tonight?" teased Clara.

"Just two! I'm not so lost as to make a spectacle of myself. Really, Clara!"

"I was only teasing, plus I knew you were aching to talk about him some more."

"Clara, you are the best of friends! I know I've talked your ear off this morning, but I've just never felt like this before or been so excited after meeting someone. He is witty and charming and makes my heart jump whenever he turns up his mouth in that half-smile he has. I find myself looking all over the street right now in the hopes we will meet him. Do you realize I purposely reminded you last night of our plans to ride this morning so he might contrive to meet us 'unexpectedly'?" Annabelle's voice trailed off in shame.

"Annabelle, look at me! Your crime is hardly worthy of that sad look. In case you didn't realize it, you're falling in love. And that's nothing to be ashamed of," Clara said gently.

Annabelle reached over to give her friend's hand an affectionate squeeze. The girls continued their slow ride home in companionable silence. Each had much to think about, but Clara's thoughts were nothing close to Annabelle's joyous feelings.

Clara's meeting with Aunt Sheila loomed ahead of her this morning. Perhaps it was time to confess all. She certainly could feel no worse than she did now, and her aunt was everything that was kind and considerate.

But how could she possibly begin to confess the whole of her tale to her aunt? To admit that she'd come to London not for the glamour and excitement of the Season but to trap a man? And not trap him in matrimony—oh no, she had only wished for his embarrassment and, worse yet, his downfall!

Would her aunt understand such deceit, and could she forgive Clara the waste of the Season? No matter how much her aunt said she enjoyed the balls, she would have to begrudge the time and money frittered away on such a thoughtless niece.

And what of Aunt Sheila's comments last night at the Farleighs' about Lord Carruthers's "high regard" for her? She must be mistaken—that was the only possible explanation. Lord Carruthers had only danced with her and come by the Clifton townhouse because of his good friendship with Uncle Marcus. Yes, that had to be the reason.

Her own feelings for Lord Carruthers had begun to frighten her some. She found herself constantly thinking about him and their time together. She did long to talk about him as Annabelle had done this morning with Mr. Smythe-Hattan. Should she perhaps consider herself what she'd just said to Annabelle about falling in love?

Clara knew she had made a fine mess of her Season. With what were now a hopeless plan and her growing feelings for Lord Carruthers, she could see no happy ending. She couldn't help but long for the safety and security of her home at Waverly Manor.

She would seek out her aunt as soon as she and Annabelle returned to Clifton House. Best to have a talk with Aunt Sheila and confess all as soon as possible. Then she could make her plans to end her Season and return home soon after her aunt's dinner party.

"Gentlemen, another fine day for a ride." Jeremy executed a neat maneuver to avoid a box lying in his path.

"We had best hurry if we're to surprise the ladies on their ride here in the park," said Dickers.

"Ladies? And what ladies would that be? I wasn't aware that we had planned to meet anyone," said Edward with a smile.

"Blast! You know I wish to see Lady Richards!"

"Calm down, cub. I was just enjoying a joke."

"Are you sure the lady would wish for your company?" Jeremy asked with a smile of his own.

"Now that is too unfair of you, Jeremy! What woman would not welcome the attentions of such a fine specimen as Dickers?" Edward added.

"Yes, but he is such a hothead at times. Certainly he's not much to look at and possessing paltry estates with indifferent lands."

"Hothead! Paltry estates!" Dickers cried. But even he laughed at these sallies as he failed to keep an angry face.

"I am glad to see we can all laugh at ourselves, since it appears the ladies are nowhere to be seen," said Jeremy.

"Perhaps they did rise with the sun and are now headed home. It would be a bit beyond forward to meet them by surprise on their very street," sighed Dickers.

"Cheer up some, old man. We can always pay a call later today. The only trouble is, I may wish to pay a call at a different young lady's home."

"What, never say you have formed an attachment without telling me!" said an affronted Dickers.

"I am sorry to have kept it from you, good sir, and I do appreciate all your efforts. But, I seem to have managed on my own," laughed Edward with a touch of smugness.

"And I suppose you knew of this!" Dickers accused Jeremy.

"No! I too am in the dark. Do tell Mr. Waters, who is the lovely lady?"

"I think I will keep a quiet countenance just now rather than speak her name aloud in the middle of the park."

"Wise, so wise," smiled Jeremy. "Perhaps you could at least tell us if we have met the lady in question?"

"Yes, you have both met her, but I will say no more while atop this beast. Let us return to my rooms for breakfast, and we can each reveal our thoughts and passions about certain ladies," Edward said, giving Jeremy a pointed look at these last words. Jeremy chose to refrain from comment on the look, but it did give him something to ponder as the gentlemen headed toward Edward's lodgings.

As the girls reached Clifton House, Annabelle gave up her hopes that Mr. Smythe-Hattan might appear at her side.

"Thank you for all you support and kind words this morning, Clara."

"You know you are welcome. Our ride was a delight, but I must confess the early hour has me yawning now. Perhaps tomorrow we could start *after* breakfast?"

"Oh, you are a slug-a-bed! Yes, we can meet mid-morning tomorrow for our ride. I will see you tonight, and let us plan to sit together for supper." And the girls gave each other fond waves as Annabelle turned her mare toward her father's townhouse. She was thankful for her groom's attendance during their ride, but she longed to see another man.

Clara had enjoyed the morning's exercise, but she was glad to be home and alone with her thoughts. She quickly changed from her habit into a light morning frock and sought her Aunt Sheila for a long overdue talk.

Sheila, for her part, knew of her niece's return from her ride. She had left instructions for Reilly to inform her immediately of Clara's return. She was determined to speak with her this morning.

Clara found her aunt in her morning room but grew shy as she neared the partially open door. Would her aunt understand such duplicity in her niece? Could she forgive her for her actions or would she send her packing?

"Clara, my dear, I am so glad to have you join me."

"Thank you, Aunt Sheila. Did you have a good night's sleep after our late evening?"

"Yes, I feel quite refreshed, though you must be tired with such an early start to your day."

"Yes, I have convinced Annabelle that we might want to start our ride a bit later tomorrow. I think a nap this afternoon will refresh me for tonight's ball."

"I am glad to hear that you still plan to attend the

Woodleys' ball. I was not sure of your mood for further parties at the end of last night's dinner party."

Sheila's offer to discuss the evening hung over the morning calm. Clara drew a deep, shaky breath and began.

"I owe you an apology, Aunt Sheila, though I do not think 'apology' can begin to cover my transgressions."

"My dear, whatever has you so upset? Are you hurt?"

"No, no, I am fine. But, I came to you under false pretenses for the Season. I am so very sorry, but you see, I was not completely truthful when I told Mama I wished to join Emma in town. Oh, I did wish to come here, but it was not for the purpose Mama supposed."

"You are speaking in circles, Clara. Can you not just tell me straight away without apologizing in each sentence," said Sheila gently.

"I will try. But, there is so much to tell."

"I think the beginning is always the best. Now what started you to thinking you wanted to come to town this Season above all others?"

"I told you once that I had met Lord Carruthers at the Thompsons' home. But there is so much more to that simple statement. Lord Carruthers and I had met earlier in the morning as I rode the buggy into town on a small errand. He was quite—um, well, he had been drinking too much, and I could not pull far enough off the road to avoid colliding with his curricle."

At the word "collide," Sheila gasped for breath.

"But you were not injured, I hope?"

"No, no, the buggy was merely at a slow trot and our wheels grazed. He, well, he slid from his seat after we came to a stop and just sat there on the ground." Clara's voice faltered at these words as she so vividly remembered the scene. The lock of wayward hair falling into his eyes pressed against her heart.

"I had no notion what to do and was alone in the

buggy. I was concerned he might be injured, so I came forward to see if I might help. I leaned forward to try to pull him up, but I was sadly mistaken in trying. He was much too large, and the slight movement woke the sleeping giant. He became mean and called me the most vile of names and then he leered at me."

Sheila could well imagine a young man on a country road after a night of drinking coming upon an innocent damsel such as her niece. Since it appeared Clara's dignity was damaged but not her person, Sheila found it hard not to smile as Clara continued the story.

"I left as soon as I came to my senses and rushed home. I, of course, confessed all to Mama, and she told me to put it all from my mind—that I would never see the brute again. But, she was wrong! He was my dinner partner that night at the Thompsons' and everyone fawned over him like he deserved the praises. But I knew better and would not speak to him during dinner."

"For the entire meal?" asked an amazed Sheila.

"Yes, we did not speak after I told him I refused to talk to one such as he."

"My, my. Well that certainly explains what Emily Thompson said about your being at cross-purposes at dinner that night. Did no one remark after dinner on the odd behavior?"

"Oh, the drawing room was abuzz on our non-conversation. It was simply horrible to endure, and I fled to the library. Unfortunately, Lord Carruthers saw my departure and followed me. Oh, he was all that was kind and proper in his apology—in fact he apologized several times that night. He was quite embarrassed about his behavior to me that morning."

"And did you accept his apology spoken so well?'

"Yes, but not in my heart. And that is where the real trouble begins. You see, after he left the library I could not help but feel even more affronted at his behavior. I wanted him to suffer the indignity of such a humbling experience as I had on the roadside that morning."

"What can you mean, my dear?"

"He, he, had insinuated that I was a, well, a lady of indecent morals."

Again, Sheila gasped at such words. It hardly sounded like the Jeremy she knew.

"Oh, you might be surprised at his behavior, but I tell you he all but offered me a *carte blanche* there on the road."

A dashing, inebriated lord coming upon a young girl on her own driving a buggy on a county road—the picture took on a most amusing shape in Sheila's mind.

"Perhaps he thought you were someone other than yourself, someone of a lower station?"

"Yes, but I do not allow that fact to excuse his cruel words."

"Continue with your story after he left the library."

"I felt he deserved a set-down, you see. And not just a berating from me on his poor behavior. Oh, no, I wanted more! Only humiliation among the *ton* would assuage the hurt I'd suffered on the road."

"But you are not such a mean-spirited person as this, Clara. Whatever can have come over you to believe such a thing?" There was a mildly reproving note in Sheila's tone.

"Oh, I knew you would think ill of me, and now, as I look back on my actions, I can only agree with you. I stood in the library and hatched the most fantastic of plots for his downfall. I wanted him to suffer among his friends, and I imagined all sorts of public spectacles of losing horse races, falling in the mud, and more. And then the plan came to me."

"What might this plan be?"

"Oh, it is a fine mess now, I assure you. My plan was

to have you transform me into the Season's wonder, and then I would intrigue him so he would fall under my spell, and then I could publicly embarrass him when I turned down his attentions. So, I told Mama I wanted to come to you for the Season, and I shamelessly used you and Uncle Marcus and your wonderful hospitality to affect my appalling plan."

"And what has gone wrong with your plan?"

"I have found him to be a much better man than I ever could imagine standing in the library and far above my touch. To believe he would even notice me is too silly a notion, and the audacity I had to plan his developing a *tendre* for me is comical. Who am I to think I could turn the eye of so eligible and fine a man as he?" Clara's voice trailed off in shame.

"And if I were to tell you I feel he had developed feelings for you, would that make your plan a success?"

"Oh, no, you are mistaken; I know you are," said Clara with conviction.

"But, wouldn't it mean that you had succeeded in your plan?" pressed Sheila.

"Well, it might mean I had partly succeeded, but I don't want the plan to succeed any more."

"Why not?" asked Sheila gently.

"I don't want to see him hurt," Clara whispered.

"Because you have feelings for him yourself?"

Clara nodded slowly and looked away from her aunt's kind face.

"I do, but I realize I have no expectations for anything beyond his regard for the niece of his good friend."

"Clara, you are a smart and worthy person, and you're doing yourself a horrible disservice to think so little of yourself and what you deserve. Now, first of all, I want you to start believing that you deserve the best the world has to offer. Can you do that for me?"

"What do you mean, Aunt Sheila?"

"I have known you all your life, young lady, and I want you to show me some of the intelligence and bravery you've always had. If you have feelings for Lord Carruthers, there is no reason to simply 'give up the fight,' so to speak."

"But, what about my purpose for coming here? I deceived you and wasted your time in thinking I came here to enjoy a season."

"I cannot say I condone any plan to trap a man into an embarrassing situation, but there is nothing wrong with being right there for him to find you. And haven't you enjoyed yourself up to now?"

"Yes, it has been a wonderful fortnight."

"What has made it so wonderful for you?"

"I have so enjoyed spending time with you and Uncle Marcus, and it was such a pleasant surprise to see Annabelle again. Emma and I have become even closer as friends, and I have been thrilled with the parties and fetes."

"What, no mention of the men you have met? As a not-quite-disinterested observer, you've had a splendid Season from the romantic perspective. Sir Richards has been most attentive to you, young Mr. Burroughs is certainly among your ardent admirers—now, don't turn up your nose like that! And, lest we forget Lord Carruthers, I told you last night that I believe he has feelings for you."

"But, what of my deception?"

"You've just told me that you have no intention of carrying through with your plan. If you've abandoned it without hurting anyone, then I do not see the harm. Perhaps the only casualty of your plan is yourself, or at least your perception of yourself?"

"I don't feel I can stay here, though."

"Nonsense, young lady! You may want to punish

yourself, but I will not let you be so cruel. Now, if you could erase any part of the Season, what would that be?"

"My horrible behavior," blurted Clara.

"But, my dear, no one but the two of us is aware that you had anything but the best and good intentions in coming here. Did you disgrace yourself in any way? No, I do not think so. Was Lord Carruthers made to feel the wrath of your plan? No, I do not think so. And certainly, you deserve happiness and love in your life with a man who loves and cares for you."

This last sentence she said quite gently, since Clara appeared skittish. Sheila did not want to frighten her niece from going to the Woodleys' ball this evening for she expected some very interesting developments with young Jeremy. He had appeared as a man with a purpose at the end of the Farleigh dinner, and Sheila would do all in her power to make sure the two players met again tonight.

"Yes, that is what I wish, too."

"Tell me of your feelings for Lord Carruthers."

"I find him to be everything that is wonderful," said a woeful Clara.

"My, that is high praise. What has he done that is so special?"

"He—he is kind to others, considerate of my feelings, a special friend to you and Uncle Marcus, and so much more. I find myself thinking of him always, and it leaves me feeling both fantastic and fearful."

"Are you feeling a bit more confident in yourself? Or, perhaps I should say deserving of good things? Dispel any thoughts of your plan from your mind!"

"But how am I to go about in company? I will not know what to say to Lord Carruthers without the security of the plan to support me."

"I think you know what to say in company, young

lady. You've attended many a party even in the informal county, so do not tell me you cannot find one thing to say to the man now."

"Of course, you are right, ma'am. I have begun to doubt myself at every turn, but you have not lost confidence in me. What would I do without you, dear aunt."

"You do feel better about yourself, then?"

"Yes, but I still think you should punish me for my despicable behavior and motivation for coming to London."

"Alright, I will punish you," Sheila replied, but she dissolved into laughter at the horror on poor Clara's face. "I was only teasing you, my sweet. Your 'punishment' shall be to rest an extra hour after luncheon so that you are truly refreshed for the evening. And if I could but find a large stack of correspondence for you to answer for me, I would hand it to you now."

Clara moved over to join her aunt on the settee and gave her a long and affectionate hug. Sheila noticed a small tear on Clara's cheek and quietly brushed it aside.

"You have had a difficult fortnight, haven't you, darling?"

"But, it was all of my own device, so I've no one to blame but myself. And no one but myself to make it right. If I do not take charge, then I should run home to Mama and Papa as the failure I would be."

"Should I be leery of you taking charge? I would hate to think of another plan forming in that sly mind of yours."

"Oh, Aunt Sheila, you are such a tease. No, I promise from this day forward, no, this moment forward, I will no longer plan any devious or underhanded tricks. My plans will only be my dreams, and I will act as a model of decorum. Now, does that sound proper enough for you?"

"A positive paragon, my dear. Now, run upstairs and freshen your face before your friends arrive."

"My, it is getting late, and they promised to call before luncheon."

Clara stood and walked to the door, but turned back to her aunt with a fond smile.

"I don't know how to thank you, Aunt Sheila. You have relieved my mind of a terrible burden, and I am only sorry I didn't come to you sooner."

"You are welcome, Clara. Now put it all from your mind and let nature take its course for the rest of your Season."

After Clara left the room, Sheila smiled to herself and then chuckled out loud at the confessions of her niece. What a scamp that girl was! To think she had planned the lovesick downfall of the unsuspecting Jeremy—what a delightful story.

"A fine meal," said Jeremy. "My compliments to your cook."

"I'll be sure to pass on your sentiments," smiled Edward.

"Our friend here appears to be lost in thought." Jeremy nodded his head at Dickers, who stared out the window.

"I'd say he's a thousand years away from here. Perhaps he's finally caught in love's tentacles."

"Surely not tentacles. No, no, I think soft embrace is much more the thing."

Dickers turned back to the table as the two men enjoyed their laugh. Not realizing he was the object of their amusement, he joined with them in the laughter.

"Dickers, you are in deep trouble."

"Whatever can you mean, Edward?"

"We've sat here talking about you, laughing at you and finally imagining you in the clutches of an octopus, and you can only look at us and laugh."

"You're quite right," he said almost softly. "If I found myself in her clutches, I would be the happiest of men."

"I do fear our lives will change forever this Season," said Jeremy with a touch of seriousness.

"'Our' lives," asked an astonished Dickers. "Never say you put yourself in the same category?"

Jeremy looked a bit sheepish but slowly nodded his head in agreement.

"Saints be praised," whooped Dickers. "I cannot believe my ears. Now you must tell me the whole of it, for I just had the most horrible of thoughts—could two of us be interested in the same lady?"

"Put your fears to rest," smiled Edward. "For, you see, I know we three have designs on three very lovely but separate women."

"So you already knew of Jeremy's great confession? I suppose I should be miffed, but to tell the truth, I'm quite happy about it all. Gad, I'm positively giddy!"

"Perhaps we should meet at the club later today, and I'll punch the giddiness, as you say, right out of you. A few rounds of fisticuffs will bring you to rights," Jeremy said, raising his fists in challenge.

"Ha! I accept your feeble excuse for a fight and will knock you down before you take your second breath," laughed Dickers.

"Shall we get back to the ladies?" asked Edward. "I do believe we have much to discuss."

"First off, I am in the dark about each of your chosen ones. Enlighten me, gentlemen," said Dickers.

"I guess we both owe a debt to my fair, departed Colette," said Jeremy.

"Never say that you've actually fallen for your . . . your . . ." Dickers's voice trailed off in disbelief.

"No, no," laughed Jeremy. "I only meant our breakup sent me off to the country to soak my sorrows in home brew and then to meet a lovely lady."

"And is she here for the Season?"

"Yes, a very fortunate event indeed. She came here with her good friend, who has caught Edward's eye. I speak of Miss Clara Edwards and Miss Emma Thompson."

"Capital, I say! They are lovely ladies. And do they return your regard?" Dickers asked.

The silence spoke volumes.

"Ah, well, I see I have some work ahead of me to see you both blissfully settled," Dickers decided.

"Now, none of your shenanigans! We'll do this ourselves," said Edward.

"It's not that we don't appreciate your help, but don't you see that it would be better if we both found our happiness on our own, just as you did?" added Jeremy.

"But you've had opportunity and come up short of the mark."

"No!" both men shouted in unison. They then laughed at the look of hurt on Dickers's face.

"You must let us do this ourselves," Jeremy said quietly in a voice that brooked no arguing. Dickers relented but would not give up entirely.

"Well, you cannot complain if I watch from the sidelines and cheer you on to victory."

"You know we welcome your good wishes and support," said Edward.

"So, what are you plans to captivate these women?" asked Dickers.

His question was met with silence and sheepish grins.

"We haven't a clue," admitted Edward.

"Speak for yourself," said Jeremy. "I have a brilliant plan, but I just haven't thought it through completely yet."

"We'll help—tell us what you have so far," Dickers asked eagerly.

"Yes, I am most anxious to hear this plan," Edward said with a smile.

"Well, I, uh—oh, blast! I don't have a thing in mind." Jeremy joined in their good-natured laughter.

"Would I be remiss in offering some suggestions on wooing and courtship, gentlemen?" Dickers asked.

"And what makes you the authority?" asked Jeremy.

"Nothing at all except my spectacular success last night," crowed Dickers amidst the groans of his companions.

"Might I suggest that we have won half our battle by simply finding these women?" suggested Edward. "I think the rest will take care of itself as we go through the Season. I for one am looking forward with much eagerness to tonight's ball. I managed to secure the promise of a dance with Miss Thompson, and I intend to make it the supper dance. Now, perhaps the six of us could enjoy a lively meal, and we can further our causes?"

"An excellent idea and enough of a plan for me," said Jeremy. "I must leave you now to meet my man of business. Dickers, do not forget our meeting this afternoon."

"I'll be waiting to knock you out!" boasted Dickers as the gentlemen rose to take their leave.

"You look just lovely, my dear."

"Thank you, Marcus," Sheila replied. "I had hoped to enjoy a new ballgown, but I haven't taken the time for myself lately. I am happy to say I convinced Clara to purchase a few new frocks. She wears a particularly lovely ivory silk tonight for the Woodley ball."

"Do you feel she is enjoying her Season?"

"Well, I think she will find tonight a bit better than the last few evenings."

"What is so special about tonight?"

"It's not so much that tonight is special but that she won't have the burdens weighing on her that have made her so unhappy the past few days."

"Whatever are you talking about? Has someone made her unhappy?"

"Oh, it's more of her own making, but we straightened it out this afternoon."

"Is there something we should be concerned about? Has she done anything to hurt her chances of making a good match?"

"Oh, no, nothing like that. She had the silly notion to use her Season to teach someone a lesson. Apparently she suffered an insult from the man on the road while at home at Waverly Manor. She thought she could serve up a bit of punishment by causing the gentleman to suffer an embarrassment here in town. We had a lovely talk, though, and I do think she will just enjoy herself without trying to engineer anyone's downfall."

"Well I must say you ladies keep me entertained. I trust the gentleman is none the wiser?"

"No, he has no notion of his narrow escape, but I am sure it will make a lively story for their grandchildren!"

"Never say she has now formed an attachment to the man who insulted her!"

"Yes, her love cannot be denied, though I don't think Clara realizes she is in love just yet. But, I am sure a few more weeks of the Season will bring them together most happily. I encouraged her to simply enjoy herself and leave the planning to nature."

"Such a wise woman I married."

"Oh, Marcus, you are too silly. Now, would you please ring for Lizzie to help me pin this trim? I think it might be the last ball for this gown."

Marcus complied and then said, "Such a tattered and worn dress certainly deserves a new bauble."

"Oh, Marcus, what have you done?" But Sheila was thrilled to see the box he held out for her.

"You have spent so much time with Clara this Season, and I knew I wanted to give you something just for yourself." The sapphire and diamond earbobs and necklace perfectly complemented Sheila's blue silk gown.

"You are such a dear man to think of me so sweetly," Sheila said, and she gave him a light kiss as Lizzie entered the room.

SIXTEEN

SUPPER WITH FRIENDS

Jeremy smiled to himself as the dance came to an end. This night offered such promise, and the lovely woman across from him formed the center of his attentions. He had easily found her in the crowded ballroom and immediately left his friends to secure a dance. A smile had lit her face at his greeting, and his heart tumbled.

For her part, the lady was just as anxious for the evening. Seeing him approach her as soon as he entered the ballroom was an unhoped-for beginning. He looked splendid in his black evening clothes, and she could not keep the excitement and anticipation from her eyes and face.

Sheila had watched Clara and Jeremy since they'd greeted each other earlier in the evening and felt very hopeful for the pair. Each one appeared relaxed and almost glowing in his or her appearance. Yes, they made a lovely couple, and wouldn't she have loved to be an audience to that roadside first meeting?

Jeremy held his arm for Clara as he prepared to return her to her aunt. Her fingers lightly fell on the material, and he had to restrain himself from putting his other hand over hers.

"Thank you for a lovely dance, Miss Edwards."

"Oh, you are most welcome, Lord Carruthers," Clara said with another of her wide smiles.

"You seem more at ease tonight, Miss Edwards. It is a pleasure to see your smile."

"Yes, I am truly enjoying the Season, and Aunt Sheila and Uncle Marcus have made it a wonderful time for me."

"Might I also have the pleasure of the supper dance?"

"I would like that very much, Lord Carruthers."

Jeremy nodded "hello" to Sheila and settled Miss Edwards before moving off to the card room. He was anxious to think more about her, and a mindless game of cards would provide an admirable cover.

He found the card room busy with the older men who did not favor dancing but wanted to escort their wives or daughters. Or perhaps the wives and daughters demanded the escort? He joined a table that looked fairly flat and was soon lost in thought.

Edward had the promise from Miss Thompson for the much-sought-after supper dance, and he really felt no interest in the rest of the evening until then. Short of strolling through the garden, though, he would have to mingle amongst the guests. He knew his presence as a pillar next to the dancers would not go unnoticed.

Miss Thompson had seemed genuinely happy when he requested the dance. *So, at least she does not hold me in aversion,* he thought with just a small amount of seriousness. They would have a pleasant repast with friends and perhaps even dance again later in the night. Two dances would show his marked attention, but he was more than willing to become the talk of the *ton* for the lady.

The more he learned about her, the more he realized that she intrigued him completely. No, captivated him was more the word. And he was surprised at the speed at which he'd come to that conclusion. He'd only met the young woman two days ago—well, two and a half if one wanted to be precise. And yet he knew immediately that they would make a wonderful couple. Funny how that worked, and he'd never been one to believe in love at first sight.

He hoped that she would find him as interesting as he found her. So far she seemed more interested in young Farleigh, and he did not appreciate the competition. He would draw on his experience, and, he hoped, greater skill with the ladies to cut out his rival. Their dance last evening had been a delight, and he hoped each time they met would only be better.

So, what to do with himself right now? He scanned the room for a diversion and soon spotted Sir Richards in conversation with two others. He moved toward the threesome and joined their discussion on politics.

"What a lovely dress, Clara."

"Thank you, Emma." Clara smoothed away a tiny wrinkle in the ivory silk.

"Let us sit together for supper. Charlotte promised to join us, too."

"That would be lovely, and we'll make room for Annabelle. Who is your partner tonight?"

"Mr. Waters asked me as soon as Mama and I entered the ballroom. He was most attentive and gracious, and I think Mama likes him."

"But, how do you feel about him?"

"Oh, I find him most imposing."

"Well, imposing is not a very promising start. Do you find him attractive in an imposing sort of way?"

"Oh, well, certainly attractive, and he was very kind when we danced at the Farleighs' last evening. We chatted most amiably, and I felt so comfortable with him, too. He does have the most engaging smile, when he chooses to use it."

"Do you find him a bit stuffy?"

"No, no, I would not say stuffy. He is quiet, circumspect even, but he can be lively in his conversations, too. He was so appealing in the story he told about himself while we danced. And he was ever so kind earlier tonight, and I do enjoy a man who is gracious."

"Is Mr. Farleigh no longer the center of your attentions, then?"

"I don't quite know why, but no, he is not. I had so looked forward to seeing him last night, and it was pleasant. But that is all it was—pleasant. I gave it quite a bit of thought today and decided I had been a bit swept off my feet by my first London beau. Is that silly of me?" Emma asked shyly.

"No, not silly at all. And quite mature of you to realize it for what it was. Mr. Farleigh will always be a fine friend for you, I'm sure."

"Oh, I should think so, especially as Charlotte seems so taken with him. I imagine we'll be seeing quite a bit of the two of them together."

"And I saw Elisa Farleigh almost leading poor Mr. Burroughs across the room when we arrived. She seems to have made her preference known to all, and I don't think the gentleman has the gumption to say 'nay' to her," laughed Clara.

"Well, choosing partners tonight must be a trait for the Farleigh family. Melissa looked in transports dancing just now in the arms of your former beau, Sir Richards."

"Now, he was never my 'beau,' Emma Thompson! You are a positive sneak sometimes."

"I only called him yours since he did single you out on occasion for dancing. But, you seemed to have found another interest. And it is just as well, since Melissa confided to me earlier this evening that Sir Richards signed her card for the supper dance and invited her for a carriage ride tomorrow and for the next day."

"It is too bad our supper table can't extend to hold this entire company of new couples."

"I think we'll have a lively enough group with just the eight of us tonight," said Emma.

"I know I will certainly enjoy our supper this evening, and I plan to make a point of sitting near to your Mr. Waters," Clara said with a wide smile.

"Did you fare well with the cards tonight, Jeremy?" Marcus asked.

"Middling I'm afraid," Jeremy replied. "My mind wandered some, so when the group broke apart, I felt it best to stay away from another table."

"Always good to know when it's not your night. Perhaps you'll do better with the dancing?" Marcus said with a wink.

"I certainly hope so, sir. I have enjoyed this Season like no other."

"High praise, indeed, and I think that can only mean a lady has caught your eye."

"Yes, but I am not sure I have caught hers," Jeremy laughed lightly.

"Any woman would be delighted to have you call on her."

"Well, if she is, I will be sure to let you know."

"You appear to be enjoying your Season more than my niece."

"What? Has she been unhappy?" Jeremy had trouble hiding his alarm at hearing Marcus's words.

"Well, according to my, wife she's been in knots over a plan she hatched in the country to bring a certain gentleman to his knees. Something about a slight on the road and the need to pay him back the insult she suffered. Apparently, the plan didn't go well, and she's found herself enamored of him now that they're in town. What a silly notion for such a practical girl."

"Enamored of him, you say." Jeremy barely spoke a whisper.

"Yes, and so Sheila convinced her it was best to just forget her plan and proceed with the Season. I haven't seen enough of Clara tonight to know if she is enjoying herself. Perhaps I'll ask her to dance. No, no, much too direct. Why don't you dance with her and make sure she has put all thoughts of this plan out of her mind?"

"As is happens, we are partnered for the supper dance. I think it best if I make no mention of this plan you speak of—I'll just see if she seems to be doing well."

"Capital! I'll let Sheila know you'll be checking on Clara."

"Oh, no, please don't give any credit to me. I would rather she not know of my participation."

Marcus nodded his agreement and excused himself to join a table just forming.

Jeremy hardly wanted Sheila to hear he knew of this plan until he could decide how he would approach Miss Edwards. He didn't know if Sheila knew the name of the scoundrel from the road, but it was obvious Marcus had no notion. What a delicious tidbit of information had just fallen into his lap!

He could only wonder how she had hoped to embarrass him for the insult she felt from their first meeting. That she still thought about it and felt the need to avenge herself, so to speak, gave him considerable pause. If he hadn't met her again at dinner that night, he would have barely given the morning's event a second thought. Apparently, she had given it much more than a second thought and had gone so far as to plan her entire Season on that morning.

He felt he must let her know what Marcus had told him. It would be unfair to tease her without revealing it, no matter how much enjoyment he might find. Perhaps he could find a way to let her actually achieve the goal she'd sought when coming to London? That notion might not serve, though, since he wasn't precisely sure what that goal had been, and besides Marcus had said Sheila had convinced her to drop the plan.

She would be embarrassed now if he suddenly brought up that morning and what Marcus had told him. So, he would need to move slowly and carefully with this knowledge, and tonight would not be the right place. No, for tonight he would put her at her ease during their dance and supper. Perhaps tomorrow they could go driving in the park and talk some during the carriage ride. He might casually mention his conversation with Marcus. It would be far better to discuss it in private than on the dance floor or at supper.

He had best leave the card room and rejoin the partygoers. The supper dance would begin soon, and he did not want to be late in finding Miss Edwards to claim their dance.

She hadn't seen Lord Carruthers for some time now. Just as Clara began to wonder if he might have left the party, she spotted him across the room. She slowly let out her breath but hadn't even realized that she'd held it for the last several seconds.

Clara had to admit to herself that she truly looked forward to their next dance. The evening had begun so wonderfully for her, and she knew in her heart it could only improve. Aunt Sheila had said again this morning that she felt Lord Carruthers had feelings for her. If only it could be true.

The music came to an end, and it would soon be time for the supper dance. She saw Lord Carruthers start to move across the room toward where she sat with her aunt. Why, she felt like a green girl at her first assembly! She would have to still her beating heart, or perhaps she was the only one who could hear its loud thump.

"Ladies, you look as lovely as the flowers in this room," Jeremy said.

"What a poet you've become, Lord Carruthers," said Sheila with an arched brow.

"Yes, my old schoolmaster would be proud. I believe this dance is ours, Miss Edwards."

"Yes, thank you sir." Clara rose from her chair.

"Enjoy yourselves, and Jeremy, have you seen my errant husband?" Sheila asked.

"The card room, ma'am, but I'm sure he'll join you soon."

"If only for some of the Woodleys' lovely supper," she said with a smile.

"Miss Edwards?" He held out his arm to Clara.

Clara placed her hand on his arm as he guided her to the fast crowding dance floor. She saw Emma with her Mr. Waters and Annabelle across the room with Mr. Smythe-Hattan. Annabelle and Dickers seemed to have become a couple quite quickly, but she supposed Annabelle knew her own mind. She was certainly the most sophisticated of Clara's friends, with her years on the Continent. And there was Reggie Farleigh, dancing with Charlotte, so they would surely have a lively table at supper.

"You seem a bit preoccupied, Miss Edwards."

"Oh, forgive me, Lord Carruthers. I did not mean to ignore you, but I was just noticing all our friends on the dance floor together."

"Any interesting pairings?"

"Oh, you are teasing me! You would never want me to gossip, would you?"

"Remove such thoughts from your mind! I am just surprised and gladdened to see my friends so happily partnered tonight."

"Very well said, sir. And you will be seeing them up close as soon as the dance ends, since we ladies already made plans to sit together for supper."

"Then my next hour will be spent in lively and lovely company. I do look forward to it, Miss Edwards."

The intensity of his gaze gave Clara some pause, but it was everything that was proper in a gentleman. As the figures of the dance separated them, Clara hoped that gaze followed her.

Jeremy was happy to see Clara enjoying herself this evening. Knowing what he now did, her mood swings of the past few days made more sense to him. Since her schemes were a thing of the past, he could only envision more wonderful nights such as this one. How long did a gentleman wait before declaring himself, he wondered?

But, no, he was probably moving too quickly. While he knew his heart and had heard from Marcus that Miss Edwards may have romantic feelings for him, the young lady herself was in the dark as to his intentions. He would have to woo her more beyond these occasional dances. Yes, that ride in the park tomorrow, and then he would have more time to see her at Sheila's dinner party the following evening.

"Miss Edwards, might I invite you to join me in a carriage ride tomorrow after luncheon? It promises to be a lovely day."

"Oh, thank you, Lord Carruthers, but I am afraid I must decline. I had a note this morning from my mother, and she and Papa arrive in town tomorrow. I do not feel I can be absent from home."

"I understand completely. What brings your parents to town?"

"Nothing in particular, I'm sure. They had planned all along to join me for part of the Season—well, at least Mama did, and she told Papa that she had no intention of dancing by herself! I am sure he will find much to do while in town and only teases Mama to vex her," she said with a smile.

"I just realized I know very little about your home life. Do you have any brothers or sisters?"

"Just my brother, Harry, who is up at Oxford for his final year. I do miss him since he's gone away to school. It's made life at home sadly flat."

"No one to share in your schemes." He laughed and regretted the words as soon as he uttered them. He'd had no intention of talking about her plan gone awry, and the words had tumbled out in all innocence. The stricken look on her face told him she still had misgivings about her actions. He hurried forward to try to mend his faux pas.

"I know I had much fun with my sisters growing up," he said. "There are three of them, all younger, but the two oldest are just a few years behind me. We tramped through the estate like gypsies as children, played pirate on the lake with a rowboat, and generally drove my parents to drink."

His prattle had seemed to draw her away from his

earlier words, and her face looked more composed. He even saw the corners of her mouth turn up in a smile at his last words.

"Are your sisters in town?"

"No, they've all married and settled in the country. They were mad to come to London for their first Seasons, but they each found a man with estates to manage in the country. My middle sister, Sarah, occasionally comes to town but not usually during the Season."

"Do you see them often?"

"Several times a year, when I visit the country."

Gad, but would he never stop saying the wrong thing? She did not seem to notice his reference to "the country," so perhaps he refined on it too much. He was glad when they again parted with the dance.

She had noticed his more-than-usual chattiness tonight, but she barely gave it a thought. Since her plan had met its demise, it was such a pleasant change to now feel somewhat carefree. This night no longer had to figure into her plan, and she could simply enjoy the party. And Clara found it a delicious sensation to give herself over to, well, to herself.

Lord Carruthers had occupied her thoughts all day since her talk with Sheila earlier in the morning. She imagined herself and Lord Carruthers dancing, chatting comfortably at supper, and even strolling in a garden.

These sensations were all new to Clara, but it was now so easy for her to recognize why her plan had troubled her so. Causing hurt to one you held in regard made no sense and had left her in much distress. She found her thoughts of him now too easily turned to dreams that left her breathless.

Clara gave Lord Carruthers one of her loveliest smiles as the dance brought them together again. He happily held her at his side for the final figures and then executed a simple bow over her hand. Anyone looking at them would have seen a romance in full sway.

And, of course, Sheila had watched them as unobtrusively as possible for their entire dance. Yes, they seemed to be getting along just fine—well more than fine, based on the smiles on their faces. They had regained their footing from the Marsdens' ball three days earlier, and it was certainly gratifying to see Jeremy so happily settled after all these years.

She watched them move toward the supper table with their friends and chanced to look around for Marcus. She spied him across the room speaking with their host and rose from her chair to join them. She expected it would be too much to hope they sat at a table near to Clara's.

Jeremy guided Clara to a chair as their friends crowded around the table to find their seats. Platters of food adorned the table, and Annabelle wasted no time filling her own plate with the first course before taking her seat. Dickers watched in amused fascination as he stood by her chair.

Clara nodded to a footman to fill her plate and reached for her champagne glass for a small sip. The cool liquid did nothing to calm her nervousness. Amid her friends, new and old, Clara had hoped to feel at ease with Lord Carruthers so near. She took several deep breaths as she lowered the glass.

Jeremy, for his part, had never felt so alive and vibrant. He looked into his future and saw a wonderful life with this amazing woman at his side for innumerable dinners to come. He, too, found his hand on the champagne glass, but it was to slow his excitement rather than calm nerves.

Charlotte and Reggie were the last to join the table, and their laughter caught the group's attention.

"What has you so amused?" asked Emma.

"I had to practically fight off three men for the honor of dining with this lovely lady tonight," Reggie explained. "I never realized I would have to put my life on the line here in a ballroom."

"It was never so bad as that!" exclaimed Charlotte.

"Well, the first man had the temerity to accost us on the dance floor as the music ended. Then, two others blocked our way and insisted Miss March join them at their table. I kindly pointed out to them that I had already spoken for the pleasure of the lady's company for dinner."

"And that settled the matter?" asked Edward.

"I wish I could say my fierce countenance frightened the halfwits away, but I must confess it took Miss March's firm tone to set them to rights. They would only accept it from her that I had not captured her for the night."

"Now, it was nothing of the sort," laughed Charlotte. "Those men had already turned to walk away when I told them I would not welcome their brash company again."

"To be pushed out of the circle so harshly!" laughed Emma.

"She was everything that was proper, which I cannot say for the gentlemen," defended Reggie.

"Let us not refine on it any longer," said Annabelle. "We are all together here to enjoy this delicious meal and fine company."

"I fear the fair Lady Richards has eyes for naught but the food on this table," laughed Dickers. "She is ready to call for the next course but cannot whilst you have yet to start your first. So, please be seated!"

Annabelle's pout with fork arrested brought laughter to the entire table. Charlotte gracefully took the chair Reggie held for her, while Jeremy raised his glass to the table.

"I propose a toast, my friends, to our excellent company, this fine evening, and many more good times together to come for us all."

"Well said!"

"Bravo!"

"How true, good sir."

Clara turned her eyes to Jeremy as he finished his words and caught the full impact of his intense gaze directed at her. She did not shy away from his stare, for that was all she could call it. His eyes fairly pierced into hers, and she returned the look with a strength she hadn't known she possessed.

Jeremy brought his glass to Clara's and lightly touched the rim. His head dipped ever so slightly in a silent bow. She smiled widely and sipped a small taste of champagne—best not to drink too quickly with this charming and exciting man at her side.

"Emma tells me your parents arrive tomorrow, Clara," said Annabelle.

"Yes, er, they should be here in time for luncheon," Clara said a bit distractedly.

"How delightful for you," said Charlotte.

"I am glad they will join me for a part of the Season. They've not recently taken the time to come up to town."

"What about your parents, Charlotte? Will they be here this Season?" asked Reggie.

"Papa's working in Italy this year, so I won't see them back in England until Christmas. I am staying with Aunt Maria and Uncle Phillip until they return."

"Have you any plans to visit them in Italy?" asked Edward.

"I would certainly love it, but it is not very easy to find

someone to travel with me. My aunt would love to, but she won't leave Uncle Phillip, and he won't leave the House of Lords. So, unless we ladies would like to make the journey, I think my reunion with Mama and Papa will have to wait."

"I can sympathize with you in your travel dilemma," said Annabelle. "I don't know how many times I wanted to dash off while on the Continent with my father, but he would hear nothing of it. Unless I had proper chaperones, I had to be content to stay with him."

"But you saw so many grand cities with your father," said Clara.

"Oh, yes, it was a wonderful time, but I did get restless far too often. I just don't have the temperament to wait around."

Edward and Jeremy exchanged amused glances. If ever two people were made for each other, it looked to be Dickers and Lady Richards. He never sat still for anything, and she just confessed to the same.

Sheila had a perfect view of Clara's supper table, but unfortunately Clara and Jeremy had their backs to her. While she could easily see the group appeared to be having a fine time, she could not watch their two faces and judge for herself. She sighed quietly but could do nothing to solve her problem.

She was glad to have Clara's parents join them on the morrow. Having Marie here would be a wonderful treat as well as someone else to talk with Clara. While Sheila was fairly sure her meeting with Clara this morning had put to rest all of the foolishness, there might be something else that Clara had not mentioned. A mother's familiar face could be just the soothing presence to dislodge any more lingering "confessions" from the little schemer!

* * *

Meanwhile at the table uppermost in Sheila's mind, their plates were now cleared, but the champagne continued to flow freely.

Jeremy found himself wondering how and when he could approach Clara about her now-abandoned plan. He dearly wanted to see her tomorrow, but the ride in the park seemed unlikely with her parents arriving.

Might he simply impose on his friendship with Marcus and ask to meet him tomorrow at his home? Or perhaps the two of them could go for an early morning ride, and Jeremy would continue a conversation with Marcus in his study. Ask him about his new horse or an investment opportunity? But no, arriving in riding clothes would mean he could not join the family in the drawing room. So riding was not an option.

He fell back on the idea of arranging to call on Marcus later in the morning. They always found plenty to discuss, and he might find a way to see Clara. Better still, if Sheila chanced on his arrival, he felt certain she would invite him to join the family for luncheon. He felt a bit unfair using Marcus in this manner, but he was sure the man would understand if he knew his reasons.

Jeremy would also be happy to meet Clara's parents should they arrive while he was at the Clifton townhouse. A casual meeting, as a friend of the family, would place him on an easy footing with Mr. Edwards. Why, her parents might have already arrived by the time Jeremy made his appearance. Then he could certainly manage an afternoon ride with Clara. Yes, arranging to call on Marcus tomorrow was a capital idea! He would seek out the man in the card room later tonight.

Edward found his thoughts centering on Miss Emma Thompson as she sat at his side throughout the meal.

He had been a bit uncertain when Farleigh joined the table with Miss March. How would Miss Thompson feel seated across from the man she had often danced and dined with as her own partner?

From all appearances, she had no qualms about the situation. Had he read too much into their friendship, or had it simply fizzled? Farleigh seemed most taken with Miss March, and she certainly seemed to dote on him.

Now if he only knew Miss Thompson's preference, he might breathe more easily. For all his discouraging months in searching for this young woman, finding her brought an entirely new set of frustrations. Would she care for him? How was he to further their acquaintance? What would her family and friends think of him? Why was he suddenly so unsure of himself?

Edward recalled their conversation while dancing at the Farleigh dinner. He'd actually told her his mother called him a wastrel! This young woman certainly brought out the odd confessions from him, but he found it quite wonderful to talk with someone who genuinely seemed interested in what he said. He planned to call on her in the morning and perhaps send flowers in the afternoon. Yes, he definitely wanted her to be sure of his interest and regard, and he would have the patience to wait for such a sign from her.

Clara had been sorry to turn down Lord Carruthers's invitation for a ride tomorrow. She so wished to see her parents, but now she could not help but feel they'd chosen a poor time to arrive!

It occurred to Clara that she might not see him until Aunt Sheila's dinner party two days hence. Oh, why hadn't she suggested the following day for their ride? It would not do for her to mention such a thing tonight, and she could only hope it would occur to Lord Carruthers.

And why this sudden urge to see him tomorrow when he sat next to her right now? Oh, why try to deny it any longer! She had already admitted to herself that she cared for him, but it was useless to hide the truth. She truly loved him with all her heart, and any time apart was just a chance to dream about him and their next meeting.

She could not help recalling Aunt Sheila's comments about Lord Carruthers. Even if he did show her a marked regard, Clara just would not believe it was anything more than simple kindness to the niece of his good friend.

Perhaps she should talk with Aunt Sheila in the morning and confess this latest development in her topsy-turvy Season. How could she admit her feelings out loud when to even say them silently to herself sounded silly and conceited?

Clara chanced a look at his profile and found him smiling at Emma and Mr. Waters. They had all seemed to enjoy the evening as much as she did, but Clara was sorry she hadn't sat next to Mr. Waters. She had so wanted to learn more about the man who had captivated Emma so easily.

Emma did feel quite captivated. Their last dance and this time at the supper table had been wonderful. Mr. Waters was a charming partner and found ways to make her feel special. She especially thrilled at the way he looked at her—a mix of kindness and regard with a touch of special feelings, she hoped.

She looked forward to their next meeting tomorrow. He'd confided his intentions to call on her in the morning, and she hoped he would arrive by himself. It would be perfect to have some time somewhat alone with him—she was sure she could ask her mother to step out of the drawing room for a few minutes to confer with the cook. Just thinking of Mr. Waters made her heart race!

They heard the strains of music as the orchestra began a quiet selection to announce the end of supper. And while the prospect of more dancing always delighted, the intimate atmosphere of their table would soon be over.

Edward was the first to stand and help Miss Thompson from her chair. The other couples followed his cue with plans for a future meeting or a carriage ride hastily discussed. Clara found herself partnered with Mr. Farleigh and quickly lost sight of Lord Carruthers as the dancers moved out of the supper room.

Jeremy relaxed comfortably in the card room and was glad he'd not signed a dance card for any partners after supper. The better to simply remember the first half of the evening as he slowly sipped his port.

He reveled in the memories and thoughts for the future. It amazed him that life could be so good now when he had arrogantly assumed it already was the best it could be. He smiled a bit and wondered what Edward's mother would call this stage of his affair. He was certainly past being mystified!

He looked forward to tomorrow and to calling on Marcus. The day presented so many unknown but hoped-for opportunities, and he couldn't begin to think how it might end. Certainly not with a short, ten-minute chat with Marcus followed by a swift exit. Perish the thought!

He would have to give more thought to his time for a private conversation with Miss Edwards. He felt certain he could find a way to spend a few minutes with her, even if it were only a stroll in the Clifton gardens.

With the family's arrival at any time, it would be best to stay close to home.

Their conversation would prove to be quite enjoyable for him. He would start with a very casual reference to that first meeting on the road. They could laugh about it now, and it would not arouse her suspicions. Then he might say he was glad she held no grudge against him for his rude behavior. That statement might give her pause. Could he then ask her whether her plans for the Season were going well? No, that would cause her some unease, and he merely wanted to tease her.

Best to simply confess at once what Marcus had told him. Once she recovered from the embarrassment of his knowing, he would feel free to tease. Until then, he would keep a close counsel on his words.

He spotted Marcus entering the room and fairly bolted from his chair.

Sheila had simply not enjoyed the second half of the evening. Jeremy quickly disappeared after supper, and Clara was engaged for every single dance. She'd had no opportunity to speak with her two players, and so she had no notion of how the drama progressed. Such frustration had her wringing her hands in a most unladylike fashion by the time the orchestra began their last selection.

She would have to be content with the carriage ride home to ply Clara with questions about her evening. And while the ride afforded her the best in terms of privacy, it often provided for limited conversation, since Clara could be counted on to fall asleep at the first turn in the road. Sheila could have screamed!

She saw Clara approaching her on the arm of Sir Richards. They seemed in high spirits for so late in the evening, and her hopes rose a bit for her conversation during the carriage ride.

"Thank you ever so much, Sir Richards. It was a lovely dance. We will miss you the rest of the Season," Clara said.

"The pleasure was mine. You were, as always, a wonderful partner." He executed a small bow over her hand and turned to pay his respects to Sheila.

"Are you leaving us?" asked Sheila.

"Yes, I leave at the end of the week for a month on the Continent with my father. It will be just a short trip to establish myself, and then I'll return to town for the summer."

"Do say you will be able to attend my small dinner party before you leave."

"But of course, Lady Clifton. It would hardly be an advantageous start for my diplomatic career were I to snub our leading hostess," he said with a wide smile.

"You do carry on, young man," laughed Sheila. "I am sure you'll do just fine in your career."

Marcus joined them, and the Clifton household said their goodbyes and offered thanks to their host and hostess as they headed toward the door.

SEVENTEEN

SHEILA'S DINNER PARTY

Jeremy threw another cravat into the growing heap and sighed in frustration. He must be a bit nervous on this night of such importance—more like a schoolboy off to his first party in long pants!

He smiled and took a sip of brandy as he thought back to the events of yesterday afternoon. Things could certainly have gone better, but then he had left the Clifton house with his invitation to tonight's dinner still intact. So, all was not lost. Now where had he gone wrong yesterday?

He'd arrived at the appointed time with Marcus, just an hour or so before luncheon, and was shown into Marcus's study. They'd discussed their business, and Jeremy had the shipping company papers with him. While he might have made the business call as a cover for his amorous intentions, he put Marcus's time to good use.

As they neared the conclusion of their talk, he'd often found his mind wandering as to how he would find his Clara. He couldn't very well go drifting about the upper floors or hovering in the dining room. Perhaps he could ask a question about the party tomorrow night—that tack might bring Sheila into the conversation, since Marcus was hardly the social organizer of the household. And with Sheila at his side, he knew Clara would not be hard to reach.

"Where is your mind?" Marcus asked. "I've asked you twice now—what are your plans for investing?"

"What? Oh, my apologies, Marcus. I seem to have wandered off. What was it you asked?"

"Out with it—why are you really here? These papers were hardly complicated. You normally would glance at them for a few minutes and then scribble instructions for your man, Farrell, to handle. We've spent nearly an hour discussing each detail. Are you so lost in your business sense?" he asked a bit sarcastically.

Jeremy's stricken face was something of a surprise for Marcus. Perhaps he'd come down too harshly on him just now.

"What's the trouble, my boy?" he asked kindly.

Jeremy sighed raggedly and ran his hand through his hair as he abruptly rose from his chair. He hadn't realized how preoccupied he was talking with Marcus, and he owed the man an explanation. So, no more games.

"I've come here today under false pretenses. You're right about the shipping papers—they were just a ruse to get me in the door."

"But you know you always have an open invitation to our home. You don't need to invent an excuse."

"I don't know what I need. No, strike that, I know precisely what I need," Jeremy replied. His hand stopped in mid-flight as he gathered himself. But how to begin?

"Yes, you were saying," smiled Marcus. He could not imagine what would make the man pace so.

"Your niece, Miss Edwards, is a lovely girl."

"Ah, I begin to understand."

"Yes, I thought you might when I mentioned her name."

"How do you feel about her?"

"She is wonderful, and I love her," he said simply.

"My, that's quite a confession. How does she feel about you?"

"I'm certain she returns my feelings—certain of it."

"You don't sound entirely convinced."

"That's why I wanted to see her today. Yesterday, when I invited her for a carriage ride this afternoon, she refused, since her parents were due to arrive today. I couldn't very well insist that she see me."

"So, you used me to get access to her."

"Well, yes, I just had to speak with her. I didn't want a day to go by when I would not see her. I have to know she cares for me," he said fiercely.

Marcus was still a bit stunned by the news and Jeremy's fervor in his statements. *My, my, he thought, what would Sheila have to say about this development?*

"Well, you must stay for luncheon," Marcus suggested. "I mentioned to Sheila this morning that we were meeting, so I am sure she has set a place for you. Would you like that?"

"Yes! It is what I hoped for in timing my arrival at this hour," Jeremy said a bit sheepishly.

"I see I've played right into your hands," Marcus said, with a smile and no trace of irritation.

"I don't mean to make you an unwilling accomplice to my plans, sir."

"Nonsense! You are my good friend, and I wish you all the best in your pursuit of Clara. She is a lovely girl, despite some odd starts here and there."

At Jeremy's puzzled expression, Marcus continued, "I refer to her plan to bring down some poor, unsuspecting gentleman. She seems such a charming young woman, so such antics do surprise me."

"Perhaps I'd best tell you something that I think will ease your mind of any misunderstanding about Miss Edwards's character. I am afraid, though, it will not reflect too well on mine."

Marcus again wore a puzzled expression as Jeremy leaned against the mantel to begin his story.

"Clara, dear, I have wonderful news." Sheila hurried into the morning room waving a piece of paper.

"Yes, ma'am," said Clara, looking up from her book.

"Your parents are just minutes from their arrival! I have a note here from your groom who travels with them. They sent him ahead on a speedy horse to let us know they are near."

"Oh, I am so glad they will be here soon. I hadn't realized until now just how much I've missed them while I've been away from home."

"I will put luncheon back a bit to give them a chance to settle in if they wish. Oh, that does remind me—we may have another guest join us for luncheon."

"Who might that be?"

"Marcus mentioned that he had a business appointment late this morning, so I expect he will invite him to dine with us. It is Lord Carruthers, my dear."

Clara let out a gasp, but her mouth turned up in a small smile.

"I take it the news does not disturb you then?"

"No, it is always quite nice to see Lord Carruthers."

"You are much too coy, young lady. Were you, by chance, expecting him?"

"Oh no, not at all! He asked me last evening to go for a carriage ride this afternoon, but I had to decline since Mama and Papa arrive today. I couldn't begin to think he is here now in hopes of meeting me?"

"No, nothing of the sort, I'm sure," said an amused Sheila.

Her mild sarcasm was entirely lost on Clara, who was preoccupied with a mixture of excitement, anticipation, and trepidation. Might she see Jeremy at luncheon and have her dear parents with her, too? She could not keep the smile on her face from spilling into a giggle as she dropped a kiss on her aunt's cheek.

"I'd best go tidy my hair before luncheon," and Clara left the room.

Sheila laughed out loud at her niece's starry-eyed gaze and wondered how Marcus fared with Jeremy in their meeting.

"You actually sat through an entire dinner enduring her absolute silence? You're both mad!" laughed Marcus.

"Yes, it does look that way in hindsight, but I assure you I was more than willing to speak with her," Jeremy replied. "She'd obviously divined that response as the best punishment for my exceptionally churlish behavior that morning."

"I do agree with you on that point—you were an absolute boor to have treated her so shabbily on the road."

"I feel we've gotten past the unfortunate incident now. Our relationship here in town has become quite enjoyable, but I want so much more. She is charming and witty and intelligent and so lovely my heart almost stops beating when I see her across a crowded room."

"You sound like a man in love. I congratulate you on your good fortune and fine future."

"But, I am not there yet. I know she looks upon me with favor, but is it more than that?"

"Well, according to Sheila, Clara will soon realize she loves the man she once planned for a downfall. Could that time be today?"

"That is my plan, my prayer. I cannot continue in this state of suspense any longer. If we cannot go for a drive today, then I will suggest a walk in your gardens. I must tell her I know of her confounded plan and hope that she will forever overlook our sorry beginning and let me love her for all eternity!"

A noise from down the hallway permeated the study doors, and both men turned toward the disturbance.

"That sounds like it is coming from the front hall—perhaps Clara's parents have arrived."

The knock on the door sounded just as he finished speaking, and Marcus gave a command to enter.

Matthew, the head footman, entered the room, and the noise level increased substantially.

"The Edwardses have arrived, my lord, and Lady Clifton bade me to inform you."

"Thank you, Matthew. Please tell her I will join her shortly." Marcus turned back to Jeremy as the door closed. "Shall you come with me?"

The simple invitation posed a challenge to the young man, and he eagerly moved to the door to grasp it. Yes he would meet his hoped-for future in-laws this day, and Marcus saw no fear or indifference in his face.

Clara paused at the top of the stairs as the two men entered the front hall. The sight that greeted her caused such joy and happiness in her heart—her dear parents meeting the man she loved.

Yes, she now fully admitted without any hesitation that she loved Jeremy with all her being. Curiously, her fears and apprehension had disappeared as quickly as she traveled down the stairs.

Clara's mother enveloped her daughter in a hug and showered kisses on her brow.

"Darling, you look wonderful. That dress is beautiful and such a lovely color and material."

"Oh, thank you, Mama. Aunt Sheila found me such beautiful clothes. I am so happy to see you both." She turned to her father to give him an affectionate hug.

"My dear, we are equally happy to see you. I am also quite elated to step out of that bouncing coach," said Mr. Edwards with a smile.

"It has been some time since you've visited us here in town, and we're delighted to have you. Luncheon will be ready soon, or I can put it back a bit so you can settle yourselves." said Sheila.

"Oh, we're famished, so please don't delay on our account. We had a light breakfast this morning at the Weathers Inn," Marie said.

"Let us move into the drawing room then, while we wait for the nod from Reilly for luncheon. Marcus has a delightful Italian vintage for you to sample."

Jeremy carefully gauged his pace to meet Clara as she moved forward. Either by design or happenstance, the two sisters paired off, as did their spouses. He had a clear field to greet Clara.

"It is a pleasure to see you again, Miss Edwards." He extended his arm to her to escort her into the drawing room.

"Thank you, Lord Carruthers. I understand from my aunt that you met with Uncle Marcus this morning to discuss some business."

"Yes, I did seek his advice, and I found his words to be of great help." But Jeremy was hardly speaking about business.

"Do you have any business dealings together?"

"No, we don't share any investments but we have common interests and goals. We often confer on new ideas and trends."

"You make it sound interesting but a bit complex," said Clara as she settled on a chair by the picture window.

"I do enjoy the challenge, and I help to keep it simple by concentrating only on the areas I enjoy."

"That sounds sensible and allows you more time for other activities."

"Such as calling on beautiful young ladies," he said with a look down to her in the chair.

Clara glanced up to meet his eyes and saw kindness and warmth. She felt so at ease in his presence, and it was a delightful change to meet him in such an intimate setting as her aunt and uncle's home.

When Reilly entered the room to announce luncheon, Clara again found herself on Lord Carruthers's arm for the short walk into the dining room. Sheila had seated them together on one side of the table across from her parents. It all seemed so right.

Jeremy enjoyed the family atmosphere in this meal. With such a small group, they talked across the table and told amusing stories. As a bachelor, he was alone for so many of his meals at home. Sharing the table today made him all the more sure of his intentions towards Clara.

"How long are you staying in town, Papa?" Clara asked.

"As long as your mother wants. I told her that she would soon find the rounds of parties boring and dull, but she assures me that I have it all wrong."

"Now, Harold, you are much too ridiculous!" Marie Edwards said. "You were the one who wanted to add an extra fortnight onto this trip after all the Season's festivities wind down. I had to beg you to stay in town for more than a week when we visited last time. So, don't you accuse me of dragging you out of your comfortable country chair."

"It's not every day our daughter agrees to a Season in town."

"Amen to that!" laughed Sheila.

"Have we met before, Lord Carruthers? You do look familiar to me," said Marie.

Clara gave a small gasp at this question and turned a stricken face to her mother. Jeremy had a momentary pause but decided honesty was for the best. Hopefully, he wouldn't have to be too honest and tell the entire tale!

"I was at the Thompsons' dinner just before the Season, ma'am. I believe we met there."

"Ah, yes, now I do remember. Emma Thompson confided to me how excited she was to have a new young man at her table. But, do I recall—yes, you were seated next to Clara at dinner?"

The two young people looked at each other in surprise, then in amusement, and finally outright laughter. There was no avoiding it now, thought Jeremy.

"I believe Lord Carruthers is trying to skip that topic, Mama, to save me some embarrassment. I was quite rude to him during the meal, and he had to suffer through my silence," laughed Clara.

"Never say this is the bounder who crashed into you on the road that morning!" blurted an astounded Harold Edwards.

"Oh, Papa, it was a mere grazing rather than a crash, and I was fine," Clara replied.

"Please accept my apologies, sir—it was entirely my fault," added Jeremy.

They spoke in unison and with such sincerity that

Mr. Edwards was a bit taken aback by the passion of their words.

"They appear to have reconciled over the mishap," said Sheila smoothly.

Clara threw her a grateful look and turned her head to her parents to nod in agreement.

"Yes, it does seem to be old history now," Marie said with some skepticism in her voice.

"Thank you both for your consideration," Jeremy offered humbly. What a way to be remembered by her parents!

"Shall we finish our cakes in the drawing room?" asked Sheila.

"Thank you, dear, but I would like to change out of my traveling clothes now that we've eaten. I think I'll save the sweets for later if you don't mind," Marie replied.

"Of course, Marie. You know you can treat our home as if it were your own."

They had finished the meal, and the Edwardses excused themselves to freshen up from their trip.

Jeremy saw his opportunity to steal some time with Clara. But how should he approach her?

"Jeremy, why don't you and Clara take a stroll in the garden. It's a beautiful afternoon," Marcus suggested.

"What a lovely idea, Marcus."

Jeremy could hardly keep the grin off his face as he turned to acknowledge Marcus's suggestion. How could he repay such a sly one?

"Would you care for a short walk, Miss Edwards?"

"Yes, thank you, I would enjoy it very much. It would feel good to be in the sunshine after our cool morning."

They began their walk in silence with neither one of them knowing what to say or how to begin. While they knew they cared for each other, they hadn't yet found a comfortable footing for familiar conversation.

With the reminder of their first meeting so fresh in their minds, both Clara and Jeremy longed to find a way to forever remove that rift. Jeremy wished this were all behind them, but continued delays would not bring them any closer to that goal or to each other.

"I do wish to apologize for my poor behavior that day. I would erase it all were it only in my power."

"Oh, Lord Carruthers, you needn't apologize again. My actions were hardly something of which I can be proud."

"I don't want the memory of it to haunt us each time we meet. And apart from your deplorable conduct at dinner, I can find no other fault with your behavior," he said with a grin.

"My deplorable conduct! Why, you were the . . ." and her voice trailed off as she caught sight of his face. He had such a look that she caught her breath—but such a look of what?

"I hope you know I take full responsibility for that day."

"We shall just put it behind us."

"Ah, but you see, I know of a plan that came out of that day."

"Whatever do you m-mean?" Clara could not stop the catch in her voice as she asked the question. How could he know? She couldn't confess her plan to him—that would be just too embarrassing!

He saw the expressions running across her face and wanted to end her agitation. He had to tell her he knew. So, he related the story of his conversation with Marcus the night before at the Woodley Ball. He left out the part where Marcus had said she'd become enamored of him, though. No need to let her know everything!

She turned wide eyes to him and started to speak. He reached up and gently put his fingers over her mouth with a quiet shush.

"I came here today to find a way to talk with you. My meeting with Marcus was just a ruse so that I wouldn't look too obvious. I had to let you know I'd found out about your plan even though Marcus said you'd abandoned it."

"But aren't you furious with me?" she asked forlornly. What must he think of her for trying to make him fall in love with her just so she could humiliate and jilt him?

"No, of course not! How could I be mad at you? I was a perfect boor and deserved a set-down. You are one of the first people to stand up to me and put me in my place. I could never be mad at you."

They had stopped walking by now and turned to face each other. Her hand still rested on his arm, and his hand lingered near her face. He slowly placed it on her shoulder and moved it behind her neck to draw her toward him.

"But I was horrible to you, or at least I planned to be," she whispered.

"Sometimes our plans don't work out as we expect." He kissed her ever so gently on her soft lips.

He could feel her melt into him, and it was a wonderful sensation. *And sometimes a plan works out just as we'd hoped,* he thought to himself. He slowly pulled away but continued to hold her near.

"What could you have planned that would be so awful?" he asked softly. He said it rhetorically rather than from any true desire to know.

She gasped and stepped back. He didn't know! Surely, he would be horrified if he found out her true intent.

"Clara, Miss Edwards, please tell me what is the matter!"

"I must go see if my mother needs me. Please forgive me, Lord Carruthers." She turned and fled into the house before he could follow her.

Thinking back on the events now, Jeremy still could not fathom why she had run. He had been on the verge of kissing her again and instead found himself with his arms wrapped around air. What could have upset her?

He'd reentered the house intent on following her but knew it was not possible. He'd slowed his steps as he left the drawing room and found Marcus and Mr. Edwards staring at Clara's retreating back.

Marcus had waylaid him, and Jeremy had taken the opportunity to speak privately with Mr. Edwards. He'd never asked for someone's hand, but he smiled to recall how easy it had been. He knew he had Marcus to thank for its going so well.

And now dinner was at hand, and he could linger no longer. His cravat was impeccable, his shoes like mirrors, and his every hair in place. While he might have to tread lightly with his Clara when they first met, he would make it a successful evening. He wondered if she looked forward to tonight with as much joy and anticipation as he felt.

She caressed the bouquet from Jeremy and struggled to hold back tears. She would lose him forever tonight. She felt like a criminal going to solitary confinement rather than a young woman preparing to meet the man of her dreams.

The day had been so perfect yesterday. She tingled when she remembered his kiss, and the tears finally welled in her eyes with the realization that it would be but a memory.

Clara jumped at the sound of the knock at the door. Perhaps if she were silent, whoever it was would think she'd already gone downstairs. After all, it was almost time for their guests to arrive.

The knock came again, and more loudly this time. She heard her mother call her name, and Clara knew she had to respond. She quickly wiped her eyes with the back of her hand.

"Come in, Mama."

"Oh, good, you are all ready to go downstairs. But darling, whatever is the matter?"

"Nothing, Mama. I am fine."

"Now don't you try to fob me off with such a silly statement. You're nothing of the sort."

Clara stood to walk toward the door, and the bouquet fell to the floor. She let out a small cry and quickly stooped to pick it up.

Marie Edwards knew of the sender and his conversation with her husband yesterday. She'd also had a very interesting conversation with her sister this morning. She'd purposefully stayed away from Clara this afternoon because she did not want to let on that she knew of the imminent proposal. Clearly that tack had been in error.

As Clara rose from the floor, her mother embraced her and held her tightly.

"Tell me what's wrong, darling. We'll find a way to make it right."

"I don't think you can, Mama. I've made such a mess of th-things." Curiously, her tears were gone.

"Is it something to do with a certain Lord Carruthers? Don't look so surprised! It was plain as day at luncheon yesterday that you care for him. Why, you could barely take your eyes off of him long enough to say hello to your father and me."

"Now, that's not true!"

"I'm only teasing you, but I was speaking the truth when I said I knew you cared for him."

"Oh, it is more than that, Mama. I love him with all my heart, and I'll never see him again after tonight."

"Why do you say such nonsense? The Season has barely started."

"I can't face him, and to see him dancing and talking with others would be too painful."

"Perhaps you'd best tell me the *whole* story, young lady. You seem to have gotten yourself into a fine mess, or so you think."

"I treated Lord Carruthers unfairly when I came to town. I wanted to teach him a lesson for the way he'd so rudely accosted me on the lane that day outside Waverly Manor. I'd concocted this elaborate plan to make him fall in love with me so I could spurn him when he declared himself.

"I know it was a silly schoolgirl notion to think I would be able to catch the eye of one so fine. But, I made such a muddle of it, and he found out! But, he has no idea I planned something so horrible. I just know he would want nothing to do with me if he knew the whole truth."

"Darling, I think you're being too hard on yourself. You've done nothing wrong nor have you hurt Lord Carruthers or embarrassed him amongst his friends."

"But don't you see that it won't matter when he finds out that I had such mean intentions?"

"Yes, you set out with a plan that you now regret, but it is all behind you. I know you harbor no such intentions toward the man now."

"You make it all sound so simple," Clara said in a small voice.

"No, it may not all be simple for you, but you can't stop trying just because something is hard or you think you might fail. You can't go through life only striving for goals that are within easy reach."

"But, he'll hate me."

"You'll have to take that chance. You wouldn't be any better off than you are now, so why don't you fight for him?"

"Fight for him?"

"Enjoy your evening with your friends, dance with your Lord Carruthers, and let him know how you feel."

"What? I can't tell him I love him!"

"No, of course not, but you can let him know in more subtle ways than words. Caress his arm as he escorts you, look deeply into his eyes when he speaks, and let him lead you onto the terrace after you dance."

"Mama, I'm shocked!"

"Oh tosh, young lady. You want this man and you have to let him know it."

"But, I still have to tell him the original intentions in my plan."

"Yes, but perhaps not as you greet him in the drawing room just now."

Clara smiled at her mother's jest and began to feel a bit of hope. She did want this man and loved him dearly, so why shouldn't she put herself forward rather than simply give up?

"And perhaps you've learned your lesson about these plans you and your brother seem to delight in making?"

"Oh, yes, no more plans for me."

"Do you feel ready to come downstairs? I'm sure a few guests have arrived by now."

"Yes, Mama, and thank you for helping me." Clara gave her an embrace as the ladies moved to leave the room.

EIGHTEEN

TERRACE TWOSOME

"Ladies, please join me in the salon while we leave the gentlemen to their cigars and port."

The guests had been small in number due to the last minute cancellations of the Farleigh ladies and a few of the gentlemen. The unexpectedly damp weather had left many in their circle of friends feeling poorly.

While she missed their company and wished them a speedy recovery, she found she preferred smaller dinner parties after so many years of entertaining. She had more time to enjoy herself without constantly worrying about how the guests fared.

So far, the evening had been a delight. The pre-dinner conversations in the drawing room were lively, and it was quite apparent that Clara was not the only young woman who'd caught the eye of an eligible man.

She was so happy to see that Emma's Season seemed complete with the marked attentions of Mr. Waters. Her earlier alliance with Mr. Farleigh had appeared to end quickly, and she felt this new pairing would surely prove to be long lasting.

And the aforementioned Mr. Farleigh hadn't suffered long, as he was now quite captivated with Miss March. The Fair Incomparable had set her sights on the dashing man, and he hadn't a chance. The girls had wanted dance cards for the evening, and she saw Mr. Farleigh scribbling madly on Charlotte's card before dinner. Sheila had seated them next to each other at dinner quite by chance, and she feared their other partners never had a moment to speak with either of them!

Clara had helped with the last-minute rearrangements to dinner's seating cards, and Sheila saw that matchmaking had certainly played a hand. Along with Reggie Farleigh and Charlotte March's cozy seating, Clara had placed herself right next to Jeremy! Sheila had to applaud her audacity, and had given her a smile and a wink as they'd seated themselves at the table.

Clara had also placed Lady Annabelle Richards next to Dickers Smythe-Hattan, and, judging by the adoration in his eyes, they too would form a lasting attachment. With so much romance in the air, Sheila felt it would be a wonder if there weren't an engagement announced before the night had ended!

Now that the ladies were alone in the salon, the thinness of the company was quite apparent. Why, with Colonel Clarkston's bad leg for dancing, they wouldn't be able to form two sets. Perhaps she'd need to suggest an alternative. She motioned to Marie, who quickly joined her on the settee.

"Dear, I think we might have to forego the dancing."

"Oh, the girls will be so disappointed. And I must admit I had my eye on my handsome husband for a dance or two of my own!"

"With the Colonel not dancing, we are a man short in the second set."

"Well, I think that will be fine. Not everyone wants to dance each set, so the odd number will let us have a rest."

"What are you two whispering about with such serious faces?" asked Emily.

"I was trying to convince Sheila that we do have enough company for dancing," Marie replied.

"Oh, never say you're thinking of sending home the musicians! Even I was looking forward to it tonight with all our good friends."

"Well, of course, then. I bow to your wishes, and we shall dance!"

Clara and Emma found themselves in the corner, and Clara couldn't help but remember a similar evening at the Thompsons'. She'd felt so lost and alone that night, and rather lonely, too. Now, she hoped and prayed her destiny lay with the same man who'd occupied her thoughts so differently on that earlier evening.

"Emma, may I ask you something?"

"Of course, dear, anything you want."

"Have you found the right man for you in Mr. Waters?"

"Oh, yes, he's everything I could want," she whispered a bit breathlessly. "I didn't have a moment to tell you earlier, but he called this morning."

"Were you able to talk with him?"

"Actually, he arrived late and many people had already come and gone. We had quite a bit of time to talk privately while Mother entertained the last few stragglers."

"Has he, um, kissed you?"

"Clara Edwards!"

"Keep your voice down."

"Then don't ask such shocking questions!"

"Well, has he?"

"Almost."

"What does that mean?"

"He held my hands as we said good-bye this morning."

"Emma, that's hardly a kiss."

"You didn't let me finish! Mother was showing Mrs. Farleigh to the door, and then Mr. Waters stood up to take his leave. He reached down to help me stand, and we stood so close together."

"I'm still not seeing a kiss."

"Clara, will you please! He took my second hand and cradled them both in his one hand. His gaze was just compelling, and then he pulled me forward as he took a half step closer."

"Yes, what happened next?"

"He put his other hand on my shoulder for just a second, and then he moved it to hold my chin. It was almost like he didn't know where to put it."

"Did he seem nervous?"

"No, not nervous, but rather tentative. Then he said that he would like to call on me tomorrow."

"Did you say yes?"

"Of course! And as I did, he leaned forward with a breathtaking smile on his face. He was so close to me, and he smelled just wonderful."

"And?"

"We heard my mother outside the door, and it broke the spell. He stepped back and dropped his hand to his side. But, my hands were still in his one hand, and that's how Mother found us standing."

"Did she say anything?"

"No, she hurried back into the room, almost as if she'd forgotten something and didn't really see us. By the time she noticed us, Mr. Waters stood beside me, and my hands were at my sides. But, I know he was going to kiss me."

"When he calls tomorrow, will you let him kiss you then?"

"Why are you asking me such questions?"

"I was with Lord Carruthers yesterday afternoon, and he kissed me in the garden."

"Does anyone know?"

"No, but I feel just like you do. He's everything I want."

The girls looked at each other and hugged.

The gentlemen had joined the ladies, and talk soon turned to the dancing. Through the open doors of the ballroom they could hear strains of tuning instruments wafting down the stairs into the drawing room.

The ladies looked at their dance cards to see who they were paired with for the first dance. Clara really did not care with whom she danced if it wasn't Lord Carruthers. She knew such an attitude was hardly fair or even becoming. She found herself simply looking for him throughout the room, hoping to catch a glimpse.

Really, she must get hold of herself! Any display of this behavior would not find favor with her friends or family, and frankly she was appalled with herself with such selfishness.

Clara stood and gave herself a gentle shake. Her aunt would depend upon her to be a good hostess, and favoritism would never do.

Jeremy saw that little shake of Clara's shoulders and could only wonder. Perhaps she was chilled from sitting near a window, and he immediately wanted to go to her to wrap her in a warm blanket. He watched as she comfortably mingled among the guests, and he found even more to admire about her with each passing minute.

The evening had gone well so far, and he'd been happily surprised to have Clara at his side at dinner. They had laughed about that other dinner now so long ago, and Jeremy smiled as he remembered remarking what a wonderful conversationalist she had turned out to be.

He had no interest in dancing right now. He would find a way to maneuver Miss Edwards onto the terrace in lieu of the first dance. He had no recollection of where he'd signed her card, so he would simply whisk her away from whoever had that first dance.

He started to move toward Clara across the room. Best to have the advantage of proximity, since he could see Sheila shuffling others to the doorway.

Edward met him at the center of the room, and the two men stopped for a moment together.

Clara saw Jeremy coming in her direction. She was disappointed that his name was not on her dance card until the second dance. But, after her talk with Emma just now, it might prove interesting to pair with Mr. Waters for the first set.

Out of the corner of her eye, she could see the two men talking quite seriously. Jeremy appeared to be asking for something, and Mr. Waters seemed reluctant to agree. Jeremy persisted, and she then saw Mr. Waters nod abruptly with an exasperated smile on his face.

Clara turned to look for Aunt Sheila to see if she were ready to move into the ballroom. Based on the few people left in the room now, Clara realized she was behind the times.

Sheila hurried over and gathered the two gentlemen as she walked. "It is time to start our dancing, so please join us now. Can't you hear the lovely music calling you?"

"Lady Clifton, you have such a charming way of phrasing it—how could we resist. May I escort you, ma'am?" Edward asked.

Sheila took Edward's arm, and the room was soon empty except for Clara and Jeremy.

"Please, let me walk you up to the ballroom," Jeremy offered.

"Thank you, Lord Carruthers." Clara rested her hand on the arm he held for her.

"I fear we may be the last ones in the room."

"It will not matter. We don't have quite enough people to make up two full sets, so some of us will have to sit out the dances and simply enjoy the music."

"I will certainly enjoy the company." He smiled down at her.

"Yes, we do have a fine group here tonight."

Why were they speaking in such stilted tones? It would drive him mad to pass the time with her in this manner. Their dinner conversation had been so easy and relaxed, and now he felt like they had just met.

Clara felt the tension but attributed it to her own task ahead. She must talk with him again privately after her disastrous rush from the garden yesterday.

They had reached the top of the stairs, and her time for action would soon be gone. Remembering her mother's advice, Clara turned to face him.

"Lord Carruthers, might I trouble you to check a light on the terrace here? I forgot to ask the footman before dinner."

"Certainly, Miss Edwards." He turned to hold the door for her.

Clara improvised and led him to a torch at the far end of the wall. She would have to think of something quickly, since it threw off a tremendous light and looked to be in fine working order.

Jeremy was puzzled by this detour, but he took it at face value. There were a thousand things to check before a party, and he knew one couldn't always take care of them all.

"Well, I am sorry to have brought you out here. It does seem to be fine now."

"Perhaps someone else also noticed it needed attention."

"Yes! That must be the answer. We can go back in now."

She had lost her nerve again and would have run away had she dared.

Jeremy, ever the campaigner, would not let such a golden opportunity slip from his grasp. He didn't know why she'd concocted the story about the light, but he was grateful just the same.

"I don't think so."

"What?"

"I don't think we need to hurry back inside."

"But, all the guests will wonder where we are."

"They won't even miss us. You just said that some of the couples would have to sit out the dancing. Once the set fills, they won't even look for us."

"But, I was to dance with Mr. Waters—you're second on my card."

"Ah, yes. I spoke with him downstairs and asked if I might have his time instead."

"I'm sure someone will miss us."

"Oh, undoubtedly they will, but not just yet. Clara, why did you ask me out here on this dark and very secluded terrace?"

"The light, of course." But even she could see how feeble an excuse it truly was.

"Might there be something else?"

Clara surprised him when she turned to walk back to the doorway. She'd taken a few steps before he caught up with her. Then she stopped in her tracks, and he walked past.

He turned back to her and saw a mighty struggle flit across her face.

"I want to apologize for running away yesterday," she said.

"I must say, you did surprise me." He took a step toward her so that their shadows touched in the moonlight.

"I was frightened. Oh no, not of you, but of what I had done."

"What had you done?" he gently asked.

"Well, not done precisely, but planned."

"Ah, yes, the dreaded plan. That's right, I'd asked you what you'd planned to do."

"And I ran away."

"I can't help but notice that you are not running now." He took her in his arms and raised her hand to his lips to kiss it gently. Then he placed her hand on his shoulder and caressed her cheek.

"Oh, Jeremy, I've m-made such a muddle of everything." She lowered her head onto his shoulder.

"Shh, it can't be as bad as you're thinking. Please know that you can tell me anything."

She stood in the circle of his arms and held him tightly. He must forgive her—he must!

Jeremy was mad with desire for this lovely girl, and he struggled mightily to maintain himself. He mustn't hurry her confession. No matter how much self-control it required of him to simply hold her gently, he would do this. Perhaps a light brushing of his hand against her silken hair would help to quiet her scattered breathing.

His hand felt wonderful against her neck as he

touched her hair. Oh, but she didn't want to move an inch. But, as perfect as this moment was, she knew she must tell him, and tell him now. She lifted her head from his shoulder and looked into his eyes.

"I had a silly notion that I could capture your attentions here in London, and . . . and . . ." Clara's voice trailed off.

"Not so silly from where I stand," he interrupted with a laugh.

"Now be serious, there's more." But she, too, had a grin on her face.

He just couldn't resist and gathered her closer in his arms and kissed her. She responded with equal passion and wrapped her arms around his neck. He slowly lifted his mouth and trailed kisses down her neck.

"Were these the attentions you wanted to capture?"

Clara trilled a laugh at such a question. "You are not making this easy!"

He lifted his head to whisper in her ear, "You will have to learn that I can be very difficult when I choose."

Clara's arms still hugged Jeremy's neck. She unconsciously adjusted them to tighten her grip, and Jeremy's smile grew wider.

"I must say, Miss Edwards, that I will not drop you or let go. So you needn't wrestle my neck with such a hold."

"Oh my." She pulled back in embarrassment, but, she didn't lower her arms.

"You are utterly charming," he said, and his lips found hers again for another kiss.

Clara could hardly think with this marvelous and fascinating man so close and so tempting. She felt all her senses melting away as his kisses continued.

"Now . . . I . . . believe . . . you . . . were . . . telling . . . me . . . something." He punctuated each word with light kisses across her brow, her cheeks, her nose, and finally again on her lips.

"I haven't a notion what we were saying."

"You had a plan for my attentions," he prompted.

She pulled her head away from him to gaze into his eyes. She saw such a twinkle it stole her breath away. What did he know?

"Let me guess. The affronted country miss was going to give the uppity town cad the setdown of his life when he came forward to press his attentions."

"But, how could you . . . ?"

"I am right, yes?"

"Well, yes, and then I would hurt and embarrass you when you declared yourself by turning you down flat."

"My, my, Miss Edwards, you are an unforgiving one, aren't you?"

"But, I've abandoned the whole plan. I don't want to embarrass you or hurt you or . . ."

"Or what?"

How could she continue? She couldn't very well say "or turn you down" when he hadn't declared himself. She was such a fool for thinking she could ever hope to have the love of such a man as he.

He saw the uncertainty on her face, and his heart went out to her. Even now, enveloped in his arms, she was unsure. He vowed now to forever make her life one of love and constant happiness.

"Now, you haven't finished telling me the whole story. You've one last confession."

With her head down she shook it and then shook it again even harder. He moved his hand to lift her chin and raise her face to the light.

"Perhaps I can help finish it for you. You do know that I love you with all my heart?"

She shook her head from side to side, and he gently

caught her cheek with his hand. He took the opportunity to kiss her once again.

"Now, my darling girl, you do know *now* that I love you?"

Clara smiled this time and nodded vigorously.

"I feel so close to you, and I can only hope and pray that you feel some of the same for me. You make me feel complete, and I want to be with you forever. Please say that you will marry me?"

"Marry you? Oh Jeremy, are you sure?"

"You are everything I want, and my only fear is that you will not want me, love me."

"Jeremy, I love you, too, with all my heart, and yes, I will marry y—"

She didn't finish the sentence in time before he kissed her again, a long and tender kiss filled with his love and longing. Her shiver in his arms brought him back to reality.

"I think we had better go inside. You'll catch your death out here, and they're sure to have missed us by now." He'd taken off his jacket and wrapped it now around her, and then wrapped his arms around her again.

"What will my parents say? Will you speak to my father tomorrow? Tonight?"

"Now, I guess it is time for my own confession. We spoke yesterday afternoon when you left the garden. I asked him then for your hand in marriage, and thankfully, he said yes. Actually, he said the decision was up to you."

"Why, you sly schemer! And Mama didn't say a thing to me today."

"Perhaps he hasn't told her yet."

"Oh, no, I believe he told her. She gave me quite a heartfelt talk this evening just before dinner, when I was so low about how I'd treated you. I don't think she would have pushed me so hard if she were not sure of your feelings."

"Pushed you so hard?"

"To not give up."

"And here I thought I had everything under control, but now I find out that you had me right where you wanted me."

"Yes, and I hope I always will.